Don't Ask Me If I Love

DON'T ASK ME IF I LOVE

a novel by *Amos Kollek*

Published by M. Evans and Company, Inc., *New York*
AND DISTRIBUTED IN ASSOCIATION WITH
J. B. Lippincott Company, *Philadelphia and New York*

for Yigal Wilk

Contents

Part One

RAM

Chapter One

I KICKED the door shut behind me. It made a long, dull echo in the big house, and then silence prevailed again. From the pale walls of the large, luxurious hall the paintings stared at me. All Impressionists and all originals. I didn't look back at them. I crossed the hall and started climbing the stairs, unbuttoning my shirt as I walked. My uniform was all wet with sweat and it clung to my body. The idea of a cold shower made me almost gleeful. The summer was coming to an end, but it didn't have to be summer to be hot in Israel. Some part of my brain, which didn't share the obscure, exhausted numbness of the rest of my mind, remarked coldly that it didn't actually feel like coming home.

It had always been the same. Through the weeks in the camp that dragged on endlessly, I would yearn for time off. And when it came, it didn't seem to mean anything.

I heard my mother rushing from the living room to the bottom of the stairs. I could even hear her excited, heavy breathing, and in spite of myself I grimaced.

"Assaf!" she cried.

"Hi, Mom. How's life?" I said quietly, over my shoulder.

I walked into my room and closed the door behind me, without looking back. I was in a bad mood that Friday afternoon. I had been in a bad mood for many days and it made me sick of myself. I had no admiration for Hamlets and didn't think there was anything impressive about people posing as being complicated, but I couldn't seem to straighten myself out.

My family was not a typical one. We were very rich. According to the papers my father was the richest man in the country. Papers may exaggerate somewhat, but anyway you looked at it, he wasn't doing badly.

First of all, there was the bank. It belonged almost entirely to him and had branches in the four bigger cities. He started with the bank, but he didn't stop there. My father never stopped at anything. His will and energy were unlimited and they didn't let him ever stop going. He didn't believe in rest; I think he was scared of it.

During the first few years of the new state, after the bank had been well established, he built two factories for military equipment. In those he put all his money, thought, and effort. They were the only enterprises of that kind in the country, and my father, who was a keen patriot, had foreseen the vital necessity for their existence. He was of the generation that had undergone the terrors of the Nazi regime and he didn't believe in depending on anyone, or on any nation. He was a self-made man who believed only in self-made men—and in self-made countries. If Israel was to survive it had to be able to support itself and supply its own weapons. Once he made that observation there was nothing else he cared about but seeing it carried out. So he built the factories. They also earned him a lot of money. The government was not blind to any of that. It helped the project to prosper, and Israel in turn was rewarded with something to lean on on a rainy day.

In 1958 and in 1966 my father won the Israel Prize for the most resourceful and distinguished manufacturer. After the Sinai Campaign in 1956, the papers praised him as one of the main civilian contributors to its success.

We lived in a three-story house in Talbiyeh, one of the two fanciest quarters in the new city of Jerusalem. It had eleven rooms, and was richly furnished, but it wasn't extravagant.

My father didn't have to boast of anything. In a way, money didn't mean much to him, and my mother was simply modest. I stepped out of my clothes and into the bathroom off my room. I took a cold shower. It made me feel refreshed and a lot cleaner, but it still didn't make me feel good. I went back to my room and crawled between the white sheets on my bed. I tried to analyze my state of mind.

The main thing was that there had been a change. I had never been a happy type, but to a certain extent I got used to it. As far as I could remember, I had always felt guilty and disappointed. In the first eighteen years of my life these feelings had formed an undercurrent which I could accept and live with, but in the last four years they had risen to the surface and it made me restless.

People around me—both children and grownups—had always hammered into my head how lucky I was. Not every boy had so many toys, not everyone lived in such a fancy house, not everyone could go abroad every year, not everyone had such a celebrated father. Everything, people would explain to me, everything I had came to me easily because of my family. I did not deserve it and it didn't belong to me. It was just another manifestation of the inequities of the system.

This, I thought clearly, lying on my back with my eyes closed, was the essential reason for both the guilt and the disappointment. I felt that there was really something wrong with the fact that I had more than others, and I couldn't really enjoy any of it any more. The last years, especially those in the army, brought with them a shrewder outlook. I still felt guilty and I still felt disappointed, but the reasons had changed. I blamed myself now for wronging myself, not other people. I blamed myself for not doing everything I could to achieve something. You can't blame yourself for being born a certain person, in a certain position, but you can damn well blame yourself for not doing all you can to make the most of it.

I was aware that it was bothering me more and more to listen to people telling me how fantastic my father was and

how proud I should be of being privileged to be his son. There
was just one way out of this, and that was beating him at his
own game.

Maybe it would have been different, I thought dreamily
and more relaxed now, if we had been closer to each other.
But it was too late. I had to pass too many offices and too many
secretaries to reach him.

As I was falling asleep my thoughts shifted to my mother.
For the thousandth time I wondered vaguely how it was possible for two such different people to be married. My mother
was small and shy and considerate and mellow. She wasn't
really good looking, but she was efficient and clever. My father
was handsome and strong and charming. He could be the
swinging star of any social event. He was six feet tall, just like
me.

At half past seven my mother woke me up by knocking softly
on my door and told me that dinner was about to be served. I
kicked away the sheets and grunted my annoyance. I had a headache and I wasn't hungry, but attending Friday night dinners
was a tradition that even my father kept.

I slipped into some clean clothes and went down to the
dining room. As I entered, Mom was calling my father to come
to the table. She was standing by the two unlit candles with a
box of matches in her hand and an expression of everlasting
patience on her face. I knew that my father was probably sitting in his study reading the papers, and as the minutes passed
by I felt the old familiar annoyance rising in me. Mother was
telling me quietly how good it was to see me and how worried
she had been. I stuck my hands in my pockets and stared
blankly at the wall, trying to decide what the hell I was going
to do tonight and not succeeding. Then, my father came in
and sat at the head of the long wooden table. He nodded his
head at me and smiled briefly. I nodded back, not smiling, and
not sitting down. Handsome devil, I thought, shifting my gaze
from him to my mother, and hoping my face didn't reflect my
thoughts. He had a jet of black hair, icy blue eyes, and a
thinly cut mustache à la Clark Gable. His skin was tanned by

his private electric sun. He looked a lot younger than his fifty-five years.

My mother lit the candles and said the prayer. She wasn't religious but this was a habit with her. Father yawned and took a bite from a big red apple that was placed in a bowl before him. I remained standing, with my eyes fixed stupidly on the wall in front of me. When she had finished we sat down and started eating. Mom launched her traditional attack.

"O.K.," she said to me, "tell us all about what you've been doing."

I tasted the fish and disliked it immediately.

"Doing?" I spat a bone on my fork. "Haven't been doing anything."

She eyed me reproachfully. "Come on, Assaf, you know we haven't seen you for five weeks."

My father ate busily, not looking up from his plate.

I looked back at my mother's sad face and smiled at her.

"Missed me?"

"Oh, Assaf. You know we did."

We? I stuffed some potatoes in my mouth so I wouldn't have to talk. At least my headache was going away.

"Tell us what you've been doing."

I shrugged. "We've been hanging around the camp. You know how it is."

"Anyone killed?" my father asked. He looked at me briskly and then returned to the bones on his plate.

"Nobody you know."

He placed his fork slowly on his plate and then he looked up at me again. "Got any plans?" he asked, searching his mouth with his thumb.

"Plans?"

"You are being released in six weeks, aren't you?"

That had been my hope and belief. "I'll probably take it easy for a while," I said casually.

"That's not much of a plan."

I could see what he was up to. I could see it coming. Cool hand me. "I've had things planned for me the last three years," I told him flatly. "I am going to see for myself once I'm out."

His cold blue eyes were still investigating my face, making observations and writing them down. "Shouldn't waste time when you are young," he said placidly. "Those are the best years."

"They keep telling me that," I said. I looked at my watch. It was ten to nine. "Well, I've got to go."

"You haven't finished eating yet," Mom protested. "What about your dessert?"

"I'm not that hungry." I got to my feet. "I told Ram I'd pick him up at nine, so—see you."

As I was walking toward the door my mother said, "Oh that boy! I could die."

"I'll go and have a look at my papers," my father said.

Evenings in Jerusalem are cool, even in the summer. In the whole of Israel it is probably the place with the best climate. I welcomed the cold breeze that brushed my face as I stepped out of the house. I walked to the small garage where my white Triumph was parked and got into it. My father had given it to me as a present for my eighteenth birthday. It was only his time he wasn't generous with.

I pulled out slowly and then stepped on the gas and sped away. I loved driving fast. I drove crazily. I loved to hear the engine roaring and the tires screaming, and to feel the wind slap fiercely on my face. My father used to say that I was going to end up killing someone before too long, but he was a nut driver himself. Anyway, I told him, I hoped his money would be good enough to bribe the judge if and when needed. He didn't react to that.

Ram had been my best friend for fifteen years. I didn't have many others. I wasn't friendly and I could do without the company of people. When I was younger I believed that people couldn't be after anything else except my father's money.

Gradually I developed the belief that most people just weren't worth my while. I wasn't going to be an ordinary human being and so I wouldn't be interested in anyone who just happened to be around.

With Ram it was different, at least for me. There was nothing usual about him. I idolized him consciously and deliberately.

He was my age, six feet three inches tall, and very strong. He was also the best-looking guy I'd ever seen, in or outside of the movies. Someitmes it almost hurt, I thought. He was so handsome.

He had the strong, masculine beauty of a Greek statue. His hair was slightly curly and brown, the same color as his eyes. When he smiled, his teeth sparkled and glinted together with his eyes in the smooth bronze of his face. It was the most disarming smile I had seen on anyone's face, but Ram rarely used it.

He had a peculiar quality I often wondered about. He was always serious minded and solemn. A born leader, the center of any group he belonged to and yet never completely there.

Ram took everything seriously, he never played. He was a good pupil and an outstanding soldier. He had an obsession about the army. I thought I knew the reason for that. His father had been killed in 1952, in a clash with terrorists on the southern border. Ram had been five years old at that time. He told me that the last time his father had been home before his death, he stood and looked at his small son who lay quietly in his bed and said to his wife, "It's worth our while to fight so his generation can have this country free when they are old enough to understand what it means."

After that, he kissed her and went away.

Ram could not remember any of this, but years later when his mother told him about it he could picture it all in his imagination as if it had always been there, somewhere in the depths of his memory. In a strange way, it filled his mind. He admired the father he hadn't known and wished to live up to the glorious image he had of him. For Ram the homeland was a sacred cause, the fighting wasn't over yet—and he had his obligations.

Ram was a lieutenant in the paratroopers. In the summer of 1965, after we had finished high school together, he was drafted. I went to the United States with my parents. My father had to be there for his work and he persuaded me to come. He fixed it with the Defense Ministry, so that I wouldn't have to go into the army for a year. He believed that being in America was a necessary part of one's education.

"You have to see projects on a scale found only in America in order to really understand how this world is run," he said to me. "It will broaden your horizons."

I let him talk me into it. I let him talk me into it because I wasn't at all anxious to go into the army. I never enjoyed discipline and the idea of being a small, unimportant part in a huge machine didn't appeal to me. I went to the States and I regretted it. Stalling for time only meant losing time in the long run.

I went into the army a year later. After five months of training I broke both legs falling from a rock during a divisional exercise. I was sent to a hospital in Tel Aviv. It was April 1967. A month and a half later all my classmates and friends were either living or dead heroes. The Six Day War had passed me by without my hearing one single shot.

It was a very bitter pill to swallow but there was nothing I could do about it. Life went on. By the end of 1968 I was a sergeant in a paratroopers' company that was stationed in the Jordan Valley, not far from the river. Ram, who had signed for an extra year as an officer, was in the same company. He was the company commander's second-in-command.

Being a platoon sergeant made life a lot easier for me. It wasn't that Ram gave me any special treatment or rights, he just did all the work he could do, even if it wasn't strictly his job. He had an uneasy feeling about not signing up for still another term. It made him feel disloyal. But even he wanted something other than a soldier's life. Ram didn't really like the army. He wanted to study, but with other young men getting killed every day on the Suez Canal or in the Jordan Valley, it just didn't seem right to him to be on the outside. I spent many hours, during weekends in the camp, trying to prevent him from changing his mind. I pointed out to him that he could always re-enlist if the situation got really tough. It wasn't an easy job persuading Ram; he liked making his own decisions.

I had a few other friends, but they meant less to me. Sometimes I wouldn't see them for months. There was Eitan, who was cynical, and smart, and always mocking, and there was Gad who was cynical, and smart, and always mocking, too. Despite those shared traits, they were not alike. Eitan was a nice guy and Gad was a son of a bitch. At least neither one was boring.

I zoomed toward Ram's house through the almost empty streets. The tires screeched at every corner.

What could one do on vacations except drive like crazy?

Girls.

But neither Ram nor I knew anything about that subject. It was quite surprising, actually.

A good-looker like him and a rich smarty like me. That was really strange, when you came to think of it.

I drove into a small, narrow alley, and brought the car to a halt. I blew the horn.

After a few minutes I saw him coming out of the house. He jumped lightly over the gate and then over the car door into the seat beside me. I pulled away.

We drove around for a while through the main streets of the city and watched the young men walking with their arms around their girl friends and generally having a good time.

For a while we didn't talk, we just sat silently in the car.

"We're not doing so well," I commented finally. "I don't think we're doing so well."

"You don't, huh?"

"No."

He wasn't the type to reveal his moods, but I suspected he wasn't feeling too happy himself.

"Let's go to the Old City. Maybe we can start a fight or something."

Ram sighed.

"Oh, be your age," he said wearily.

I was driving to the Old City anyway. I went through Meah Shearim, the old quarters where the extreme orthodox Jewish group, the Neturey Karta, live.

As we were approaching I could see the bearded men in their heavy black suits and their big black hats, moving off the sidewalk to block the road.

"You can't go through there," Ram said. "It's Friday night."

"Watch me."

I stepped on the gas and the car shot forward in a beautiful sprint. We went through fast, almost hitting a couple of older people who weren't as quick as the rest in rushing to the sidewalks. When they were all far behind us, I slowed down a bit.

"You shouldn't have done that," Ram said, unamused.

I was still wondering vaguely why neither of us had a girl friend. I came to the conclusion that we were both scared of being turned down. It would be a blow to our self-image and reputation. It was all very stupid. I felt irritated.

"They've got the whole sidewalk," I said.

"You don't have to hurt their feelings."

"I can drive where I want. I don't stop them from driving in my neighborhood, do I?"

Ram leaned back in his seat, his face was hard.

"You're a spoiled child."

I was that.

"They don't go into the army," I said, trying to put some weight between the words. "They don't fight. They don't do a thing. This is their Holy City, but they won't do a thing for it, except keep other people from living the way they want."

"They pray."

Was he kidding me?

"That's beautiful."

"At least they believe in what they are doing. That's a hell of a lot more than I can say for you."

"Oh! Enough of that!" I said irritably.

We were driving on the wide road that goes around the walls, which was renamed after the paratroopers who conquered the city in the Six Day War. It was very beautiful. It never meant a thing to me, emotionally, but it was very beautiful. The walls were lit by dim yellow floodlights which made them look even more mysterious and old. The road was quite empty, and very quiet, and the air was fresh and clean. I suddenly felt sad and lonely and I took my foot off the accelerator and slowed down. Misplaced, displaced, and wasted, I thought to myself, secretly admiring my choice of words. What the hell am I doing in this world, anyway.

Compromising.

Not even between others' wills and my own. Just between others' wills and the general state of affairs. Never really having the power and the guts and the determination to have my own way.

Fighting the Arabs, for example. I had no interest in that. I never cared about the Arabs one way or another. I didn't think much of them. They were usually stupid and ignorant and extremely inefficient. So what? I didn't want to solve the nation's problems. I wanted to solve my own. Need they be the same?

They tell you you have to be proud of being a Jew. I didn't care if I was a Jew or a Moslem or a Christian. I didn't believe in religion. It was the oldest and most primitive invention of them all.

Don't worry, boys, someone is watching you from above. You can't go wrong. Jesus loves you.

If there was any God he must have been joking, anyway.

Then there was my father, who was harder to dismiss. He had plans for me. He wanted me to join the party, become a politician, fill the part he didn't have the time or the will to play himself. There's a lot of force behind any wish of my father's.

Compromise.

I hated the word.

Be great or small but don't be average. Win or lose but don't compromise.

What the hell is one worth if he can't have his own stupid way?

You can't ignore people, my mother would say, you cannot live in a void. A void.

"Hey," said Ram, "there's one for you."

I took a look. Quite far away there was a girl making her way toward us. I couldn't see her too clearly except for her white dress and her long yellow hair.

I scratched my cheek nervously with my forefinger.

"You are the guy who is always looking for beautiful blond girls," he said, almost smiling.

I sensed he knew I wasn't going to do anything. I wondered what was going on in his mind. I could never understand his attitude toward girls.

He was the big dream hero of the girls in school. He had the status of an almost sacred institution, as far as the girls were concerned. He never made anything out of it, though. Maybe, I thought, maybe he just didn't know how they felt.

Once, when we were in our last year of high school, I came to his flat after supper, to work on a history paper. It had been raining hard and I arrived at his place soaking wet.

As I entered the building I saw a nice wet, blond girl in a raincoat standing by the staircase, leaning patiently on the wall. I stopped for a moment to look at her because she was very pretty. She looked familiar. Then I realized she went to our high school. Her name was Sharon Or and she was considered a promising beauty. Members of my class mentioned her name quite often.

I hesitated for a minute. She looked at me and blushed slightly.

"Waiting for Ram?" I asked her finally with a sudden insight.

She blushed a bit more, but didn't say a word.

"Like to come up? I'm going up there now."

She shook her head.

I shrugged and started up the stairs.

"Give him my regards," she said abruptly, and walked out of the building.

"What is this Sharon Or business?" I asked him as I entered the room.

"What?"

I took off my coat.

"She was downstairs. Waiting, it seems, and quite wet, in fact."

Ram raised a dubious eyebrow.

"Silly girl," he said.

"Quite a looker."

He took my coat and hung it on the back of a chair. Then he placed the chair by the electric heater.

He stared at the floor for a moment.

"It's a pretty hard rain," he said.

"Yeah."

"Well, we'd better start studying."

He was hard to figure out.

The girl was getting near. She was coming slowly down the sidewalk on my side. I looked at her silently but she was staring down at the gray asphalt ahead of her. I couldn't see her face.

She had to be a tourist, I thought. Israeli girls usually didn't look like that. They usually didn't walk with their faces down. They were seldom on their own in this area at night.

I took a deep breath. I spoke just as she passed my door.

"Excuse me."

She looked up and stopped walking. I could get a good look at her face now. It was worth my while.

She didn't say a word, she just stopped walking.

I studied her, fascinated. I was always fascinated by beauty. Her features were delicate and composed: thin straight nose, full lips, pale blue eyes and dark eyebrows.

Ram cleared his throat.

"I'm glad I met you," I said, not thinking at all.

Her mouth curled up slightly.

"Did you?"

"Yes."

She didn't respond.

"I can't think of anything original," I said, rubbing my chin with the back of my hand, "because my mind has stopped working, but I would like to know you a lot better."

"Why?"

I put my hand down.

"Maybe I would like you," I said slowly, "I think."

She was silent for a moment, then she smiled.

"Sounds reasonable."

The wind blew her yellow hair in long waves around her face and shoulders.

"Are you from the States?"

"Yes."

I gazed at my hands, resting on the wheel.

O.K., I thought, so here we go.

"Will you join us? Please?"

She shook her head.

"Thank you, but I am on my way to meet someone."

I laughed softly to myself. Not because I was happy, just because sure, that's the way it had to be. (Spinoza.)

"Tough luck," Ram commented quietly. The girl looked at him for a moment and then turned back to me.

"Luck has nothing to do with it," I said, to no one in particular.

"What is your name?" she asked.

"Assaf. This is Ram."

"How do you do?" she said. "My name is Joy."

A bright, charming smile appeared on her lips.

"How do you do?" Ram said.

I turned to look at him, but he was again peering into the night with an expressionless face.

I turned back to her, sadly.

"I hope I'll see you again."

"Well," she shrugged, "my friend and I are probably going to be in a discotheque around here later on. Maybe you can happen to meet us there?"

And with a slight gesture of her hand, she turned and walked away.

We sat silently, our eyes following her tall retreating figure.

"Well, what do you think?" Ram's voice seemed to come through the clouds around me.

"Guess I'll have to get this one," I said.

"Oh God."

"I won't be needing Him."

"A discotheque?" he said dubiously.

"What?"

"Have you ever been in one?"

"Sure," I said, "I think so."

He shook his head slowly, still doubtful.

"It won't be so good."

"Why?"

"With your dancing?"

"Don't be narrow-minded."

"Anyway, how do you know which discotheque?"

"No one ever goes anywhere in the Old City on a Friday night, except to the Blue Goose, especially if he wants to dance. Don't you know anything?"

Ram winced in shocked disbelief.

"Where did you pick that up?"

"I saw an advertisement in the papers today, naturally."

"Naturally."

"I wonder what she meant by 'friend.' In English it could refer to either sex."

"Or both."

"Yes, there's always that."

I turned on the radio and closed my eyes. Frank Sinatra was singing "One for My Baby" with a slow caressing voice.

I had an uneasy feeling about Ram. I wasn't sure what he was thinking. He never talked much, not even to me.

For some reason, my thoughts trailed back to things that had happened a few months before. And it only increased my restlessness.

Chapter Two

IT was during the first weeks after I had been made a sergeant in Ram's company. We were doing our routine job of holding the line on the Jordan, and it wasn't too tough, when you had gotten used to it. It wasn't anything like the Suez Canal, which made Ram feel guilty. But I didn't share this attitude.

Then, one night, one of our command cars hit a mine and four soldiers were killed.

It happened in the early dawn. At the first pale light of sunrise, the command car was on its way, collecting the ambush groups. I sat by the pathway with the other four members of my squad. We were to be the last to be picked up, and we waited quite a while. We sat wrapped in our coats and blankets, shivering violently, and clinging to our weapons with numb, frozen fingers. I closed my eyes wearily and wished that the sun would rise faster. The freezing night was worse than the boiling day, especially when you had to lie motionlessly on the ground for nine hours. I always wondered how soldiers managed to fall asleep on ambushes. That was a trick I could never pull. The rattling of my teeth would wake me up immediately.

It was very quiet. The soldiers sat silently, rubbing their red eyes and yawning. I felt sorry for them. They still had two and a half years ahead of them.

From far away came the dim humming of the motor. I

opened my eyes and blinked at the bright rays of the sun. I
looked at my watch: it was ten minutes to five.

The soldiers got slowly to their feet and stretched themselves.
"Why does he drive so slowly? That son of a bitch," one of
them said sulkily.

Then there was a huge, shattering explosion.

I jumped to my feet. Somewhere someone screamed with
pain.

"It's the command car, isn't it?" one of the soldiers asked
stupidly.

I didn't answer, I was already running toward the sound
as fast as I could. The others followed after me, breathing
heavily from the effort and their excitement. The blast knocked
the command car a few yards in the air and it landed vertically
on the side of the path. When we got there we found ten
people lying on the ground. Six of the unit's soldiers were
only wounded but the other four were dead.

"Oh, my God," the soldier who had asked if it was the
command car way back at the pick-up point said. "Oh my
God."

"Come here and give me a hand," I told him, watching his
pale face and feeling my own stomach turn. "Don't just stand
there, goddammit."

Two days later, we crossed the river along with five more
companies of paratroopers, and went into a small village called
Saame. We blew it up. The village had been known to be
the base of the terrorists. We captured three of them, and
another nine were killed. We didn't touch any civilians, but
we blew up all their houses. By noon we were back on the
West Bank. We had no dead, and no wounded. The same
evening Ram and I went to Jerusalem. One of the soldiers
who had been killed by the mine had gone to school with us,
though he was three years younger.

We took a twenty-four-hour leave to pay a call on his parents.
Ram did not want to take the C.C.'s jeep and so we hitchhiked. We had started out late and weren't doing too well.

It was past eleven o'clock when we finally reached the old police station of Latrun.

This was the place where one of the bloodiest and most fruitless battles of the war of independence had taken place. The Israelis had not managed to take it then, but they did in June 1967. Since that time it has been just an old gray building, standing harmlessly on the road between Tel Aviv and Jerusalem.

Ram and I were quiet and unenthusiastic. This leave held no charm for us. We stood there on the side of the road, each immersed in his private unappealing thoughts, and not really caring if we got a ride or not.

Not many cars were passing at that time of evening but the first one that did, stopped for us. We got in the back of a big old Ford, and it pulled away from the curb and started going again. The driver was an elderly man, and his elderly wife sat beside him.

There was another passenger in the back seat at Ram's side. She was a girl of twenty years or so, quite dark and reasonably good looking. I wasn't paying much attention to her. I didn't know about Ram, because most of the time I was staring out the window, and ignoring everyone.

Anyway, after a while the girl seemed to have grown tired of the silence so she turned to us and started talking.

"Going to Jerusalem?"

"Yes," said Ram.

"On leave?"

"Yes." said Ram.

"Nice evening, isn't it?"

"Yes," said Ram. He was a talkative bastard.

There was a short pause. I imagined she was using it to get over her shock that neither of us seemed to seize this great opportunity. Soldiers were usually more forward with girls.

"Is it really tough in the paratroopers?" she started on another angle.

"So so," Ram said.

I stared aimlessly at the darkness outside trying to decide

whether it would be worth while to try getting some sleep. The springs in the seat were old and the ride was quite uncomfortable. I decided against it.

"I am studying at the university," the girl was saying. "I couldn't go into the army because I have to look after my mother who is very sick."

I turned and looked at her briefly. She was staring at the two of us with interest. Ram gazed at me uneasily and, getting no support, turned back to the girl.

"What are you studying?" he asked.

"Art."

"Oh."

I smiled to myself. In the front seat the elderly couple was taking in every word. Maybe they were thinking of their youth.

"I figure on studying myself next year," Ram added woodenly, because she was looking at him expectantly. "Once I am through with the army."

"Art?"

"No. Political science."

"And you?"

Silence.

"Hey."

I realized she was talking to me now, and tried to seem absorbed in the invisible landscape outside. I thought to myself that I could do without contributing to this conversation.

"I think your friend ignores me on purpose," the girl commented cheerfully to Ram.

"He has his moods."

"Oh."

The next thing I knew she was leaning toward me and tapping me lightly on the shoulder.

"Are you ignoring me, soldier?" she asked.

"I've been thinking," I said.

She looked at me encouragingly. The woman in the front seat turned to look back, and then, embarrassed when she met my gaze, turned around again. I smiled and shook my head thoughtfully.

"You are not being very polite, are you?" the girl asked.
"No."
She burst out laughing.
"You're cute."
I grimaced. I didn't like that word.
She shrugged and looked at Ram.
"Are you two old friends?"
"Yes," he said. "Quite."
"Comrades in arms," she said dreamily, "isn't that the strongest kind of friendship?"
I leaned my head against the window and went to sleep.
Twenty minutes later we said thanks to the old couple and got out of the car somewhere in the center of Jerusalem.
By that time I discovered to my surprise Ram and the girl, whose name was Gila, had become quite friendly.
Looking at the two of them as we walked her home, I realized that maybe he was even interested in this one. For a reticent person like himself he was doing quite a lot of talking. I inspected her again and still didn't find anything exciting there. But then, I had never been keen on brunettes.
I pushed these thoughts out of my head and tried to think of some good line to say to the dead soldier's parents, the following day. I couldn't think of any. After a few minutes we reached her house. We stood by the gate.
"Well, that's it," Ram said, finally.
"Thanks a lot, but I am afraid your friend has suffered."
"You are most welcome," I said.
She looked at me curiously.
"O.K.," Ram said.
She opened the gate, then hesitated.
"Good night, hope to see you sometime."
"Well," he said, "good night."
We walked away. After a short while we came to the corner where our routes parted.
"She seemed like quite a nice girl," Ram said.
"Yeah, not too bad."
"See you tomorrow then."

And each walked his own way.

The next morning we went to make our call. There were many people there, in the small flat, so it wasn't too hard. They were O.K. None of the family members was crying. They just sat there looking at their visitors as if they were slightly confused, and not quite there. But that was all.

Ram and I didn't have a lot to say. We just sat there for an hour and a half, or maybe more. Then we left.

"Don't make me pay such a call on your family," I told him as we walked out, "I don't really care for this kind of entertainment."

"You are not supposed to."

"Well. We can start going back now."

"We still have a few hours."

"Got any plans?"

"I've a few things to do," he said. "How about meeting at the gas station at six? That should leave us with enough time to make it."

"Anything you say, chief."

I was wondering about the few things he still had to do, but I didn't ask. I didn't believe in asking Ram questions.

We both were on leave the next weekend, but I didn't see him or hear from him till Saturday evening. This was quite unusual, so I finally got in my car and drove to his place.

It was past eight when I walked into his room and he was sitting there with Gila, engaged in conversation.

I was immediately sorry I had come.

"Sit down," Ram said.

I remained on my feet.

"Thanks, I think I'll be going."

"You just came."

"Just wanted to make sure you're still alive. You are. So I'm going."

Gila was looking at me apprehensively. She had on heavier make-up than she had that night in the car. She was even wearing earrings.

She didn't look bad at all.

"We were about to go to a movie," Ram said.

"Go right ahead."

"Why don't you come along?" Gila asked me coquettishly.

"I don't feel like it," I said.

She burst out laughing. It was a pleasant sound. Quite deep and not vulgar.

"What do you feel like doing?"

"Being on my own would be fine. Have a good time, children," I said, smiling at Ram. "Drop a line every now and again."

I went back home.

There was no one in the house. I fixed myself a sandwich and a soft drink and started wandering through the rooms and corridors. I looked at the paintings hanging all over, anywhere there was a wall. I enjoyed it. They were good pictures. My father had excellent taste, and he didn't mind spending his money on art. There were lots of portraits in the collection, and I liked them best. I loved doing portraits myself, and I was quite good at it. Faces. They could be complete on canvas as they would never be in real life.

I paced through the house for a long time, stopping now and then to refill my glass with Coca-Cola and ice. I wondered if Ram was getting to be a bit romantic in his old age. I wasn't sure I minded it. I wasn't sure I liked it, either.

My next leave was three weeks later. Ram, of course, came home a lot more often. As a re-enlisted officer he had a lot more privileges. But I didn't see him. On Saturday afternoon I started working on a painting. I drew a girl, standing in the sea, with water coming to her hips, and her long, pale hair blowing in the wind. It was a good drawing and I gave it more time than usual. Then I started painting. At eight o'clock I was still working on it when Ram and Gila came into my room.

I was a bit surprised to see them, and not at all pleased. I hated being disturbed whenever I was occupied in any way. That is occupied of my own free will.

I asked them to sit down. There wasn't anything else I could do. Ram was quiet but Gila was in high spirits and she asked me to go on painting.

She placed herself comfortably on my bed. I kept painting for half an hour or so and they both sat and just watched. After I was through I changed my clothes and brought a few bottles of Coke, cubes of ice, and three glasses from the kitchen.

I sat down on the floor and sipped the cold liquid into my throat. I leaned my head on the wall and closed my eyes. I was very tired.

"This is beautiful," Gila's voice said, referring to the picture.

I shrugged and drank some more. The world was going in circles around my head. It had flamboyant colors.

"It doesn't look like a real person, though."

"Real people are no fun," I said.

"At least they are real," she said logically.

I opened my eyes wearily, trying to express my disinterest with every muscle in my face. I probably didn't have enough muscles there. Gila looked at me pertly, and her eyes glowed joyfully. She was probably, I concluded, simply a happy type. Ram's face was blank, and he didn't say a word.

"How's life?" I asked him.

"All right."

There was a pause.

I looked quickly around the room. My eyes landed on the stereophonic record player at the other side. It seemed to be far away.

"Want me to put on a record?"

"No," said Gila.

I was relieved at that.

"Two soldiers were killed on the Canal today," I said to Ram just to keep the conversation going.

"I know."

"What are you going to do when you are released?"

The girl was really developing into a problem, I thought, opening the second bottle and adding some more ice to my glass. Why weren't they going? Couldn't two people have fun just by themselves?

"I'm going to write a book."

I had the feeling that she was going to say she knew it from the start, but she didn't.

"What about?"

"I'll find something."

"A novel?"

"Yeah."

I closed my eyes again.

"You don't seem very happy," she said suddenly.

I laughed.

"What is there to be happy about?" I asked indifferently.

"Everything."

"Hooh."

"This guy is a disgrace to the Israeli spirit," Ram said.

"Hooh, hooh," I said again.

It wasn't an interesting evening. After a while Gila started talking about art. She said she would have liked to study drama, but there weren't any good schools for that, unfortunately, not in Israel.

"What the hell keeps you here, then?" I asked hoping she would take the hint, but she just opened two big, black eyes.

"Oh, I love this country."

"You see," Ram said to me.

"Surprise, surprise," I said dolefully.

It was past midnight when they finally left.

Afterward I took the car and drove around town for a while, hoping maybe to bump into a movie star. There were none of them around. The streets were absolutely empty. Life in Jerusalem stopped after the second shows at the cinemas.

I went back home.

The next day we were training to fight in trenches. It was hot and windy and the thin desert sand that streamed through the air made it hard to see or breathe.

When we had our break I caught up with Ram who was climbing up the hill to take a look at the Dead Sea.

"It's beautiful, isn't it?" he said when I approached. He wiped the sweat and sand off his face with the back of his hand. I stood by his side, breathing heavily.

"Lousy weather," I said.

"Complaining again." He smiled.

"How do you like that broad?"

"Who?"

"Gila."

"Seems O.K."

I looked at him curiously. His face was impassive.

"Give me a drink out of your water flask," I said, giving up. "Mine's empty."

He took it out of his kit and handed it to me without shifting his eyes from the wilderness below.

I gulped the warm, tasteless water, and gave him back his bottle. I went back down the hill.

We started training again.

A few weeks later, quite late on a Friday night, I was sitting in my room trying to get drunk on a bottle of gin. I had an ice tray beside me and was lying on the floor, dropping pieces of ice into my glass and swallowing the drink as fast as I could. I could take gin very well. I was not so good with whiskey or vodka, but gin was my favorite hard drink. My father had dozens of bottles in his cellar. From time to time, I used to go there and take one or two and bring them to my room. He didn't mind anything, so long as it didn't mean wasting time.

The problem was, I could never manage to get really drunk, I just would become more clear headed at first, and later on, more tired, but that was all.

That night I wanted to get drunk, I couldn't think of anything better to do.

Genius, I thought, really impressive. Like the leading actor in a B film, with the bottle and the one-day-old beard. Only

the girl was missing, and the good looks. But what the hell?
You can't have everything.

Or maybe you can?

Maybe. But only after you're through with the goddam
army. You can't have your own way when that whole organiza-
tion is riding on your back. It is hard enough to have the
family to deal with.

Everybody talks about the injustice of the social order,
but from the point of view of the underprivileged. Maybe
being privileged is a form of injustice too.

The idea is, I thought drunkenly, the safest idea is to be
yourself. Do what you want and the hell with the rest. I am
me. I am the only one who is me. The whole world, as far
as I am concerned, is perceived through me and by me, and
by no one else. Therefore, I am the whole world. Simple.
Must have my own way then.

Maybe the other people are just an illusion. The only proof
of their existence is through my brain. Once I'm dead they're
gone too. Poor bastards, to depend on such a brain as mine.

Why can't this brain produce better people? The son of a
bitch.

Maybe he's making fun of me.

At around this point, there was a knock on the door.

"I'm not here."

Gila stepped into the room and closed the door behind her.

She took a long look at me and at the bottle and probably
also at the floor.

She was wearing a tight, short black dress which was rather
daring by local standards. She was quite small, but her figure
was not bad.

I took another gulp and hiccuped.

"I see what you mean," she said.

"Have a drink," I said politely, "since you're here. Where's
Ram?"

She seated herself on the floor beside me.

"Probably home."

She considered the bottle.

I sat up with a jerk.

"You mean he's not here?"

Her eyes were amused.

"Yes. That's what I mean."

She put the muzzle of the bottle to her mouth and swallowed. Then she started coughing. Israeli girls seldom drank alcohol.

I wanted to be sure I had it right.

"Why did you come?"

"I felt like seeing you."

I didn't even feel flattered.

"Told Ram?"

She shrugged.

"I don't belong to him," she said.

She wasn't even my type. She didn't look bad, with her long black hair, her almond-shaped eyes, and her thin make-up. Very Israeli. I wasn't interested in her, but that was beside the point, anyway.

"Just came to see your old friend Assaf?"

"That's right, a social call."

I took the bottle from her.

"How's the gin?"

"Terrible," she said.

I poured some more into my glass.

"Have anything particular on your mind?" I asked her.

She shrugged again.

"No. I just wanted to see you. You seem to be quite an interesting guy."

I leaned back against the wall for mental support.

"Listen," I told her, "I like Ram a hell of a lot more than I like you."

She just stared at me. Her chest was heaving up and down so that I could get a fair idea of its form, which was not bad at all and rather large.

"What has that got to do with anything?" she said.

"That's got everything to do with it."

She didn't move at all except to scratch her left ankle with her right toe, in a slow manner which I considered provocative. She had a nice pair of thin, delicate-looking legs.

I took another mouthful from my glass and stretched on the floor.

I closed my eyes. "So long," I said. "Be on your way."

I was listening carefully for the banging of the door when something warm and soft and perfumed was pushing on my mouth. By the time I opened my eyes, her tongue was pressing on my teeth, and her arms were around my neck, and she was giving me a rather professional treatment, indeed.

It is all well and good for religion to teach that temptations should be resisted, but it's still perverse. It's like refusing to eat because the food is good. I had my arm around Gila and was unzipping her dress, and then I thought better of it. Girls are a dime a dozen, I thought logically, but Rams are not. She was warm and soft against me. I pushed her away and got up. I walked to the other side of the room and sat at my desk.

She sat up, looking at me, sulkily.

I picked up a paperback that lay in front of me. I hadn't noticed it before. My mother had a habit of buying me detective stories for my vacations at home.

"I would like doing that," I said, "I really would. But I am not going to, so you'd better go. Otherwise, I'll have to kick you out, and I haven't got the energy."

She stood up and smoothed her dress. Her face was furious, but she forced a tight, thin smile.

"Bastard," she said, swaggering out of the room, leaving the door open.

I next saw Ram in camp. We were preparing for the 120-kilometer march, which was the army's funny way of celebrating the end of the NCO course. I had gone through this procedure once before, fourteen months back, when I was a trainee myself, and I hadn't liked it then.

Ram didn't mention Gila, so I didn't either. I didn't see

much of him because he was out of camp most of the time, inspecting the route we were about to take together with the C.C.

Ram loved to walk. He was considered the best navigator in the regiment.

I had a fever the day before we started the march. I was sick and in a bad mood and I didn't feel like doing anything at all. On the morning we set out my temperature was down again, but I felt weak and apathetic. I was too apathetic even to decide to stay in camp.

It was a long cruel walk on a long hot day. Three soldiers collapsed from exhaustion and had to quit before the end. When we started again the next morning, it crossed my mind for the first time that I was not going to make it. I felt hot and cold, and my limbs were aching.

Tough-luck Charley, I thought to myself, forcing my legs to keep their painful motion, and trying to calculate in the blur of my mind, how many kilometers we still had ahead of us.

A platoon sergeant can't afford to drop out. Not while his soldiers keep walking. Bad for the morale. Bad for discipline.

Where's your pride, Assaf? I thought. A big strong guy like you.

I transferred the submachine gun to the other shoulder and rubbed my forehead with the sleeve of my shirt.

It's spring, boy. What can be more beautiful than a walk in the mountains of Galilee on a bright spring day?

I stumbled on a hidden stone and I cursed indignantly, kicking it with the sole of my boot.

"Easy, Sarge." Three big soldiers passed me and strolled cheerfully forward.

Twenty more, I thought, eighteen at best. Nothing doing.

"How are you feeling?"

I looked to the left with an effort. Ram fell into pace beside me. He looked at me anxiously.

"Lousy."

"Just take it easy," he said quietly. "We're practically there."

"How practically?"

"Enough."

He smiled mysteriously.

"If you just don't stop, you'll make it."

"Simple, huh?" But I felt I was smiling.

"It is, actually," he said. "When one doesn't give up, there's not much that can beat him. It's ninety per cent a matter of will."

"What's the other ten per cent?" I wanted to know. "Sex?"

"Strength," he said, "but you shouldn't be too worried about that."

"Anything you say, chief."

When our destination appeared in sight, two hours later, Ram slapped me on the back and started pulling away.

"I'll go in front a bit," he said. "See you around."

He took a couple of huge steps and then stopped and turned back to me.

"Oh, by the way," he said.

He made a meaningless gesture with his hand.

"I finished the big affair with Gila," he added finally, with an effort.

I raised my eyebrows but didn't comment. I was having a hard time catching my breath.

"I didn't think it was right from the beginning," he said apologetically. Then he turned and moved quickly to the head of the line.

Chapter Three

THAT was as far as my thoughts went back.

As Frank Sinatra's last song for that evening's program came over the car radio, my thoughts trailed and shifted away. I liked the words.

"On a clear day you can see forever and ever and ever and evermore."

Ram's voice, from the other side of the car, snapped me back into the present and into reality.

"Really want to go to the Blue Goose?"

I sat up and switched the radio off.

"Yeah."

"We might as well get going then."

I turned the key in the ignition and put the lights on.

"Did you like her?"

"Oh, I don't care," he said. "I'll watch you."

The Blue Goose was just like the few other discotheques you find around Jerusalem. It was a long, cave-shaped room, with a small bar, a dancing floor, a few tables and not much more.

That night it was quite crowded with Israelis, Arabs, and lots of tourists.

Ram and I were pleased to find a single vacant table. We ordered two gin fizzes as we were instructed by the Arab waiter, and then turned to have a look around.

There was quite a lot of noise. A record was being played rather loudly, and most of the people were talking loudly. There were a few couples on the dance floor shaking and twisting in a most grotesque manner. Joy was nowhere to be seen. I ordered myself another drink and winked encouragingly at Ram's mask of boredom. I forced myself to look at the dancers to catch some of their brilliant technique. I was not fond of dancing. First of all, because I couldn't do it well, and secondly, because I felt silly when I did do it.

After half an hour of this Ram started tapping his fingers on the table impatiently. I was getting annoyed myself, because the drinks were very small and lousy, and there wasn't anything else to do but drink.

"Doesn't look too promising," Ram offered, at length.

"Hang on," I tried to convince myself, "never lose hope."

He stared at his watch and said nothing.

Then Joy stepped in.

She was accompanied by a dark, rather good-looking young man.

I forced a long, low whistle through my teeth.

Ram chuckled quietly to himself.

They looked around for a free table and seeing none, walked over to the dance floor and began dancing.

Looking at them irritated me. She was a snappy dancer and when she moved, her light hair bounced on her shoulders and flowed with her motions. I realized she was rather tall. Her partner was a bit shorter than she. At least I was tall.

They danced for a quarter of an hour or so and then there was a break in the music.

The dark man moved over to the bar to get drinks. Joy remained standing in one of the corners, leaning on a wall.

I finished Ram's drink and got to my feet. He looked up at me and his mouth curled playfully.

"Take it easy, pal."

I snapped my fingers and gave him a smile.

"Sure."

But I felt as nervous as a cat.

I walked over to her. The music started again.

"Good evening," I said to Joy.

"Hi."

She looked at me and smiled faintly. In the background, I could see her friend approaching us with two cocktails.

"Will you dance?" I asked her.

"Thank you."

She moved with me to the floor and started swaying her long, elastic body with the music. She looked at me through half closed eyes without much expression.

"You'll have to excuse my dancing," I said. "I never found it necessary to dance before, so I never did."

"Do you find it necessary now?"

"Your boy friend was hunting you with two enormous cocktails. I thought I'd better ask you to dance."

She showed two rows of white healthy teeth.

"He isn't my boy friend."

"Well, that does help."

"Are you a student?"

"No. I'm still in the army."

"You must be having a hard time, then?"

"I don't know," I said, considering it. "But I'll be through in a few weeks."

There was silence. I stepped on her foot.

"I'm sorry."

She just laughed.

"How long have you been in this country?"

"Over three months already."

I watched her body swinging with absolute ease and hoped whoever was in charge of the records would have the brains to put on something slower. I found it difficult to keep up with her.

"Immigrating?" I asked her.

"Not really."

"Just hanging around?"

"Are you kidding? I'm a hard-working girl."

"Doing what?"

"TWA office, in the King David Hotel."

"Where do you live?"

"At 22 El Rais Street. That's inside the walls."

"Age?"

"Twenty-two. White. Unmarried. Maybe you should take notes."

"My memory is quite good."

"Oh, well then."

The music stopped for a moment.

"Would you like to sit down?" I asked.

"Why not?"

We walked over and joined Ram at the table.

"You've met," I told them.

The dark young man appeared behind Joy.

"I've been looking for you," he said.

"I was picked up, meanwhile," she explained. "Girl can't be left on her own these days." She motioned him to a chair. "This is Ram, this is Assaf, and this is Muhammed."

She looked at us expectantly.

I wondered why I hadn't realized before. I felt helpless anger building inside me.

"How do you do?" Muhammed said politely.

Ram and I just nodded our heads slightly.

I stared disgustedly at my empty glass. Suddenly I wanted no part of all of this. I had nothing against those people, I told myself. People were not born good on one side of the border and bad on the other. It was all a matter of fate. Fate played with people, and they played with one another. That was all.

But then, we've been killing the Arabs and being killed by them for more than two decades now. Sentiments are not rational. They are not supposed to be.

And blood is thicker than water.

I tried to listen to the ongoing conversation.

Joy was saying that Muhammed was her neighbor, and that he was showing her around in Jerusalem.

I didn't comment on that. I was wondering if they had been

to bed together. They used to say Western girls were crazy
about dark men.

I looked at Ram. He was staring at me thoughtfully and
I was sure he was reading my thoughts. I turned my eyes away
from him.

Suddenly I became aware that no one was speaking, and
they were all looking at me. I glanced at Joy. She was studying
me with her pale blue eyes. I got the impression that she
wasn't too sure of what she saw there.

I looked back at Ram.

"I think we will be going," I said.

"Yes."

I rose.

Joy kept staring at me. The expression on her face betrayed
bewilderment, and I thought, maybe also hurt. Muhammed,
politely, looked at the table.

"So long."

"So long," said Ram, getting up.

"Good-bye," Joy said frozenly.

Muhammed nodded politely.

We walked out.

"You're a funny guy, you know," Ram said to me.

We got into the car. I sat at the wheel but didn't start the
engine. The goddam girl, I thought angrily, sitting in there in
her white dress like a goddam virgin.

"Let's go home."

I didn't react. I was trying to figure out what made me
leave like this, like a whipped dog with his tail between his
legs.

"You didn't have to go if you didn't want to, but since
we are out let's beat it."

I could have tried to ask her to come home with me. Maybe
she would have. You could never tell what a girl would do.

"Oh, for God's sake," Ram, who was above conflicts, and
above moods, and above girls, said disgustedly, "it won't do
any good to sit here all night."

"What's your hurry?" I asked aggressively, "got something better to do?"

"I had a rough week," he said placidly, "I could use some sleep."

That was true, I thought dully. The company commander had been on leave for the past ten days and Ram had taken his place. He had reason to be tired. I looked at his handsome, impassive face. His superior self-control and indifference irritated me suddenly. I couldn't match it.

"Let's go and get drunk."

"No."

"Let's go and look for girls then."

"No."

"Oh come on. Stop being too good to be human."

Shut up, I told myself. What's the matter with you? Do you have to ruin everything? O.K. So it's not your day, so what? Go back to your room and crawl into bed like a good boy.

"I'm going home now," Ram said, "if you don't want to drive me, I'll walk."

"Go."

He didn't even look surprised. His face remained blank. He started to get out of the car.

I tapped him on the shoulder and as he turned his face to me I hit him viciously on the mouth. My knuckles smashed into his teeth and it sent a stinging pain through my fist. I looked at my hand with genuine disbelief. The skin was bruised and covered with small drops of blood. I froze in my sitting position, holding my wrist in my left hand.

Ram half-fell through the door. He was up on his feet almost before he touched the ground. He walked slowly around the car and opened the door on my side. He looked at me with his calm, thoughtful eyes. Then he grabbed me by the collar and pulled me out. He did it easily, he was very strong. I saw his fist coming and I heard it connect dully with my jaw. The world began going around me in crazy circles. It finally slowed down when I slipped to the pavement and threw up my supper on the side of the car.

"A spoiled child," he said.

I saw a thin trickle of blood making its way slowly down his chin. He turned and walked away.

I put a weary hand on the handle and hoisted myself up. I got into the car and turned the radio on.

I woke up late in the morning. I shoved my head under the cold water and let it run for a while. Then I swallowed a couple of aspirin and went downstairs.

I was relieved to see that my parents had already eaten and the kitchen was empty. No family debates at least. I made myself a few pieces of buttered toast and a cup of tea.

Lately, whenever I spent any time with my parents, we ended up before too long on the subject of my future political career. Despite the fact that there were about thirty parties in the country, my father could see my career in his party very clearly in his mind. There was only one party that mattered, he said, and that was the Labor party. It was the only one that mattered because it was the only one that won. He had good connections with its leading figures. He always knew what was going on and followed it closely. Getting me into politics would not be difficult, it just required good planning. The only problem was that I wasn't interested.

I liked art. I liked literature. I didn't like politics.

There was nothing wrong with art and literature, my father said, but there was no power in them. A man had to be practical. He had been practical. In the thirty years that had passed since his father died and left him his small, crumbling bank in Tel Aviv, he hadn't wasted a day. It wasn't for money's sake. He had always dealt only with things that interested him. Economy, industry, defense, but he had had no time for politics. He bought a new Dodge every year. My mother had a small Dodge. Neither she nor my father would drive a German car.

Twenty-four years ago my father left Tel Aviv and moved to Jerusalem. He married my mother on the same day. She had also been an immigrant from Germany and was five years his junior. She hadn't come to the country before the war as he had. She had spent three years in a concentration camp. But there was no bitterness in her. I never heard her talk about that period in her life, and I couldn't sense any negative influence on her character. She was always gentle and kind and didn't seem to hate anyone. For her, the new country was the most wonderful thing in the world. It was a miracle. She didn't need anything more.

After I had breakfast, I went to the terrace and sat in the sun. The main thing was to make time pass.

Just six weeks.

I had lunch with my parents.

"This government," said my father, after we had sat down and started with the soup, "is no good."

"We have a very good Defense Minister," my mother protested gently.

This was one of the issues on which there was general agreement in the family.

"That's not the point," he said. "This government represents too many parties, that's the problem. It cannot hold any firm line. It cannot come to any decisions. Right now, not making decisions is worse than deciding wrong."

"You know," I said, wanting to irritate him a bit, "if you consider it objectively the Arabs have better arguments than we. The excuse that two thousand years ago there were Canaanite tribes here to whom we are doubtfully connected is only for laughs. Even according to that line the Arabs are no less entitled to this country than we."

He shook his head grimly. "Six million of this nation were killed because they were stuck in foreign countries, among foreign peoples. We came here so that never again could such a thing be. How's that for an argument?"

As he talked my mother looked at me anxiously with her sad brown eyes. I regretted I had started with that subject.

Mom served the meat and the potatoes.

"The only thing that matters," I said, "is that we're here, so we have to make the best of it."

"I talked with Barak, the party secretary, the other day. I told him you might be coming to work for him in a few weeks. He said welcome."

"He did? And what did I say?"

He regarded me blankly, unimpressed. "The steak is delicious," he said, turning to smile at my mother.

"I don't like it," I said.

"It was cooked specially for you," my mother said, with a hurt expression.

But I was getting worried. It seemed that he was really determined. In the past few weeks he had spent some time actually talking to me. He had never gone that far before. "I don't like it," I said again, louder.

"You have a future, maybe," he said kindly, "but you shouldn't waste time."

I sat silently at my place and ate the dessert. I saw a tall, blond girl in front of my eyes, whose body was swaying to unheard music.

If you want something, go get it. Otherwise—you'd better not want it.

I wiped my mouth with the napkin.

"O.K., I'm going."

"Ram again?" my mother asked.

"How'd you ever guess?"

I left the house and drove over to Ram's place. His family lived in a small flat in the neighboring quarter. His mother worked in a government office and had to support herself and her two sons. They didn't have a lot. But Ram was making some money himself, and it helped take the load off her back.

As I took the stairs, three at a time, up to their apartment, I remembered my behavior of the previous night, but I relied on Ram to be the type not to bear a grudge.

I rang the bell.

His mother opened the door. She was a tall, handsome woman with brown eyes and brown hair. She always dressed simply.

"Well," she said, "I haven't seen you for a long time."

I smiled back at her.

"I've been busy soldiering." I walked in. "Is the lieutenant around?"

"In his room I believe. Think you'll be able to find it?"

I shook my head dolefully. "Madam, you are underestimating me."

Udi, Ram's sixteen-year-old brother, appeared in the hall. He was almost as tall as his brother, though not quite so handsome. That still made him better looking than average.

"Hey, Assaf!" he said glowingly.

"Hi, old man."

Udi liked me.

"When are you going to start making movies, or writing books, or gangstering around?" he asked. "I am watching after you, boy."

"You keep that spirit, uncle," I said, starting toward Ram's room.

"Are you going to drag Ram with you into politics?" he asked behind me.

I frowned.

"I am not going into politics, and Ram is not willing to become a movie star, so I don't know what I can do."

I walked into Ram's room. He was sitting on his bed reading Dayan's *Sinai Campaign*. I moved over to the window and opened it. The air outside was dry and hot; it wasn't a pleasant day. I shut the window and sat at his desk. I picked up Ben Gurion's *Talks with Arab Leaders*.

Ram's interests were not hard to define.

I put the book down and stared out of the window. Everything was still and quiet, typical of early Saturday afternoon. Ram stopped reading and started shifting around. He looked at his hands and then put them inside his pockets and looked down at the floor.

"What's on?"

"Nothing," he said.

"Have any ideas?"

"No."

"Sorry you had to walk home last night."

"Good for my health."

"I don't know why there's never anything for us to do on vacations."

"Yes." He shrugged. "Fortunately we go back to the valley tomorrow."

I grimaced.

In our high school days Ram and I used to spend many weekends on short journeys to different parts of the country. We liked walking and had never had any trouble passing free time. The army had brought a change. We didn't have much of an urge to walk or travel after parading in full kit throughout the week. There wasn't a lot else we were capable of doing for amusement, except go to the movies every now and then. We were both outstandingly inefficient where having fun was concerned.

"I know the address of that American girl."

He laughed softly.

"I thought you were walking out on her."

"Better dead than red. She's better than nothing."

"Have a good time."

But I wasn't buying. "You come along too," I said.

He took his hands out of his pockets and waved them in despair.

"Can't you do anything alone? You really don't need me. It's her you're after, what the hell do you need me for? I'd only steal her from you, if anything."

"All right then, you can have her," I said.

He shook his head. "You're supposed to be all grown up now. What's the matter with you?"

I picked up Ben Gurion's book and looked at it with little interest.

"O.K.," I said drily, "want to see the football derby then?"

He peered at me sadly for a long moment and then decided to give up.

"All right. You win. Where does this bloody girl live?"

I smiled to myself. "I'll show you," I said sheepishly.

We had no problem in finding 22 El Rais Street, which turned out to be an Arab house, in a small narrow street in the Old City. It had an old green door, with no name on it, but I assumed it had to be the right one because there was no other entrance. I started feeling a bit stupid about the whole business and I was glad I had company even if he was a lot better looking.

"What are you waiting for?"

I knocked.

Joy, wearing a white dress but a different one, opened the door.

"It looks like you really like that color," I said.

"Oh, it's you."

"Yeah."

"Well."

"Actually, I was secretly hoping you would ask us to come in."

She shrugged.

"Please—come in."

"Thanks."

Muhammed had to be sitting there, of course, having himself a cup of coffee and looking good and at home. Although half-expecting it, I stopped midway in the door, but Ram pushed me forward, lightly, and closed the door behind us.

"Good afternoon," he said to the young Arab, and flashed his disarming smile.

Muhammed smiled back.

"Good afternoon," he said.

We were in a small, square room, furnished in Arab style, which gave it atmosphere, something you never find in Israeli apartments. There was a long, low table in the center and around it four small Arab stools. We sat down. Joy remained standing, leaning on the green door, looking down at us.

"Any of you want a cup of coffee?"

"Please," Ram said.

"I'd like tea," I said, a bit aggressively, hoping I could at least start a quarrel, if nothing else.

"O.K.," Joy said, "amuse yourselves in the meantime."

She disappeared into a small kitchen.

Muhammed put his small cup of Turkish coffee on the table and stared at us in polite curiosity.

"Are you students?"

"No," I said, "we're in the army."

"I am a student."

I didn't give a damn what he was and didn't want to know, but Ram's interest rose immediately. Such topics appealed to him.

"Where do you study?" he asked.

The Arab smiled faintly.

"Here in Jerusalem, at the Hebrew University. It is a most charming place."

"No student riots," Ram suggested.

"And no lynchings," I added.

Muhammed ignored me.

"It is a most charming place," he repeated.

"What do you study?" Ram asked.

"Political science and philosophy."

"Don't you think," I asked him, "that you profited quite some, here in Jerusalem, by losing the Six Day War?"

He looked at me and smiled again.

"No one likes to be ruled by strangers. Not even for a better education, but you do have more advanced systems than we have, and a very nice university."

"In which sometimes bombs explode," I helped him along, "killing students, and lecturers, and other such armed soldiers."

"Yes," he looked at me calmly, "that is most distressing."

"And yet," I said, smiling at him, "the rumor's that it is done by fellow students, who come from the eastern part of the city and who are seldom hurt on such occasions, and, in fact, rarely at all."

He just kept looking at me calmly. He was a cool one.

"I'm an Arab," he said finally. "And I am proud of it, but I would never plant a bomb in any place like a university. We are not all terrorists."

"You've just made me a happy man," I said. "See? It's easy."

Joy came into the room with the cups. She put them down on the table and sat down. I looked at her and she looked at Ram. I smiled to myself.

"Having fun?" she asked.

"Not much."

"Pity."

"Actually," I said, "what we had in mind, was to pick you up and drive around a bit, since it is such a beautiful day, etc."

"Especially etc.," she remarked. "So when are we going?"

This surprised me. I didn't expect to win at this round, and was filled with wonder.

"Whenever you're ready."

She smiled. "Always ready."

"And you?" Ram asked Muhammed as I knew he would. Ram wouldn't even shoot an enemy in the back.

The Arab shook his head. "No, thanks. I was about to leave when you came. I have some things to attend to."

"O.K.," I said, "so let's get the hell out."

We went out and told Muhammed good-bye, and so long, and see you, and started driving with Joy sitting in front, by my side, and Ram in the back seat.

"I have a virgin complex," Joy said suddenly, "that's why I wear white."

I drove to the western part of the city, trying to figure out which of the two possibilities this statement indicated. The girl seemed to be having a good time. She showed interest in everything we passed, and her face beamed.

We went for a short walk in the Israel Museum. ("Got all those statues from Billy Rose, just like that," she said as we went through the Art Garden. "How can you say this country's running out of miracles?")

After that, we went, on her request, to Yad Vashem, which is the memorial for the six million Jews that were murdered by the Nazis. It's in a small forest, on a hill on the outskirts of Jerusalem, and has a big library, and pictures, and all sorts of

other things in memorium. I would never choose to visit this
place since it is most depressing, and supposed to make one
feel sentimental and considerate, not the way I like feeling.
We walked around there for a long while, because Joy wanted
to see it all and seemed much more shocked and concerned
than I considered worth while some twenty-odd years after all
that had taken place. When we finally left I sighed with relief.
She shook her head. "That was awful," she said.

"Well, it's the past."

She looked at me with surprise.

"How can you say such a thing?"

I shrugged.

"It's probably easier for you," she commented as we approached the car, "you're Jewish."

It occurred to me, then, that she was Christian.

I drove to the Kennedy Memorial which is in the mountains,
a few kilometers away from Jerusalem. I was obsessed by the
newly acquired idea that Joy wasn't a Jew. The oppressor. The
girl with the virgin complex. I was suddenly wildly sexually
attracted to her.

The Kennedy Memorial is a white building in the shape of
a cut tree. It is surrounded by young forests and, when not
crowded, is most peaceful and pleasant. We walked around for
a while and then sat down on the low stone fence by the
parking lot. The sun was beginning to set.

"I like this place," Ram said.

"Kennedy was a good guy." I liked people who were young
and beautiful and intelligent and rich and successful. They
had to be good.

"Lousy son of a bitch the man who killed him."

"Yes."

"Was he well liked here?" Joy asked.

"Yes," Ram said again. "But then, I think Kennedy was a
symbol for youth all over the world," he added.

"So as not to get our hopes too high, he wasn't made to last
very long."

"I don't know about that," Joy said doubtfully. "I am not sure he was such a good President."

"What does that matter?" I said. "He had some charm, and style. He didn't give the President the image of an undertaker this faceless bore does now."

"Take it easy," Ram said.

"It's a gray world anyway," I persisted.

"I think I have to be going home," Joy said. She looked dreamily at the red sunset.

"What's the rush?"

"Well, I want to eat, and wash, and then go to some party I'm invited to."

I felt disappointed at that.

"O.K.," I said, "let's go."

When she got out of the car in front of her house, Joy said, "Why don't you go and have supper and then pick me up around nine?"

I hesitated because I had the feeling this invitation wasn't really sincere.

She put her small white hand on my arm for a brief moment. "Well?"

"O.K. If it means all that much to you."

She laughed and walked into the house.

The party we went to also took place in a house in the Old City.

The apartment belonged to a long-haired, strange-looking American named Alan. He seemed to be an old acquaintance of Joy's. As we entered, he came to us enthusiastically and kissed her fondly on the cheek. He was short, maybe thirty and had a big black mustache.

I disliked him immediately.

As we went farther into the long, dimly lit room, it became clear that many of the people there knew Joy. They hugged her or kissed her, or slapped her on the back, or just shouted at her from wherever they were sitting. The place was rather

crowded; mostly with Americans, but there were also a few
Israelis, and two or three Arabs. Somewhere, in the background of the semidarkened room, a record player loudly
played Aretha Franklin. Most of the guests were sitting on
the floor or on small chairs and smoking. One or two couples
were dancing, stumbling every now and then into the legs and
arms of those who were sprawled on the floors. No one seemed
to be saying much and through the thick, smoky air and faint
light, it was hard to get a good look at the faces. You could,
however, tell that they were by and large long-haired and
dirty and not particularly worth seeing. I realized that Ram
was not going to have the time of his life, and I wasn't even
sure about myself, though for different reasons.

"I hope I am not corrupting either of you," Joy said.

We finally found three neglected cushions in one of the
corners and crumpled onto them. She between the two of us.

"I wouldn't know," I said to Joy truthfully.

She was pressed close to me so that I could feel the warmth
of her body through her thin white dress. I didn't move at all,
waiting to see what would happen next.

A young American next to me handed Joy a cigarette and
she put it in her mouth and inhaled deeply. Then she took it
out and, putting her arm around my neck, placed it between
my lips. She closed her eyes.

"Have some grass, baby," she said in her low-pitched voice.

I took the smoke into my lungs and blew it out at length.
I looked down at her chest, moving slowly with her breathing.
Her breasts were clearly visible through the light material of
her dress, which was white silk. She didn't have anything under
it.

I moved my eyes away and looked up.

There were two couples on the floor, doing a slow shake.
One of the girls, a pretty black-haired American who was dancing with her eyes closed and her lips slightly parted in aban-
donment, started unbuttoning her blouse. Underneath, she
wore a black bra, and her tanned skin was sweating all over.
It was very hot. I put my hand out and touched Joy's neck.

She was still sitting with her eyes closed, her head leaning backward, against the wall. She opened her eyes and looked wearily ahead of her. I offered the burning butt in my hand to Ram but he shook his head.

"An officer and a gentleman," I said to Joy. She didn't react.

My hand went down and dug inside her dress. I touched the warm skin of her breast, it was smooth and soft.

"Dance?"

I looked up. A tall blond American, whom I had not noticed before, was leaning over us.

"Pleasure," Joy said.

She was up and away before I could say damn. The cigarette in my hand went out and I threw it on the floor. They started dancing. I glanced at Ram. He was watching the scene placidly, through half-closed eyes. He wasn't looking for kicks. Ram was there just to keep me company.

I shrugged helplessly, rested my chin on the palm of my hand and went back to regarding the blond couple. They were both excellent dancers and were obviously having a good time. In contrast with the phlegmatic, motionless figures around, they made a strangely vivid picture. Time went by and they kept swaying, showing no signs of fatigue.

Someone tapped me lightly on the shoulder.

"Have a joint, man."

Alan, the host, seated himself between Ram and me and offered me a freshly lit cigarette. His face twisted in a friendly grin.

I took the cigarette and stared at it for a moment. Then I dropped it on the floor and crushed it with the heel of my shoe.

Alan stared at me with utter bewilderment.

"Now why did you have to do that, man?" he asked thickly.

"That's what I felt like doing," I said happily.

He shook his head.

"You shouldn't have done that, man."

I put my hand out and slapped him lightly on the cheek with my forefinger.

"Don't call me 'man'," I said to him. "I am not one of your bloody American friends."

He just sat there and stared at me uncomprehendingly.

"Now, why did you say that?" he said, "I came here to settle."

I laughed for no reason.

"Yankee, go home."

"I am as good a Jew as you are."

I slapped him on the back and laughed some more. I saw Ram stiffen.

"Probably better," I said, "probably better."

Ram shook me by the shoulder and started getting to his feet.

"O.K., genius, we're on our way."

His face remained impassive. He held out his hand and helped me to my feet. Joy and the tall American stopped dancing and came over to us.

"What's going on?" she demanded.

She was sweating and her dress was glued to her breasts and to her hips, so that the brown color of her skin showed through.

"Oh, it's you again," I said.

She studied my face with cool, pale blue eyes.

"Take it easy, it's only a party."

I turned away from her.

"Oh, get out of my life."

I started walking out.

Behind me I heard Ram's calm voice. He was speaking to her.

"He has his moods." Pause. "That's just the way he is." Pause. "I'm really sorry about that." Pause. "I hope you'll have a good time." Quiet.

"Thank you."

Then he came after me.

Chapter Four

I WENT home and to bed without even brushing my teeth. I dreamed of a gray day in some unknown, ugly environment. Everything around was filthy and mucky and dirty. There was a strong, bad smell that came from nowhere. The thin gray walls, planted on the gray soil, added to the depressing atmosphere, even Joy added to it. She looked strange. Extremely thin, so thin, you could almost feel her bones underneath the S.S. uniform. Even the clothes were gray. It all seemed like a scene from a weird black and white movie. I couldn't remember why I was there. The uniform I saw, as it all came closer, was ripped and torn. The missing pieces of cloth uncovered deep, ugly wounds, smeared with black blood. I looked at the pale, strained face and the white, strawlike hair that hung around in disorder, and wondered whatever aroused my interest in this girl. I was about to walk away from there when an invisible sniper began to play with his rifle. He was a crack shot. The bullets went squarely into Joy's chest, making a dull, muffled sound as they crushed into the bone. I stuck my hands in my pockets and watched. She didn't fall down and didn't utter a word. Her eyes were opened wide and staring aimlessly. They were the only pretty thing about her. The shooting stopped abruptly but the sound didn't. It was not the same as before, and was growing louder and louder until it became almost painful. I looked around, irritated, but there was nothing to see. Only the gray soil and the gray wall and the gray sky. My eyes fell back on her face. Her mouth was working frantically and it occurred to me that the loud, unpleasant noise was the sound of her screaming. I vaguely considered telling her to be quieter about her problems when I observed that her popping eyes were no longer aimless and I closed my half-opened mouth and followed her gaze. There was a small hole in the wall, just by her feet, and there were furry creatures eagerly crawling out of it. The rats started tearing zealously at her shabby clothes. They had long, glittering teeth and big bloodshot eyes. There were dozens of them, and their number was increasing constantly. They were eating the uniform quickly and it soon all disappeared. Joy made a helpless gesture with her hand and attempted to cover her breasts with a transparent arm, then dropped it lifelessly at her side and gave up. The small animals now started biting at her flesh. Her screams subsided and she sunk quietly to her knees. Her eyes focused on me, no longer wide and horrified. I lowered mine a bit. A vicious-looking rat which was bigger than his companions, climbed on her knee and thrust his teeth in her genitals. A dark stream of blood poured out. The rat pulled his hairy head back and stared at me for a moment from dark wolfish eyes. Then he pushed in again and disappeared in the recess of her body.

I was relieved to wake up. I put on the light and peered out the window. The moon had disappeared already but the sun was not yet up. It was a little bit after three. I resented the obviousness of the dream. It left me with a bitter taste. I dressed and started hunting for a book, but there was nothing new on my shelf; I had read them all. I overcame an impulse to drive over to Joy's place.

I lay on my bed and waited for the sun to rise.

Sprawled in the back seat of a bus, a few hours later, I tried to catch up on my sleep. Ram was sitting next to me and reading the morning paper. Time's a-wasting, I thought bitterly. If I had enlisted when I should have, I would be chasing Joy at my leisure, between lectures at the university and swimming in the sea. Who needed the army?

Ram frowned at Nixon's picture and turned to the back page.

I remembered Gad saying that Nixon would be the end of Israel after completely ruining the United States first. He didn't even dislike the American President. He just considered him simple.

Gad was a born pessimist, he didn't believe that anything would ever turn out right.

He isn't doing so bad for himself right now though, I thought grimly, doing his second year in the university while you are stuck here guarding that stupid river.

Gad claimed he was studying economics in order to be rich. He didn't really care so much for money, he said, but there was nothing else to do except live well while you could. Anyway, nothing could possibly last long. With that stream of Russian arms and Chinese arms supporting the weaker side.

I tried to brush my thoughts away. Gad held no charm for me. He had a good mind but it was always calculating and scheming and plotting. I didn't like him.

In three weeks, I said to myself, it will be all over. Ram and I were supposed to get a three-week leave before our discharge. It was a custom in the army. It was supposed to help the soldier find a job and get settled in civilian life. What's three weeks against three years?

I sat up in my seat and leaned on the window sill, looking at the bare landscape we were passing. The light brown color of the soil dominated the scene but there were also increasing amounts of green. From time to time, we passed groups of Arab villagers who stood by the road and followed us with their dark, sulky eyes. I was never sure if all of them really hated us. The young, half-naked brown children often cursed at us as we drove along, but sometimes they would wave and show their big white teeth in what could easily be taken for a friendly smile. But then, those were the smaller kids.

"I wonder if the Russians are really going to move soldiers

into this area," Ram said from behind his newspaper. "If they do, we could be in a spot."

"Can't expect the Arabs to fight the whole of Israel by themselves." I said. "They've only got seven countries around here."

"On the other hand, Russia is farther from here than from Czechoslovakia."

"If we could be independent," I said, "if we didn't have to crawl to the Americans for every breath or air, they wouldn't stand a chance, even if they could bring the whole Russian army."

"Oh, they won't beat us," he said confidently, "they could just make life a lot harder."

"Make it a five years' service. You'd love it."

"Wouldn't you?"

"Anything you say, chief."

We arrived in the camp early and went to our residence. It was before ten. The soldiers were not due before eleven, and weren't supposed to go on duty until after lunch.

The camp was set on an old Jordanian base, about two miles west of the river. It consisted of a number of long asbestos huts, of the same color as the sand. They were usually teeming and swarming with flies and mosquitoes and always hot as long as the sun was out. Life fell into a routine that was only disturbed when one of our posts was attacked by guerrillas, or when we had to chase them through the hills to the caves. Gradually, that too became a routine. We would lose some soldiers but they lost many more. I often wondered to my self why they repeated the same mistakes over and over. They were always caught and killed in the same manner. They learned little from experience. That was lucky because there were always more of them than of us.

I went to my room, stretched on my bed and waited for the time to pass. After a while, Ram appeared and sat on one of the beds. He stared quietly at the ceiling for a long time, while neither of us talked. Outside the big trucks unloaded the freshly returned soldiers. Their voices, discussing their girl friends of the previous night, filled the air and finally faded away as they strolled to their huts.

Ram got up and shook himself back to life.

"Have everyone in the yard by eleven-thirty, will you?" he said and walked out of the room.

I turned on my small radio, and went to sleep.

After lunch, the company was gathered outside the mess hall, and Yoav, the company commander, made his usual short speech. He outlined the scheduled activities for the next days. There was nothing extraordinary about any of them.

Thus, another week started.

In the evening, Ram took the company for a 10-kilometer run. He used to do that every Sunday, if there wasn't anything more important to do. Ram was the best long-distance runner in the regiment. I was sitting alone in the canteen with a bar of chocolate and a few bottles of Coke, when he gathered the men outside in the yard. There were about forty of them there, the upper parts of their bodies bare, all the soldiers that weren't on duty that night.

"O.K.," Ram was saying quietly, "all the lame and sick can fall out."

No one did.

I raised my eyebrows, and took a big swig; Ram's methods often surprised me.

"Let's go then."

He turned, and started running into the darkness. The three lines of men soon disappeared after him.

Ram believed that soldiers with six months of army behind them could be trusted with some free choice in matters that weren't strictly operational. He didn't force soldiers to run 10 kilometers if they said they were sick. After all, people could feel sick, he told me. It had even happened to him.

In his recruiting days, when his platoon had done the traditional 8-kilometer "white circle," for the first time, Ram hardly made it. He had been lying on his bunk, coughing and sweating, when the squad commander called everyone out.

Ram cursed under his breath as he got to his feet. He disliked any kind of evasion. Soldiers were not supposed to have an easy time. He had liked making the extra effort that was a part of army life. But he knew he was finished for the day. There was no sense in overlooking the fact that he just wasn't well.

He got out of the tent and joined the rest of the soldiers. Most faces revealed displeasure. The "white circle," the sandy pathway circling the camp, was not well liked by the young recruits.

"O.K. Let's start hearing about all your sicknesses," the corporal said scornfully, "but it won't help you, nobody's staying here who isn't dead."

Ram, listening to the jeering voice, disapproved of its owner and of its owner's attitude. He thought about it as they started running and he still had it in the back of his mind when they were doing the last few hundred meters. He could see the faint light coming through the window of the supply room and he fixed his eyes on it, and tried to empty his mind of any other thought. When we get to the light, he thought obscurely, trying to wet his dry lips with his dry tongue, we will stop, that can't be too hard. When they reached the light and stopped, he ran a few meters more into the small group of eucalyptus trees, puked out his lunch and then lay on his back on the dry, brown leaves and closed his eyes. A corporal who discovered him there an hour later, walked him to the sickroom. He remained there for two days till his fever was down and he was back to normal again. Ram told me he had felt very silly about that incident. He disliked weaknesses in himself.

I was sitting in the canteen when the group of runners returned. A few minutes later, after Ram had relieved them, he walked in.

"Give me a big gulp from that thing and I'm gone," he said cheerfully as he approached me. "What would Coca-Cola ever do without you?"

"They'd give up," I said as he picked the sixth and last

bottle from my table and emptied it. "Not all of it, for God's sake, not all of it."

"I'm going to visit the northern posts," he announced, ignoring my protest. "Want to come?"

"Are you kidding me? It's way past my bedtime."

He shrugged. "Well, don't say I didn't give you the chance."

"Much obliged, but I'd rather go to sleep."

"O.K."

He started moving away, and stopped.

"Want to do me a favor?"

"No."

"See that the cook has hot coffee when the ambush squads are back."

"Yes, sir."

"Well, see you."

Ram was going out a lot on patrols and night reconnaissances. His impending release made him intensify his efforts and activities to the maximum. He couldn't stand the thought of resting. I, on the other hand, was having myself a relatively easy time. As a platoon sergeant, there wasn't a great deal I had to do. And what I didn't have to do, I didn't do.

"I am willing to bet you ten to one," Ruthi, the company clerk, said to me, "that he will sign up as a career officer, before his time is up."

We were sitting in the canteen on a late Friday evening, listening to the old music that blared from an old, crackling record player. The company commander had picked it up earlier in the evening, along with a few records and a couple of female guests, from a mysterious distant camp. The whole company, including the officers, had remained on our base. There had been rumors that some activity could be expected. Most soldiers were on guard duty or laying in ambush. Those of the cadre who weren't otherwise occupied, were gathered in the canteen, having a reasonably good time.

"Not Ram," I said. "I've been watching over him."

"Brother," she said, "so have I."

Ruthi had been with our company for the last three months. She was a pretty girl with blue eyes and short black hair. The soldiers liked her. In the small world of weary, bored men, her presence had a magical effect on morale. It gave the people the feeling they were not altogether cut off from their previous normal way of life.

We sat in a corner and watched the C.C. and another officer tangoing vigorously with two of the unknown girls. It was an amusing sight. The C.C. was six feet four with a neck that would have looked big on a bull. The fragile-looking girl he was holding gently, careful not to break her, completely disappeared in his huge arms.

The captain was one of the soldiers whom the chief of staff had commended for bravery and leadership during the Six Days War. He had personally destroyed two machine-gun posts during the fighting in Gaza and then led his men into the bunkers, suffering no casualties. He had been a lieutenant at the time, and was promoted soon afterward. He was one of those men who were expected to be generals at thirty-five, if they ever lived to be twenty-five in the first place. I didn't particularly like the C.C., but I admired his courage. He and Ram were good friends and had great respect for each other. I knew the captain was pressing Ram not to leave the army. Occasionally, I was afraid he was going to succeed with that mission. The trouble with this kind of man, I thought, looking at the broad shouldered officer who was smiling jovially down at his partner, squeezing her delicately with his massive powerful hands, the trouble with these men is that they identify so much with the army. There must be something wrong with a person who wants only to be a soldier.

"How do you like him?" I asked Ruthi, pointing to the captain's swaying figure with my thumb.

"I don't know," she said indifferently, "he's O.K."

"Maybe you could have the next dance with him."

"Don't guess I will."

"Still waiting for the special someone?"

"Maybe."

Ram had taken the C.C.'s jeep earlier in the evening and gone on a private checking patrol of his own. I was feeling that this was the cause of Ruthi's irritation, but didn't bother to ask.

"Have some Coke," I told her.

The C.C. and his girl passed by our table as they danced. He winked at me. "Got the champagne ready for your party?" he asked.

Ram and I were to celebrate the occasion of our discharge in the usual manner by buying drinks for everybody and making a sad speech.

"We're still raising the money for it."

He laughed and danced away toward the other side of the room.

I opened another bottle.

"Well, well, what do you know," said Ruthi, whistling quietly through her teeth. Ram, with his submachine gun hanging loosely on his shoulder, was coming through the door, gently pushing a young Arab of seventeen or eighteen in front of him. The Arab was in khaki clothes and barefoot. He looked rather scared.

The C.C. stopped dancing and walked over to where Ram and his prisoner were standing, as did the rest of us.

It turned out that Ram had spotted his prisoner some two kilometers north of the camp. As he turned on his searchlight, ready to open fire, he realized that the man was unarmed. So, instead of shooting, he started the motor and chased him with the jeep. Ram was a crazy driver when he chose to be, and he caught the fleeing man.

The C.C. said the prisoner would have to stay in the camp for the night. In the morning, he would be transferred to headquarters. The young Arab insisted that he had been on his way to visit his family, when he was captured.

I asked Ram to sit down and help himself to a drink, but he said he had to do something about the young Arab first, and that he would come back later. After Ram left with his prisoner, the C.C. started dancing again and I sat back at the table with Ruthi, continuing to waste soft drinks.

Ram took his Arab to the small cell that served as the camp's prison. It was in the same shack as the guardroom. He locked him in there, and freed the soldier who had been put in the previous day for a discipline offense.

Afterward, he went into the guardroom and told the soldier who was on duty there to look after the prisoner and give him something to eat. When he was through with that, Ram came back to the canteen. It was past twelve when he joined us at the table. He sat down and put his submachine gun under the table. Finishing one of my nearly empty bottles, he looked at me wearily.

"So how are you making out with my girl friend here?" he asked.

"I don't know," I said gloomily. "I don't seem to be getting anywhere."

"You mean you've already finished your day's work?" Ruthi asked Ram sardonically, opening big blue, wondering eyes.

"Almost."

"Think you can really spend some time here?"

"A bit."

"Then, will you dance with me, officer, sir?"

He smiled.

"You know I never dance," he said apologetically.

"Well then," she said, "it looks like I'll have to ask the C.C. himself, after all."

Ram looked down at the table. His face was tired. When he looked up at her again she was staring steadily at the dance floor. Her fingers tapped on the table to the rhythm of the music, but her face was hard.

No one spoke. We all sat and watched the dancers. I thought to myself it was lucky the next day was Saturday. I was getting rather tired.

Finally, Ram picked up his weapon and got to his feet.

"I'll go and see if everyone is on his watch and then I'll

hit the sack," he said to both of us and to no one in particular. "See you around."

He walked away.

Ruthi looked at his retreating back and put a bottle to her mouth. She drank and then slammed it angrily on the table.

"That man!" she said with sudden fury. "You can't get to him. I don't know what's driving him. Dammit. I can't get to him at all."

"O.K.," I said. "Take it easy."

"I don't understand that guy," she went on with her monologue. "What kick does he get out of life? What kick does he get out of all this? I don't believe he enjoys any damn thing, except doing his goddam duty, saving his country, and keeping everyone happy. He gets on my nerves."

"Drink some more, it's Friday night, remember? Everyone should have a good time."

"You know," she said, "do you know that he is the only goddam officer in this camp who never tried to make me?"

"Tough luck."

"It tastes lousy, actually," she said, putting down another empty bottle with disgust. "I don't understand him."

I shrugged.

"Why don't you go and tell him?"

She laughed.

"Oh, God," she said. "I am beginning to feel unhappy. I should go to sleep."

"Haven't danced with the C.C. yet."

"Oh, screw him."

"Now, is that any way to talk?"

She rose to her feet.

"Well."

I got up too.

"Wait," I said. "I'll accompany you. A young lady shouldn't walk all alone in the streets at night."

"That's so true," she said icily.

The shack in which she lived was on the other side of the

camp. We walked slowly on the sand paths among the asbestos huts. After a while Ruthi said, "It's funny how peaceful and secure this place seems. It almost gives you the feeling there has never been a Fatah."

Then she laughed.

"Well, I guess," she said, "that while Ram is out there checking the guards, this place is safe."

"Probably."

"I really like that guy," she said, "but it irritates me so much that he seems to have no feelings."

"For God's sake. Can't you change the subject for two seconds."

Her face was darker than the night.

"You're another one," she said venomously.

"You don't say."

"Go to hell!"

"Actually," I mused, "I don't even think you're right about Ram."

"What?"

"You know Rotman?"

"Our Rotman?"

"That's the man. Let me tell you a story about Ram and Rotman."

I was wondering contemptuously what made me so talkative all of a sudden, but I carried on just the same. I told Ruthi my story.

A few weeks after I got into the company we left the camp and started a month of field exercise. It was a relatively hard time with little sleep and no leaves. On the last night we parachuted onto the seashore, and then we had to walk to the camp. It was a distance of about 50 kilometers and there was supposed to be a competition between the three platoons to see which of them would get all its men to the camp first.

The first 45 kilometers went pretty well. They were hectic, but we were walking fast and making good time. Then, all of a sudden one soldier sat down on the ground and said he couldn't walk any more. Rotman was one of the biggest men in the company. He wasn't just big, he was also tough. He was a damned good soldier when he wanted to be, but he seldom cared. He was a difficult guy to handle, undisciplined and aggressive. When he was in one of his bleak, melancholic moods, which was quite often, he would give his superiors a real hard time. Ram had been in charge of our platoon that night as our second lieutenant was in the hospital with a broken leg. He looked back over his shoulder to discover the source of some unexpected complaining. Observing Rotman's figure sitting in the middle of the path, he quickly walked back.

"What's the matter?"

"I can't walk any more, sir."

Rotman looked at Ram with a grim, indifferent expression.

"What the hell's the matter with you?"

Rotman shook his head.

"Can't walk any more," he repeated.

Ram looked at the small cunning eyes and his anger rose. He was sure this was just a show. He grabbed the big, husky man by the collar and pulled him to his feet.

"You walk."

"I cannot move, sir."

Around them, the soldiers began to gather and halt, looking curiously at the scene.

Ram spun around, angrily.

"You carry on," he said to the soldiers. "Don't anyone stop."

He waited till they moved away, then turned back to Rotman.

"Now you walk too."

"I really hate to refuse, sir," the other said calmly, "but I just can't move any more."

Ram cooled himself down.

"Why not?" he asked quietly.

"My stomach hurts, and my legs."

I stopped alongside them. Ram turned to me briskly.

"See that no one slows down."

"All right," he returned to Rotman, quite calmly, "you can't walk, I'll carry you then."

He caught the soldier by his feet and by his shoulders, and with a sudden effort hoisted him over his back. Rotman wasn't exactly a lightweight, but neither was Ram, and straightening his back, Ram half-ran, half-walked until he reached the head of the line of men.

"O.K.," he told the weary, astonished soldiers who stared at him, "I know you're tired. So am I. It's a quarter past seven now. At eight we'll be in the camp. Then you can rest."

He turned his back to them and, bracing himself, started moving again, half-walking and half-running as before. The rest followed him, impressed, and trying not to lag behind. I brought up the rear for a while, but after we covered about three more kilometers I moved forward and caught up with Ram. His face was red and he was sweating all over, but he didn't slow down.

"Why kill yourself?" I said. "Let the soldiers carry him."

"Don't let's waste time," he said curtly.

I knew he wanted to win the competition, and I knew he was furious at the strong guy he was carrying. That could make him quite unbreakable, but carrying eighty-five kilos for five kilometers was a tough task, even for Ram.

"I feel sick," Rotman said quietly.

I believed him. He couldn't have been having a good time. Ram's shoulders were bony and hard.

"Shut up."

We kept on.

For the last kilometer I carried Rotman myself and it nearly broke me, although I had never been weak. But we were walking very fast. Our platoon was the first to reach the base and that improved our mood. On the last few hundred meters, between the gate and our tents, we even managed to sing at the top of our voices.

At the end of the day, the soldiers of the platoon got a free evening. Ram didn't feel like leaving the camp so I hitchhiked to Netania alone and went to see a movie.

Ram sat in the canteen for a while. Then, around ten, he decided that there was nothing better to do than go to sleep.

He started walking toward the encampment. As he was passing by the platoon's camp, he heard loud voices from one of the tents arguing. He stopped by and listened.

"What was all that show for?" a voice asked.

"Wanted to teach our great big officer a lesson. Educate him a bit," Rotman said. "He finished the officers' course as a distinguished cadet, so he thinks he's a god."

"Oh, come on. He is a good officer."

"So?"

There was silence.

"I am surprised at you," someone said sardonically, "that you of all people should break down like that."

Rotman laughed softly.

"Could have walked another 50 kilometers easily. What for? Guy wanted his men to be first, so I figured out I might as well spoil his party. Childish thing, competition."

"We did win though."

"How could I guess he'd carry me the whole way? Guy likes punishing himself."

He was quiet for a moment.

"I don't like officers," he added simply.

Ram walked slowly away. He stopped and leaned against a tall eucalyptus tree, surprised at the bitterness he felt. Maybe he's right, he thought. Maybe I'm just trying too hard. Rotman was no fool, the bastard. But then, what's the use in doing anything if you're not doing the best you can?

Anyway, you can't change your character; nobody ever changes. You can only think you change, but that is all. Stupid thinking, he told himself irritated, you better go to sleep. That's the best thing you can do right now.

There was a faint sound of footsteps and he forced his eyes to open. The fly of the tent had been turned aside and a tall figure emerged and started walking on the path toward him. Ram watched him silently. The soldier kept advancing in his direction, humming in a low voice. When Ram spoke, Rotman still did not see him because of the dark.

"Rotman."

The big figure flinched. Then it stopped and looked hesitantly around.

"Rotman."

The wandering gaze fell on Ram's face in the shadow of the tree.

"Yes, sir."

Ram straightened himself and dropped his arms down to his hips. He stared curiously at the set, tense face beside him.

"How are you feeling?"

"What?" He seemed surprised. "O.K., I'm O.K. now."

"Feet don't hurt any more?"

"No."

"And the stomach?"

"No, sir." His voice regained its usual placidness. "I am feeling fine now."

Ram looked at him thoughtfully.

"Well, that's good," he said softly.

Then, he swung his right arm back and drove his fist into the soldier's stomach. His expression still remained thoughtful and curious as Rotman took two steps back and doubled up. He opened his mouth in a desperate attempt to breathe. Ram hit him in the jaw, putting all his weight behind the blow. Rotman crumbled and fell to the ground. Ram bent over him and looked down.

"It's against army rules, actually," he said thoughtfully.

He got no answer to that.

"So you see," I said, concluding my story, "even Ram's a sentimental baby sometimes."

Ruthi looked at me dubiously.

"Did he complain?"

"Who, Rotman? No. He isn't that type. Ram told me he wasn't worried about that, he was just worried he wouldn't be able to hit him hard enough to prevent him from getting up and hitting back." I laughed for no good reason. "Rotman is a toughy himself."

"It seems."

We reached her hut and stopped by the door. She looked

rather good just then, in the dark, although I never went much for girls in uniform. Joy's image, in her light white dress appeared before my eyes and insisted on staying there.

I grimaced.

"Well, then, I guess I'll go to bed," Ruthi said.

"If you don't invite me, I won't join you," I said, "so I'm going to my room."

She frowned.

"You didn't really give it much of a try, did you?"

"I sensed the uselessness of such an attempt."

"Did you?"

She fished her key out, and turned to the door.

"Good night."

"Flights of angels," I said.

As I walked away, Eitan's stupid remark that one always misses the army once he's out of it floated into my mind. It irritated me for a moment, until I reminded myself that he had said it sarcastically. Eitan never meant anything he said. He had a good sense of humor, that's why I liked him. He said that the Israeli situation was getting to stupid to be taken seriously. Once you started thinking seriously you could find yourself concluding that we couldn't beat the Russians. Nor the Chinese.

Life was O.K. so long as you didn't think.

Eitan had been an officer in the tank corps. Now he was studying art in Jerusalem. A strange combination. I passed by Ram's shack. There was light coming from his window, so I stepped into his room. He was sitting on his bed with a newspaper, trying to fill in a crossword puzzle. His two roommates were still in the canteen. I sat on one of the empty beds.

"A philosopher, starting with B, five letters."

"Try Bacon," I suggested.

"Looks reasonable."

He wrote it down and lapsed into silence again. From time to time he added something with his pencil, never lifting his face.

"Do you really like doing that?" I asked, curious.

"It's not so bad."

I shrugged.

"Freud's term for sexual energy?"

"Try libido."

"That works."

"Ruthi says you irritate her."

His eyebrows went up.

"Why?"

"Not expressing yourself openly."

"Oh." He wrote something down. "She's a nice girl, though."

"I think I'll go to sleep," I said. "I drank too much Coke."

He put his paper down and looked at me.

"You have only two more weeks to go," he said. "You must be counting the minutes."

"I'm holding my breath. How much do you have?"

"Oh, the same."

"Yeah, well, I'll be going."

I moved toward the door. He suddenly got up and walked after me.

"Let's hear some clever opinions," he said, to my utter surprise. "Do you think it's really the right thing for me to study political science?" He was smiling, half-apologetically, but his eyes were keen, and his brow a bit wrinkled. It embarrassed me to realize that I wasn't sure what to say.

He strolled back to his bed and sat down.

"If I stay in the army, I'll probably get killed some day."

He drew a circle on the sheet with his thumb and then smoothed it with his palm.

"You don't last long in this sort of profession. The funny thing is, I don't think I want to die."

He looked up at me apologetically.

"It is awfully stupid," he said curiously.

I leaned on the door and stuck my hands in my pockets.

"One can always go back to the army," I said. "What's the rush? After a year or two out you will be able to see for yourself. Studying can't do you anything but good. The army is an awfully limiting institution."

He stared at his hands. I had an uneasy feeling that I hadn't said what he was hoping to hear, but I couldn't put my finger on it. When he looked at me again, his face had its usual blank expression.

"Well," he said, "it doesn't matter. I'd better go to sleep. I don't think I'm functioning too well right now." He started unbuttoning his shirt.

"O.K."

I opened the door.

"Still thinking about this girl, Joy?"

"Not much," I said.

Ram's body was strong and brown and muscular. He had two small pale scars, on his chest, a souvenir from the war.

"I think she is very nice."

"I don't know," I said. "Good night."

He smiled briefly.

"Sweet dreams."

I walked to my room and went to bed. I didn't have sweet dreams. I was under the spell of words I had never expected to hear. They filled my mind. When did he ever talk in that manner? I couldn't think of any such occasion, ever. Except maybe, that time when he told me about the war. Ram did not like telling stories, and I thought he knew the subject was not pleasant to me. We did get to talk about the war one time, though. He had been in one of his rare talkative moods, sitting in his room late one night. So he talked.

His company had been stationed for about two weeks somewhere along the southern border, before they finally received the order to move. Those two weeks had been the hardest part of it all. They were nerve-wracking because the soldiers didn't know what was going to happen. Ram, a very new officer, had tried to put all his time and efforts into training and organizing his platoon. There was not much sense, he reasoned, in trying to guess the future. They would have to solve their future problems when the time came. Throughout the two weeks, almost every day, the company commander said that the war was due to begin at any minute. And with every day that passed the soldiers grew more doubtful. If they were really supposed to fight, what were they waiting for? The newspapers and radio discussed the possibility of the negotiations for a peace solution and of wakening the conscience of the world and the United Nations, a conscience which, every fool knew, was nonexistent. Many people had been making speeches, and many promises. They all amounted to a big, fat zero. What were they waiting for?

Ram, sitting on the sandy ground by himself, one warm June night, had been calculating indignantly what it had been that took the enthusiasm out of him. He didn't really like any of this. He didn't want to fight, he didn't want to kill. He didn't want to get killed. He would have liked it to go on forever in the training camp, where it was just make-believe. The fact is, second lieutenant, he told himself, that you are completely phony. And you don't even know it yourself any more. That's no way to talk to an officer, he thought sarcastically. Where are your manners? Let's be polite with ourselves, he went on, maybe we'll be dead soon.

Early next morning Ram's company went across the border and started advancing into the desert. He sat in the half-track, not nervous and not worried any more. He was almost happy. No more bullshit. This was finally it. Finally the war.

The word didn't seem to have meaning, in the beginning. They moved deeper and deeper into the sands without meeting any real resistance. From time to time there were single bursts of fire aimed at them, and far away they could see small, retreating figures. But none of it had any real meaning so far; maybe because none of the soldiers had been hurt.

The town of Han Yunis surrendered after offering only token resistance. As the long line of Israeli motorized forces passed through the main streets of the city, Ram found himself musing that maybe the whole war would be as easy as it had been so far. Through his thoughts he heard the menacing hammering of a machine gun and he jerked up and looked around. A bowed figure in khaki was standing in one of the courtyards, behind a low concrete wall. The figure silhouetted against a large white flat held its long, gleaming weapon and was operating it smoothly, aiming straight at them. Ram grabbed his machine gun and fired two short bursts of fire. The speed and efficiency of his own movement surprised him. The figure collapsed on the wall immediately, dropping the machine gun on the ground. Ram turned his gaze back to the track. Got to be more careful, he told himself somberly, white flags or not. One of the soldiers caught his eye. A very comfortable soldier, leaning luxuriously on the metal wall of the track, and dozing in perfect indifference.

An indifferent bastard.

Ram knelt toward him and shook him violently by the sleeve of his shirt.

"It's not bedtime yet!" he shouted over the screaming of the motor. The soldier moved from his position by the track's side and leaned heavily on Ram's arm, pouring on it a stream of red, hot fluid. All the soldiers watched him wordlessly. Then, hoisting him to his former position, Ram pulled back, wiping his hand on his shirt. He looked sideways again, digging his fingers into the deadly piece of metal in his hand. The white flags could be seen everywhere. Frightened faces peered out from behind them.

"Don't rest," he told his men, feeling hot fury inside himself. "Shoot anything that moves."

But at it turned out, they left the town without further interruptions and moved on.

All the way to Gaza they did not meet with any genuine fighting. They didn't see many enemy soldiers and those they saw were on the run. They couldn't possibly lose, the opponent was not up to fighting them. They had expected trouble on entering Gaza, and didn't meet with it. But they still had the posts on the surrounding hills to conquer. It was not an appealing task, but they did have the advantage of surprising the enemy. The Egyptians were entrenched with their backs facing Ram's company. When they realized the Israelis were behind them, it was already too late and they started running.

Ram stormed forward in front of his men, shooting nonstop and not looking back to see how they were advancing. It was simple. There was no need to think of anything. He hoped he hadn't left the others enough time to think, either.

When he reached the advance positions, he found them deserted. All the other positions were deserted too.

Afterward they went slowly into the smoking trenches. There were a lot of corpses lying around. He walked at the head of a row of men, watching every burnt Egyptian body with great care, never moving his finger from the trigger. But none of the figures showed any sign of life.

He stopped when he reached the end of the trench. The soldiers were spread around, looking down as they walked. Ram turned and started moving again when his gaze fell on one of the corpses he had passed before. His mouth went dry. The Egyptian soldier was still lying in the same place and in the same position. Only now his eyes were open. The finger on the trigger was white, and the barrel of the Kalachnikov was pointed directly at Ram's face.

Ram breathed slowly as he moved his right hand with the submachine gun for what seemed to him an infinite length of time. Then, there was a brisk, humming sound, somewhere behind him. The Egyptian's face was suddenly covered with blood, and he loosened his grip on his weapon. It slid soundlessly into the sand.

Ram turned his head with an effort and looked back. On the slope near him, one of his soldiers was fitting a new magazine into his rifle.

"He was going to shoot you," the soldier said excitedly.

"I know," Ram said.

He wiped his cold face with his sleeve and breathed deeply. You almost managed, he thought to himself, almost.

He climbed slowly out of the trench, and slapped the soldier lightly on his arm.

"Thanks."

He was surprised to see the sudden embarrassment on the soldier's still excited face. He didn't say a word.

Ram started walking slowly up the hill. He saw the tall, stout figure of the C.C. moving toward him from the other direction.

"How does it look to you?" the C.C. asked.

They stood on the hillside, looking around them. The wide area below had fallen into a deceptive silence. Far away there were dim sounds of explosions.

"I don't know. We couldn't have gotten all of them, but I don't see anyone around now."

The C.C. reached in his pocket and produced a clean, neatly folded handkerchief. Ram wondered vaguely where he had gotten that carefully ironed, delicate-looking, piece of white cloth. The company commander was not married. It must be his mother, Ram concluded, feeling a strange, absurd need to burst out laughing. Wonder what his mother looks like, he thought; he must have been an awfully large baby. The C.C. mopped his brow. He must be having a hard time, Ram thought. He had only been appointed to his new post a few weeks before. It couldn't have been easy to become acquainted with your first company at a time like this. He felt great respect for the big, self-assured man.

"We have finished our part here," the C.C. said. "We have to wait till we get the order to move. Meanwhile, you better let your men get some rest."

Ram nodded. His eyes wandered to the slope above them and fell on two dark pits on the hillside, a few dozen yards from where they were standing.

"Anyone checked these holes?"

The C.C. shrugged. "I don't know."

"I'll go and have a look," Ram said, "I think that could have been their command post." Then he checked his sub-machine gun, filled all the magazines with bullets, and started climbing up the hill.

It was past six o'clock, and the sun had begun to set. It

colored the sky in the west with deep red, and Ram, walking up the hill, marveled at its beauty. He didn't want to shift his eyes away from the flamboyant cheerful colors.

Turning his eyes back to the two caves, he became alert. He approached the opening soundlessly and stood by it for a few seconds, listening. He thought he heard a low rustle but it could easily have been the wind. He took his last grenade and threw it in. After waiting a few seconds, he followed it, shooting two bursts of fire as he entered. Nothing happened. It took his eyes some time to get used to the darkness inside but he couldn't see anything suspicious.

He refilled the magazine of his gun and stepped out of the first cave. He approached the second one and sprayed it with bullets, then he pressed himself against the wall outside and waited. Again nothing happened. He stepped in and took a careful look around, but there was nothing of interest to be seen.

It must have served some purpose, he thought, hanging his submachine gun on his shoulder and starting down. There were unused cartridges and empty boxes in there, but that was all. That didn't seem important. The sun had disappeared over the horizon, throwing a peculiar, unnatural light upon the houses and streets of the town. Closer to him, the soldiers were sprawled on the ground. The light breeze brought with it the dim sound of their voices.

Ram raised his hand and pushed back a curl of brown hair that fell in his eyes. He suddenly felt the burden of the whole day and a weariness that seemed to draw him to the ground. You're growing old, Ram thought contemptuously, better go down and get some rest.

He heard a low, metallic sound behind him and started turning around. The roar of an automatic weapon drummed in his ears, and then he felt a sudden burning pain that spun him halfway back.

Ram sank slowly to his feet and then fell on his face and lay on the ground. With an effort he dug his fingers into the slippery sand and stopped himself from rolling down. He breathed hard. His submachine gun thrust against his ribs.

Can't even move it away, he thought.

Can't even have one lousy shot.

Where had he been hiding all that time?

You'll probably never know, he thought, doesn't matter now, anyway. Not any more.

Can't get to my feet.

He let himself roll down a bit and turn on his back, careful not to lose his grip on the sand.

At least we can have a look at the sky.

He lay with his eyes open, looking up.

Well, that's it, that's the way it had to be.

Can't really come as a surprise to you.

But it does, he thought.

As his fingers suddenly relaxed and straightened, his eyes shut and the crimson sky blurred and went away.

He started rolling down the hill.

I had been going through this over and over again, trying to imagine the scene in my mind. It was somehow painful to me, and yet I couldn't resist it. It held a strange fascination. The picture of Ram lying motionless at the bottom of the hill kept coming back to my mind. It was always the same.

The only actual traces of the wound were the two small, pale scars. The doctor had said he used the luck of a lifetime, getting away with it as easily as that. But Ram was not happy about it. The war lasted six days, and he missed more than five of them. I assumed that that was one of the main reasons he decided to sign up for another year's service. He thought he still owed the army something for not being with his platoon throughout the whole war.

It was peculiar for Ram to say all this, I thought, to talk about not wanting to die. It made me feel restless.

You had to live fast, I thought, as long as you could. A good-looking blonde would help a lot.

Saturday dragged on long and boring. I spent some of it playing chess with Ram. I won, but it still didn't make the day shorter. Most of the soldiers sat in their rooms and played Shesh-Besh from morning till night, but I didn't like that game. I went to bed early that evening on the assumption that sleep helps time pass more quickly, but I couldn't fall asleep. It was too damn hot.

It was that night, lying awake in my bed, that I thought seriously for the first time of writing a book. The idea appealed to me. It could be a challenge. With a bit of luck it could get me started in a big way.

It seemed better than politics.

I racked my brain but couldn't think of any satisfying plot. I welcomed sleep when I felt it taking hold of me. It prevented me from having to admit defeat.

The next morning, Ram took a group of soldiers on a long day's reconnaissance. We walked the sandpath along the river. There had been some vague information of a possible penetration by one or two groups of Arabs the night before. It didn't have much credibility as the source was not considered reliable, but we walked cautiously, just the same. Ram and I walked in the lead, with him carrying the small wireless communication instrument and acknowledging our position every now and then. The bald wilderness of the Judean hills made an eye-catching view but I wasn't interested in it any more. I had seen it before.

"You know," I said to Ram, "this could be good scenery for making a movie, if you're not so dumb as to use the usual heroic stuff for a plot. Some modern Israeli story, about young people, but with no heroes; that would really make a hit."

"I thought you were going to write novels, or study political science, or something."

"What's the matter with movies?"

"Just thought one thing at a time might do."

"I don't know."

We kept walking. The sun was climbing to the top of the sky, making our throats turn dry.

"Figure there's any of them around?"

"I don't think so," he said.

"Two more years," a soldier behind me was saying to his friend. "I've got exactly two more years and I'm through, can you believe that?"

After the army, I thought, life is going to be like one big holiday.

"Yeah. Why come here and be killed," I said. "It's strange no one wants to die and yet everyone does. It is unnatural."

"Why? End up like you started. Just complete a whole circle, what's unnatural about it?"

"Then why be at all? Millions of years pass without your existence. Then all of a sudden you appear for a few years and vanish again. The whole process is unnecessary."

"I don't consider philosophy—just facts," Ram said.

"Unless you deprive the idea of time of its meaning. Then there is only the existing and the nonexisting. That makes us belong to the winning side. We exist."

Ram chuckled quietly. "Is that practical?"

"No, but then neither is our walking here. At least, not to me."

"You'll be court-martialed and shot at dawn, Sergeant. I'm afraid I can't help you."

"Actually," I said, "I wouldn't mind being on the seashore right now."

"What the hell for?"

"Have ice cream and watch all the girls in their bikinis. One of them could fall for me by mistake. Everything's possible. Just need statistics and good will on your side."

He didn't bother to comment.

I took my water flask out and had a gulp. Ram spoke into his communication instrument. He gave our position, said there was nothing to report, and hung it back on his shoulder.

"Not that I have anything against what we're doing here," I said, "being patriotic, and all that. I just wish to state that maybe we don't have as much fun as some men our age have. If you care to look at it that way."

"Maybe it's still better than taking drugs and smoking grass," he said, "Maybe it's more meaningful."

"Yeah, O.K.," I said, "but those are not the only things you can do for a good time. The main thing is to be free to choose how to spend your time, so you don't have the feeling someone else is to be blamed for messing it up for you."

"You'd rather have yourself to blame, huh?"

"Sure, I'd rather."

"Maybe it's because you don't have the feeling that you belong."

"Yeah. Maybe it's because I don't have the feeling that I belong. What do I belong to? I am me, that's all."

"Well, don't worry. You have a lifetime ahead of you, and knowing you, you will probably screw it up.

"Just because I am not crazy about sacrificing myself for the benefit of my country?"

He smiled thinly.

"Not at all. Just because you're a spoiled crazy bastard."

"Thanks."

"Don't mention it."

I took my helmet off and shook my hair.

"I'm going to start growing my hair now. I hate it short."

"Put the helmet on," he said, "you are supposed to set an example, goddammit."

So I put it back on.

"Yeah," I said, "that's freedom for you."

There was a sudden burst of fire. It came from behind a line of tall, thick bushes, on the left side of the path. I threw myself automatically on the ground, feeling my heart beating faster, and at the same time hearing a remote, calm part of my brain remarking that this was a surprise, for a change. I glanced quickly back. All the soldiers were stretched on the ground, preparing to shoot. It didn't look as if anyone had been hurt.

"Spread!" I yelled. "Get under cover and shoot!"

I opened fire and rolled on the sand until I got behind a big hillock on the side of the path. I kept shooting, telling myself to be careful not to hit Ram. I had a notion he might try a private assault on the invisible enemy. I didn't see him.

At my side, the heavy machine gun started roaring, and then a bazooka shell exploded neatly on the bushes where the ambushers were hiding. It was a beautiful hit, and I heard a loud scream of agony, coming from that direction. Rotman did a good job there. Two small figures emerged from behind the bushes and started running away. The machine gun nailed them almost at once, and they fell lifeless to the sand. I studied the area intensely but didn't see anything moving. The shooting stopped and silence again prevailed. I got slowly up, half-expecting to be shot at, but nothing happened. I walked toward the bushes. There were four men lying there, dressed in khaki clothes. They were all dead, except one whose face was covered with blood but who still moved. I put a bullet in his chest and he froze in a lifeless knot on the ground. I started walking back. The rest of the soldiers were gathered on the path, and one or two of them were kneeling down. For the first time since the shooting had started, my brain was beginning to function normally. Then my thoughts froze again. I walked slowly to where the soldiers were silently standing and I looked down.

Ram's face had not changed in his death. It was calm and restful like a mask and his eyes were closed. He lay on his back, with the submachine gun still in his hand. On his shirt, near the center of his chest, a red stain was slowly growing larger.

The soldiers stood motionless around me and no one spoke. I stuck my hands in my pockets and breathed slowly and looked.

Chapter Five

ON the morning of the last day before I was going to be released, I was lying on my bed in my room, not doing anything. I had nothing to do. For all practical purposes, I was through with the company and with the army. After our farewell party, which had been planned for the coming evening, was canceled, the C.C. told me I was free to go home. There was nothing more for me to do in the camp. I was not anxious to go home. I was in no hurry. My room seemed quite comfortable now that there were no more duties forced upon me. It was pleasant to lie down on the bed without rushing or worrying about being bothered. It was as good as a holiday. There were the long days and long nights to think and make plans and drink up the cold Coke bottles. I was having a good time.

I lay down and looked at the ceiling. I was enjoying the clarity with which my mind was operating. It was like looking into the brain of someone else and seeing all his thoughts. It was like being in space and looking down at the people on the earth, observing all their movements without being seen by them. It was an uplifting feeling. Then three fat, small officers from the engineering corps walked into the void talking loudly, gesturing widely with their hands. The smallest and fattest of them was a major, and he had already seen his best days. The other two were lieutenants. Our camp was due to undergo some reconstruction. But still, I thought, they could have come a day later. I shifted my eyes back to the ceiling, and tried to catch up with my previous train of thought, but it was running away, leaving nothing behind it.

I was still uselessly racking my mind, feeling cold and hostile, when the three men stopped by my bed and looked down at me. The fluent bubbling of their voices fell off and died completely. I welcomed the silence.

"Sergeant."

I moved my eyes unwillingly from the ceiling to him. The major was balding and ugly, his face was distorted. He was looking at me with animosity.

"What?"

His face turned velvet red. He swallowed his Adam's apple, it disappeared behind the fat plaits under his chin.

"What?" he repeated after me.

I thought it was a stupid question and I lost interest. On the ceiling above me, a small green lizard was crawling toward the corner. I watched it curiously.

"Sergeant."

The lizard slipped down and fell on the floor by my bed. He missed the major by inches. But then, he probably hadn't expected such a high-pitched scream.

I looked back at the elderly, plump man.

"Stand up when I talk to you," he ordered hoarsely.

"Oh that," I said, with a sudden towering need to laugh. "Oh that," I repeated, smiling at him. I was beginning to enjoy myself again. "Go to hell, why don't you?"

The upshot of this was thirty-five days in military prison. It was a light penalty, considering the offense, but I had a few factors in my favor. After all, it was supposed to be my last day in the army and I had a clear record of three years of service behind me.

That hadn't been the important thing, though. What had counted, I thought, walking to the guardroom with the embarrassed sentry, feeling almost sorry for his embarrassment, was that the officer who had acted as judge in my case had been the regiment commander. The regiment commander didn't like the small fat major from the Engineering Corps. He didn't like the Engineering Corps altogether. He also didn't like fat, small officers. He was six feet three himself, and very slim. He could outrun most of his soldiers on the "white circle." I stayed in the guardroom two days before they transferred me to the military prison. The sentry didn't lock my cell after he put me in and he didn't check to see if I really stayed there. He had been a soldier in my platoon for two months. He didn't like having me as a prisoner.

The first thing that happened, after I got off the truck in the military prison near Acre, was that I got a haircut. It was the shortest one I ever had, but there were not many mirrors in the jail. That made it less effective.

I didn't have a bad time there. It gave me a peculiar pleasure that I wouldn't have normally expected to get from such a place. I like the rough treatment of the military policemen who served as jailers. I acted rough toward them, too. They were for the most part poorly educated men of low intelligence. I liked listening to their conversations with the prisoners and among themselves. It gave me an undisturbed sense of superiority.

Life in a military prison is not very hard for soldiers who are there for the first time. The jailers wait for your next term in before they really start giving you a bad time. I had no intention of being there for a second term. I would have found it hard to get locked up again even if I wanted to. I hadn't any more soldiering to do. My service was over. Except for those thirty-five days.

The days passed while I peeled potatoes and washed the huge pots, or did various odd jobs. We fixed the long wire fence, and removed the stones and dirt that the MPs would manage to find. It was fun because I had no obligation to like anyone or pretend to like anyone. They didn't expect you to be friendly to the other prisoners or to the jailers. You didn't have to justify any feelings of dissatisfaction to yourself. You were not supposed to be satisfied.

Sometimes we went on marches. That was the part I liked best of all. The MPs would come along with us, because we were not free men. Marching was supposed to be a form of punishment. It was supposed to be hard on us. But the jailers had to come along too. And it was no fun for them. Recruits in the Military Police Corps don't get a lot of physical training, and they have almost none at all once they finish their three months of initial training. The marches were no holiday for our jailers. When we really got going they would be left behind breathless.

I had little time to think, and I avoided it whenever I could. I made no plans, and I didn't count the days that passed. There didn't seem to be a lot to look forward to. I couldn't figure out anything I would like doing, once I got home.

It was that way for the first three weeks.

My attitude changed during my last days in prison.

One of my tent mates was a big, dark Yemenite, from the tank corps. I had never talked to him, but I watched him often, because he smiled constantly, showing pearly white teeth in his darkly tanned face.

His smile irritated me.

"What makes you so happy, brother?"

I was surprised when I started talking to him one evening after we had our meal. I hadn't intended to talk to anyone. I liked being closed up within myself. I didn't care about making friends or enemies.

"I'm thinking," he said, smiling, "and my thoughts make me smile."

I sat down on the bunk opposite him.

O.K. boy, you did your piece of talking for the day, now go to sleep.

"Maybe you could treat me to some of your thoughts. I'd like smiling."

He shook his head, grinning slackly at me.

"No you wouldn't. Your kick is frowning."

That took me completely by surprise, and I burst out laughing.

"How did you work that out?"

He shrugged.

"That's as obvious as the Russians in Egypt. That's probably why you are here."

A wise guy, I thought bitterly to myself. What do you know?

"Why are you here? Because you like smiling?"

"No." He had a calm, deep, caressing voice. "Because I was stupid. That is why I'm smiling, probably."

I stared at him.

"Why are you here?" I repeated, irritated by my interest. "I mean what did you do?"

"I struck my squad commander," he said still smiling, "twice on both cheeks. It made them red," he added.

I believed that. With those thick, brown arms, he couldn't have been weak.

"A new soldier, huh?"

"Four months. Fresh meat."

"Not a good way to start."

"No."

There was a silence.

I waited for him to ask what I was in for, but he just sat there, motionless.

Behind us, a cigarette passed from hand to hand. One of the soldiers, a driver, was telling about his different romantic adventures. He probably added a few. Drivers in the army usually have remarkable imaginations. There were many of them in our tent.

"I was relatively impolite to a major," I said. "I wasn't treating him so good."

The big Yemenite nodded.

"That probably wasn't a clever thing to do, either."

Now I smiled.

"But I don't have two years and eight months ahead of me."

"That doesn't make any difference. Civilian life is not basically different from the army. Wherever you are, you never gain anything by becoming a loser. When you punish yourself, you don't punish the world." He smiled softly. "You just punish yourself."

Simple, I thought reluctantly, isn't it?

"You worked it out, huh?"

"Yeah," he said earnestly. "I had time to work it out. It wasn't hard. When you have to do something that implies either winning or losing, you'd better win." He raised his hand to his mouth and yawned. "You should try it once."

A small, vicious dwarf was hammering painfully way up in the back of my head. I couldn't stop him. I had no power over him.

"Why did you slap him?"

"Who, the squad commander? He gave me an extra four hours of guard duty. That was after I had already done four hours. He said I was a good color for being on duty at night. That was probably the only thing my color was good for, he added."

I whistled softly.

"That's very strange," I said, "I never heard of any other such incident. They are usually pretty decent in the army."

"I know," he said. "That was why I hit him. That was also why it was wrong."

"I see," I said, wondering

"I'll be out tomorrow," he said.

I looked up at him. I didn't say a word.

"A waste of time, this place," he said.

The hammering in the back of my head stopped gradually. There were only single, occasional dim knocks.

"I'll get myself some sleep," he said.

"Yes."

Lying on my bunk that night, I saw it all clearly in my head. There was no vagueness or uncertainty about it, at all. It had been there all along, I thought. There wasn't any other way. You could make the best out of your world, or the worst. But have it the way you want it, as far as you can.

The people around me here, I thought, those who laughed,

those who cursed and those who were silent, they didn't rebel
against anything, they had no cause. They were just too stupid
to keep out of trouble. There is nothing in the world, I
thought, deeper than what you can taste or feel, smell or see.
You can only take what you can grasp in your hand.

The cards are against you, you can see that. You are only
what you are. That's why you can't accept it.

Only way is, win as much as you can, as long as you can.

Make the best out of it.

The book, I thought, that was the first thing to do. That,
and Joy. But first the book.

It will be a quick way to ascend. Just write it the right way.
It shouldn't be difficult. There will be no need to search for
a story. It's right there, inside you. I could see all of it in the
crystal clearness of my mind. It was simple.

From then on I started counting the days to my release. It
made the time go slower.

I left the prison after thirty-two days. They had taken off
the days I had been in the guardroom in the camp. One day
was for traveling.

Three days afterward, I was discharged from the army.

Part Two

ASSAF

Chapter Six

I was lifting weights in my room, when my mother knocked carefully on the door.

"Yeah?"

"Dinner is ready," she said softly, not opening the door.

"O.K."

"Will you come down?" she asked softly.

"In a minute."

"All right."

I heard her retreating footsteps.

Everybody around was talking to me softly, ever since my homecoming three weeks before. Even my father was patient and rather pleasant. I occasionally caught him exchanging meaningful looks with my mother who was quieter and more tolerant than ever. There was a tense expression on their faces whenever they spoke to me. I thought that maybe they were worried.

I spent almost all of my time in my room, behind an ever closed door. I had a portable typewriter and a pile of white, smooth sheets of paper lying on my desk. They had remained white and smooth throughout the three weeks, except those that had been crumpled and tossed into the wastebasket. I found it hard to get started. I couldn't concentrate. I did a lot of physical exercise. I specialized in weights. I worked with them for a few hours every day. It was an effective way of releasing energy.

I was supposed to be in the university for those three weeks. The year had started officially on the twenty-fourth of October, four days before I got out of prison. My mother had signed me up for economics, after she and my father had had a long talk. I didn't want to go to the university. I didn't care about economics. I wanted to write my novel. But I didn't do that either.

I put on a red, flowery shirt and looked at the mirror. My hair had almost reached its normal length again. I intended to let it grow a lot longer.

I kicked my tennis shoes off and went downstairs.

My parents were already sitting at the table. My father was really coming home more than usual lately. I couldn't remember when in the past I had had dinner with my whole family as often as in the last few weeks.

I was seeing him almost every other day.

I sat down and stared at my plate which was loaded with a large, juicy steak.

"Please, everybody start," my mother said in her low caressing voice.

She looked at me with her sad brown eyes.

Everybody started and thought to himself that the meat was pretty good. Having meat for every meal, in the fighting State of Israel, was not bad living.

"How's it going?" my father asked. He was chewing his piece of calf with visible pleasure.

"How's what going?"

"How are you doing, generally?"

"Beautifully," I said. I wiped my mouth with my sleeve.

My mother lowered her eyes to her empty plate. My father straightened up in his chair and looked directly at me.

"You'd feel a lot better if you were doing something," he said.

"I'm playing with weights," I said, "probably too much."

I rolled up my right sleeve, and contracted a muscle.

"See?"

He switched back to eating after giving my mother a brisk look that meant "I did my best, didn't I?"

About an hour later, when I was doing my exercises to the beat of some hip music that blared from the radio, he knocked on the door and walked into my room without waiting for an invitation. He turned off the radio and sat down on the chair near my desk.

"O.K." he said. "Sit down, relax and let's talk."

I shrugged; "Well, why not?"

I went and sat on the floor at the other end of the room.

I looked at him. He was staring back at me, lighting himself a big Havana cigar, self-assured and at ease. As always, I felt respect, despite myself.

"Look," he said finally, puffing a big cloud of smoke, "tell me what you have in mind, and I'll tell you what I have in mind, and then let's see if we can find a way to make the two work together."

"I don't have much in mind, right now."

He took the cigar out of his mouth and stared at me.

"Let's not waste time," he said curtly.

It was then that he really got to me. Hadn't I made up my mind to win? Why waste time? One, two, three, go.

"I haven't got it so clear in my head yet, but I want to be a writer, and I want to make movies. Those two can probably interact well. It's possible I will want to go into politics one day but that day hasn't arrived yet. I don't like the business, and I don't feel that sociable, either."

"O.K.," he said. " I have nothing against your writing or making movies. Meanwhile you might as well start studying. It never hurts to learn. When you have a clear plan with which studying interferes, or with which you might need help, come to me and we'll talk."

"Yes, sir. Thank you kindly, sir."

His eyes fell on the typewriter in front of him.

"Have you started anything?"

"No."

He returned the cigar to his mouth.

"Does what I say make sense to you?"

"You always make sense."

"Yes, I make my living that way," he said. "So we have an agreement?"

"Why not?"

He got to his feet and walked to the door.

"O.K., then, I'll be seeing you."

Don't make it sound so much like a threat, I thought.

He walked out, leaving a gray cloud of smoke behind him.

Actually what he had suggested did sound reasonable. Studying wouldn't have to take more than a couple of hours a week. Except for exams. It was worth spending those few hours to keep everyone warm and happy. What's wrong with having a B.A. or an M.A. or a Ph.D. anyway? Might even come in handy.

I picked up the car and took a ride around town. There were a lot of girls in the streets and some of them looked pretty good. At least from a distance. The image of Joy popped to my mind but I tried not to think about her.

"You might even fall for her," I warned myself.

You can't afford to let yourself fall for anyone.

The only way is to play it cool, just like in the movies.

Then you've got a chance.

Maybe.

I was going through Katamon at fifty miles an hour when a girl waved at me. Katamon is one of the poorer sections of the city. It is inhabited mainly by people who came from North Africa or the Arab countries. It is considered lower class and undesirable by the Europeans. But then girls don't have to be high society for what I wanted. I stopped the car, slamming hard on the brakes and nearly running her over.

"Yes, doll."

I put on my mechanical, meaningless smile.

She was full and pretty and vulgar-looking, but I liked her. I thought she would make a good screw.

"Going to town?" she asked.

I stuck my head out of the window so that it almost touched the full breasts that were stuffed into her cheap, red dress.

"Anywhere you say, doll."

She laughed.

"You're funny."

She walked around and stepped into the car.

I stepped on the gas.

"What's your name?"

"Zehava."

"Beautiful."

Zehava, in Hebrew, is similar to Goldilocks, but only dark girls carry this name, for some strange reason.

"I am Assaf."

"You're from Jerusalem?" she asked.

"Yeah, sure."

"Never seen you around."

"Yeah, that's too bad, isn't it? Any special reason you want to go to town, doll?"

She giggled.

The perfume she wore hadn't been imported from Paris but it was very strong, so it made its point just the same.

"Going to visit a girl friend. Why do you ask?"

"Well, how about you and me going for a beautiful ride, and the hell with your girl friend?"

"Like where?" she asked.

"Oh? Out of town, doll. Doesn't matter. This being a warm, dreamlike night, and with the moon full and all that."

"You're funny," she said again.

"No, I am poetic. But not funny, doll."

"All right," she said, leaning back in her seat, "let's go. I like driving."

I know, sister.

I drove the car through the outskirts of town and then out. She worked as a hairdresser eight hours a day. She adored Raquel Welch. (What an actress!) She loved dancing.

She had to share a room with her eight brothers and sisters. That was a drag.

There were many other things she told me while we were driving into the night, but I wasn't listening. I could have guessed them all, probably, had I wanted to. But I didn't want to. I didn't want to hear her talk.

The legs that were crossed and resting neatly on the seat beside me were brown and very nice. I glanced at them from time to time, thinking that I really didn't dislike her at all.

Actually, what did the people in my neighborhood have against Oriental Jews? They are a bit less educated on the whole. So what? That isn't their fault, after all. Give them better schools and fewer children per family and they'll catch up in no time. They are also a bit poorer, on the whole. Maybe more than a bit. But didn't I hear you say that it's not the money that makes the man, it's not the money that really counts?

Just the soul.

Probably one of the major reasons for there being no deeper division between the European and Oriental Jews was Israel's constant need for self-defense. You cannot divide the soldiers who fight into classes. In Israel everyone gets a fair chance to die a brave man, and that unites the people. I stopped the car on a side road and turned off the engine.

"O.K.," I said to the girl beside me, "no need to use all the petrol."

She stretched and didn't say a word.

"Don't you think it's a terrific night?"

"It's nice," she allowed.

I leaned over and kissed her fashionably on the mouth. She had warm, full lips, which were quite willing and rather pleasant. After a while, her tongue started brushing my teeth and that really got me worked up. I pulled her to me and undid the buttons of her dress. I was having trouble with the hook of her bra, when she pushed me forcefully away.

"No!" she said simply.

To Assaf the Great.

I pulled back and leaned on the door on my side of the car.

"What's the matter?" I asked politely.

"I don't want it like that," she said seriously.

"Like what? I love you. I'm crazy about you."

"Don't be funny," she said in a small voice. She began quietly buttoning her dress.

"What's wrong with sex?" I tried. "That's what it's all about. This is the twentieth century, remember? You don't need those formalities any more. Time's awasting."

"No. I don't want it like that."

I stared at her coldly, trying to figure out if there was anything to lose. Then, making up my mind, I leaned forward and pushed her down on the seat, going after her with all my strength. I lay on her pushing her dress up, but she was too powerful and too strong-minded. She drummed on my face with her fists like a lightweight pro. I had hardly reached for her panties when I gave up.

"O.K.," I said, rising to a sitting position. "The war is over."

She breathed hard, but didn't say anything. I looked at the mirror to see if my ears were swelling up. They weren't yet, but they had a funny pink color. I started the engine.

"Where are you going?"

"I'm taking you home."

I kept my thin, mocking smile as we rode along, but I wasn't impressing myself with it.

"I'm not a prostitute," she said hollowly.

"I didn't think you were."

"It's even worse, then."

She's really taking it seriously, I thought. She isn't joking.

"Don't get excited," I said.

"Just because you have this car, that doesn't make you the king of the world."

"That's right."

"I thought you were a nice guy."

I was beginning to get tired of the conversation.

"I'm not a nice guy. Don't worry."

We finally reached the big apartment building where she

lived and I stopped the car gratefully. She seemed in no hurry
to get out.

"Well, that's that, doll."

I wanted to go home.

"Wasn't a success, was it?" she asked me.

"Not particularly."

"That should teach you a lesson."

"I have to go home now," I said, "or my mother will start
hollering for the police. She gets nervous when I'm not
around."

"Funny."

She got out unhurriedly.

"Could you close the door?"

She did.

"Thanks."

"Good night."

She walked away, swaying and bouncing. She had a good
figure. I pulled away.

Chapter Seven

THE next morning I went to the university and attended an hour of a lecture on the basic principles of economics. There was a large number of students in the vast lecture hall, all eagerly writing down wisdom which seemed to pour from the lecturer's mouth. It made me nervous. I felt out of place. I concluded that this was no way of handling the school. The way to handle it was to find someone who would keep me informed about exams and papers. I looked around the room and saw no familiar faces, but it was hard to get a decent look. When the bell finally rang, I went to the door and stood there watching the exiting students. A few minutes passed before I spotted our former company clerk, Ruthi. I was close to missing her despite the fact that she almost brushed against me on her way out. She wore a chic black dress and had her hair up. Her ears were armed with large, green earrings, and in her hand she carried an important-looking bag. Every inch of her implied serious-mindedness and elegance. I hardly recognized her. She didn't see me, so I tapped her on her nose as she passed by.

"You too, Brutus?"

She turned and winced in surprise.

"Well," she said at length, "look who's here."

It occurred to me for the first time how good-looking she was. The khaki uniform had done her an injustice.

"Say, since when are you such a looker?"

She raised a thin, painted eyebrow.

"I never thought you could flatter."

I grimaced sadly.

"Let's have tea at the cafeteria," I said, "and I'll tell you what I want you to do."

"O.K."

We waited in line at the cafeteria for a few million years. Then we carried our cups to one of the corner tables, and sat down triumphantly.

"This is awfully crowded," she commented. "Why do you come here?"

"My first time," I said lightly. "Listen, what's new in the company?"

"I wouldn't know. I left soon after you disappeared. Got an earlier discharge in order to study."

I nodded.

"How was jail?"

"All right, thank you."

"I was glad to be discharged," she said, drinking slowly from her paper cup, careful not to spill any of the tea on her dress. "I know I liked it quite a lot once, but I would have hated to stay longer, now."

"Personally," I said, "I don't see what people see in economics. It's such a bore."

"Might come in handy."

"Yes, that's what he says."

"Who?"

"Some guy. You don't know him."

I emptied my cup in four hearty gulps.

"I thought you were from Tel Aviv," I said.

"I am, but I like it here. I have a nice, cozy room."

"With a big double bed."

She wrinkled her nose.

"No. Actually I share it with another girl, and we both have tiny little beds that can hardly contain us."

I shook my head disapprovingly.

"O.K.," I said. "So listen to this."

And I went into a long explanation of what I wanted her to do. I asked her to keep good summaries of the lectures and also to keep me up to date on what was expected of me as a student, but only the essential details.

"That doesn't seem too hard," she said.

"I'd be extremely grateful."

"How are Ram's parents taking it?"

"There's only a mother. She'll survive, but that's about all. She'll never be happy."

She stared at her cup, without seeing it.

"That's horrible."

"He was a fool to sign up for an extra year. He was asking for it."

She looked up, bewildered.

"What are you talking about?"

"Doesn't matter," I said lightly. I smiled at her. "How old are you?"

"Twenty."

She crumpled her empty cup and carefully stuffed it into the brassy ashtray.

"Why?" she asked.

"Just wanted to know."

"Well, I've got to go. I have another lecture."

"Drop in, anytime, or give me a call. We're in the phone book."

"I might," she said, getting up.

I watched Ruthi walking gracefully between the tables and couldn't see the girl in uniform any more. She didn't even look familiar, but I felt relatively close to her. As close as I felt to anyone.

I drove home and went up to my room and locked the door behind me.

I sat down at my desk and decided that this was it. It was time to start doing something, if I was ever going to.

I listed for myself the reasons for wanting to write a novel: (a) I wanted to be famous, (b) To be famous for work that necessitated brains, (c) To prove to myself and others that I could do it, (d) To make money, (e) It would be useful for other later occupations like making movies, (f) To get the girls, (g) To influence people, (h) To express ideas I had in my head, (i) I liked writing, and (j) I thought maybe I could manage to do it. These arguments impressed me as rather sound.

What else?

Number one rule: write in English, even if you can't spell butter. A best-selling author in Hebrew hardly makes a living and is forever unknown outside his country, unless he gets hijacked or wins a beauty contest, which doesn't often happen. In fact, it never happens. The book, I thought, should be the story of a young man. He could be a lot like me, only with a few tragic love affairs. In the weakest parts of the plot, in the gaps, you could put a bit of philosophy. It never hurts to have a little bit of philosophy whenever you want to impress people.

And massacre religion. The old bitch.

My leading character would believe that one should have as much money as one can get. One should have as much sex as one can get. It is most unnatural to think that we are born with such desires just to ignore or overcome them. I typed down this wisdom as part of a monologue the hero of the book delivers to a girl he has picked up in a nightclub. Long, seemingly clever monologues are a specialty of the hero's seduction technique. He knows them by heart and can give them offhandedly. He knows when not to use them: when the girl in question is either too clever or too dumb. One night he picks up a girl who is too clever and she is not impressed; she is just bored. He didn't expect her to be clever when he picked her up. That is why he is hooked.

I left the story there, feeling satisfied with the six, double-spaced, neatly typed pages of notes I had written. I even felt good about the headache it had given me. I thought perhaps my new brilliance was pressing on my brain. After mixing two aspirins with a Coca-Cola, I put on a clean shirt, and went to visit Ram's mother.

I was relieved to find an elderly lady there who was also paying a visit. I didn't like to go there by myself. It always seemed to me that there were things I was expected to say. When there was no one else there except me I didn't know what to say.

As I entered, Ram's mother nodded and asked me to come into the small living room and sit down. The elderly visitor was chatting about contemporary events and political opinions. She made zestful gestures with her hands to emphasize her points. Ram's mother was very calm and attentive, but I suspected she didn't have much interest in the conversation.

I looked around the room. There was a small picture of Ram leaning on a flower vase on a cupboard. He was in uniform and smiling broadly at the camera. I didn't like the picture.

The old lady was explaining why Israel should never give one inch of the occupied territories back. I had heard the arguments many times, and mostly from people of similar age. The older generation was tough. They still have vivid memories of the persecutions and the pogroms in the foreign countries they had come from. They had known darker and more bitter days and they were distrustful and disillusioned. But they were not the ones who had to back hard politics on the borders.

I tried not to be drawn into the discussion. I didn't like that type of conversation. I thought it was useless.

The old lady gave me a hopeful look from time to time, because she was running out of arguments. I avoided her eyes remorselessly and waited for the time to pass by.

Udi came into the room, carrying a dish of chocolate candies. He had a strained expression on his face, and seemed to look older. He was quiet and reserved, but he smiled at me as he put the dish down on the table, right in front of me.

"Hi," he said.

"How are you?"

"All right. You can start eating," he said, his smile widening and then gradually fading away as he sat by his mother. He knew chocolate was my favorite food.

"Thank you. Yeah, sure, I will."

I put three pieces in my mouth and nearly choked. He looked at me curiously. His brown eyes were familiar; they rested on my face permanently. I moved in my seat, uneasily.

"How is school?" I asked him.

"Boring."

"It will pass."

"Yes, everything passes."

"How's it in the university?" his mother asked me.

"O.K."

I looked away from her, and took another candy.

"When are you going to be famous?" Udi asked me.

"What?"

"When are you going to be famous?"

"Who said I am going to be famous?"

"I think so."

"Well, then you should know," I said, wondering what the hell we were talking about.

"I thought maybe you'd give me a part, when you make a movie."

"I don't know," I said dubiously, incredulous, "I don't know if I am going to make any."

"You will."

His mother looked at me peculiarly.

"Udi has always been enthusiastic about your future," she said. "I think he believes strongly in your abilities."

I was getting embarrassed.

"I am sure his judgment never fails him," I said.

"Seldom," she said seriously.

"Ram used to say you might be a writer."

"Ram also used to say I was a spoiled child," I told her, and he was probably more accurate about that."

"They are not mutually exclusive," Udi grinned at me.

How did we ever get to this topic, I thought. What is it to them, anyway?

I fixed my stare sullenly on the table, picking the chocolates from the dish one after the other, and chewing them dully.

"We shouldn't give anything back," the other guest said suddenly, as if it just occurred to her again, "not one yard."

How would you work it out, I thought wearily, when small children can get blown up on their way to school without the world's giving a damn. We have to find a way to put an end to that.

"We have no other alternative except being strong," the elderly lady said. "These people we are dealing with don't understand any language other than killing. Only yesterday they blew up that supermarket in Tel Aviv. Three women were killed." She laughed soundlessly. "Freedom Fighters for the Liberation of Palestine. I wouldn't call them fighters."

"There will be peace, one day," Ram's mother said indifferently, "But it's going to take a lot of time till that day comes."

"Yes," the old lady said.

"Don't you think so?" Ram's mother asked me, without much interest.

I shrugged.

"It's probably not going to be in my time," I said searching my mind for a reasonable answer and finding it strangely difficult, "so I try not to bother myself about it."

"I don't know," she said. "You are still young."

"Peace needs a generation that doesn't have the bitterness of war in its heart on both sides of the border," I said uncertainly, feeling I should say something more, feeling I should try to explain something, but not knowing what it was. "Otherwise, it won't work. You can't just impose peace on people," I said, "who hate, and know why they hate. That's what I think," I added lamely.

"Maybe," she said, looking aimlessly out the window. "I don't know."

I put another candy into my mouth. There weren't any more.

"I see I have to go and get more chocolate," Udi said, and smiled.

I rose to my feet apologetically.

Ram's mother shifted her aimless gaze from the window to my face.

"I am glad you came," she said.

"Yeah, well good-bye," I said, "and thanks for the chocolate."

The elderly lady smiled at me in a grandmotherly way from behind her rimless glasses.

Udi walked with me to the door.

"I am looking forward to the army so much," he said fervently, looking for a brief moment like a young boy again. "I wish I could go already."

"Yeah," I said slowly, "the army is not so bad."

"But, it won't run away," I added, opening the door.

"I know," he said disconsolately, "but school drags on so slowly."

I stepped out.

"Come visit sometime, if you feel like it. I can beat you in chess, or something."

"I will," he said.

I came home and found the living room filled with American businessmen who had come over for a cocktail. There was a lot of loud talk, strong perfume, cigar smoke, and liquor. I joined in and grabbed a bottle of gin for myself. I walked around the place, not introducing myself and not talking to anyone. I began drinking, welcoming the warmth and brightness that poured into my head with the alcohol. Around me, people were having a good time. Why not me?

I sat down heavily on one of the couches, and took a healthy bite from the remains of a piece of cake on a plate near my feet. I poured another drink from my quickly emptying bottle. A very bleached blonde of forty-odd years placed herself by my side. She looked at me in a way that reminded me of an old-fashioned movie.

"And who are you, young man?"

"Assaf," I said. "Why?"

"And why not?" she said in a husky, lingering drawl, that must have been Texas. "Are you the son of the owner?"

"I guess. I don't know."

I looked at her flamboyantly made-up face, waiting for my mind to click and empty itself of everything but the alcohol. She extended a soft, fleshy hand.

"Well, I'm glad to meet you."

"Sure, sure."

I squeezed her fingers briefly.

"Have a drink," I said.

I found a neglected glass and poured her a generous shot. I placed it carefully in her hand. She sat there, plunked in her place, eying me constantly. Maybe she is getting hooked, I thought drunkenly, the old bag.

"Thanks," she said, raising the glass to her lips. "Cheers."

"To Texas," I said.

She laughed. I gave her one of my smiles which aren't so bad when the lights are not too bright. At the other side of the room I saw my mother's anxious eyes staring at me out of a worried face, but she had a few million dollars' worth of a man planted beside her. I gave her a cheerful wink, and switched back to my companion.

"Your father is most charming," she said coquettishly.

"Yes. Of course."

"That guy over there," she said, pointing with a red-painted fingernail, "is my husband."

She grinned ruefully.

"That must be tough," I said sympathetically.

She looked at me with surprise, so I smiled at her again, though my face muscles were getting tired.

"Irreverent."

I emptied my glass and put it on the floor.

"I didn't catch your name."

From the other side of the room, my mother's blurred image was floating unsteadily toward me.

"Shirley Jacobson," the painted lady by my side said nasally.

She put a long thin cigarette in her mouth and waited. I picked up a lighter from the other side of the table and lit her cigarette, being careful not to set her nose on fire. My eyes weren't functioning at their absolute best.

I stooped and picked up the near-empty bottle.

"Well, Mrs. Jacobson-Shirley," I said, shaking the bottle and smiling at it dreamily, "I'll be going up to my room, but you are most welcome to join me for another gulp."

I stood up. She was looking at me with a steady, inquisitive stare and was about to speak when my mother floated across the room like a big cloud and appeared at my side.

"Assaf, are you behaving yourself?"

She was wearing an expensive, silver dress, which was unusual, since she was a chaste, timid woman who never put great emphasis on her appearance. I learned later that she had received the dress from one of the guests present, so she felt obliged to wear it.

"Yes, Mother," I said.

I took another drink.

She looked worriedly around the room. Most people were far gone by now, as there was no shortage of liquor, and no reason to stop them from drinking. Only the two or three Israelis present were as sober as judges, but that's just the way Israelis are.

"Well, then," I said, "I'm going upstairs. Good night, Mrs. Jacobson."

"Good night, sweet," she said, giving my mother a sugar-coated smile.

I padded away through the room, looking it over and thinking it was actually a nice place when there was no one there. It was a large L-shaped room, where my father had the majority of his best paintings scattered among the many lamps and mirrors. There was an elaborate bar on one side, and on the other there was a terrace that overlooked the mountainside and its old olive trees. It made a picturesque view.

As I moved along, my gaze fell on my father's face. I was surprised to see the disinterested expression on it. He sat in an armchair, in the midst of a laughing, bubbling crowd at the far end of the room. His eyes, cold and bored, wandered aimlessly about the scene, inside a mask of indifference. They met mine and rested there for a moment. I bowed my head politely. He bowed in return, slightly amused, and winked at me, boyishly.

I walked out.

Safe in my room, I put on the radio and sat on the floor with the bottle. The eight o'clock news came on reported in a low, metallic voice. Three men were killed by a bomb in Tiberias. The National Front has proudly announced its responsibility for the deed. The Russian Premier has warned Israel that unless her aggressiveness stopped . . .

I turned it off with a yawn and returned to my drinking, still half expecting to hear a soft, fleshy knock on the door. After half an hour I gave up and, having no drinks left, went to bed.

I woke the next morning with a revolting headache and generally feeling low. I made myself a pot of tea and scrambled eggs, and threw it up into the sink, five minutes later. I walked around, barefoot, looking for a fellow human being but there was no one there. The place was empty. The world was empty. I felt like a goddamned useless American; empty.

That brought me back to my room with a firm decision to repent. I took a look in the phone book. The TWA office really was inside the King David Hotel. I walked into the office blinking my red eyes, my hands shoved deep inside my pockets. I spotted the white dress immediately. She sat at a table writing on a sheet of paper. I walked over and stood staring down at her.

Finally, she looked up. She gave a light nod with her head to acknowledge that I was there. Her yellow hair was tied with a white ribbon. Even her teeth were white.

"So," she said, "it's you."

I didn't say anything.

"Please sit down."

"I'm O.K. standing," I said.

"Would you like to book a flight?"

I shifted my weight from one foot to the other, my eyes unable to stop blinking.

"No," I said. "I would like to book you for supper, if you're available."

She shrugged.

"Why not?"

"O.K. then."

"Where is Ram?" she asked, smoothing her hair absent-mindedly. "I thought you two were inseparable, something like ' 'til death do us part'."

I stared at her face and I liked her. My eyes stopped blinking and narrowed steadily. I put on a very thin smile.

"How did you ever guess?"

Her face froze and she put her pen slowly on the desk before her.

I shrugged.

"Still living in the same place?" I asked her.

"Yes."

"Eight-thirty. O.K.?"

"Eight-thirty," she said uncertainly.

"Well."

She took hold of the pen again, with very pale, thin fingers, looked at it and placed it on the edge of the desk. It slipped down.

"I didn't get what you said about Ram."

I stooped and picked up the pen. I placed it in front of her.

"He got shot, two months ago," I said, "killed in action, as the saying goes."

She looked at me and then at her long white fingers.

"Eight-thirty, then," I said.

I took my hands out of my pockets and wiped them on my shirt.

"Yes."

"Maybe you won't wear white."

"All right," she said, "all right."

I stuck my hands back in their holsters and walked out.

Joy wore a short, low-cut red dress. When she opened the door for me, her hair fell in waves on her neck. She wore enormous silver earrings, and for the first time was heavily made-up. Her eyes looked big and experienced, with her dark painted eyelashes. Her lips were as red as Campari. She had a remote expression on her face, not an entirely happy one, but she was absolutely stunning.

"I have forsaken my virgin outfit especially for you."

"It doesn't look so bad."

"Yes, most seductive," she said. Her breasts moved slightly with her breathing.

"Well," she said, at length, "how about supper? I am hungry."

"Yeah," I said, "I guess."

We went to eat in the only Chinese restaurant in town, the Mandarin. It was a rather expensive place, but the food was good.

"Your father is very rich, isn't he?" Joy said to me, after we had ordered the meal.

"Yeah."

She smiled.

"What's funny?" I asked.

"Nothing."

"What brought you to this country?" I asked, pouring red wine into her glass and then into mine. "Pity?"

"Envy would be closer."

"The decline and fall of America?"

"Mmmmm," she said, drinking.

"Life is not what it used to be, there," I smiled. "Something went wrong."

"Not bad for an Israeli."

"I was there three years ago. But I meet lots of Americans and they all sing the same song."

"Oh yes?"

"Yeah, yeah."

"Then it's too bad," she said thoughtfully, "isn't it?"

The waiter brought the dishes, said "tong tong" or something similar, and took off.

"So one day you decided that you had had it with the American way of life, and you packed up your toothbrush and came to Israel to look for meaning."

She didn't smile.

"No," she said calmly, "I packed my toothbrush and went to England."

I raised an eyebrow.

"Surprise, surprise."

"I have a sister in London," she said through the chop suey. "She's married to an Englishman. So after I had three years of psychology at Berkeley, and got good and fed up, I went to London and lived with them for a while. I got a good job as a secretary, and everything was O.K."

"But then?"

She smiled.

"Yes," she said, "it still didn't have much meaning, so I packed up again."

"So you came to the land of the Bible to look for meaning and see all the heroes with your own blue eyes."

"Sort of."

I laughed softly.

"You're wasted here," I said, "my being no hero and not giving a damn one way or another, anyway."

"You're all talk."

I sipped some more wine. Help the Israeli industry.

"How do you find it here? Touching?"

She eyed me calmly.

"You are having a hard time," she said, "but it is a better country than most."

"How about the poor Arab kids we are supposedly murdering in their sleep every night," I said, smiling. "Please have a heart."

"It's a pity that some people feel the need to be cynical."

"I'm sorry. Stick around for a while and see what happens to you. Three months is nothing."

"I am very sorry about Ram," she said.

"Yes. Aren't we all?"

"Maybe it's better than being killed by the National Guard."

"Oh," I said aggressively, belligerently, "the hell with that."

She didn't comment on that. We had our tea in silence.

"Want anything else?" I asked.

"No, thank you."

I called for the bill and when it arrived I paid and we left. I drove to her place.

"Want to come in?" she asked.

"Yes."

"Well, let's go then."

We walked in and she put on the lights in the room and motioned for me to sit down.

"Please," she said quietly, "I won't be a minute. I'll just slip out of this dress."

She went out.

I took a look around the room, although there was not much there to look at. It was neat and clean, with little furniture. I walked down the small hall and came to her bedroom. The door was open, and she was standing with her back to me, slipping on a robe. Her figure was slim and perfect. She wasn't wearing a bra.

She turned around and saw me standing there. I hoped my eyes weren't excessively big, but I was blushing.

"Oh," she said. "Seen everything? I am afraid it's not much of an apartment, but I like it."

"Yes, what I saw was sort of O.K.," I said, breathing deeply, "not bad at all."

She smiled, shaking her hair loose. She had that peculiar smile that seemed to say that something had amused her, though she didn't care to say what. Her eyes glinted mischievously and then the smile was gone. I put my hands in my pockets, and waited.

"Well, let's go back to the other room. That is where I entertain my guests."

She brushed softly by me, as she went out, turning the light off.

The room was immersed in darkness. I walked after her.

Joy placed herself on one of her small Arab stools and stretched.

The delicately curved form of her body outlined itself visibly under the red cloth of her robe. I leaned against the wall and watched her. She crossed her legs and clapped her hands with sudden vigor.

"Well," she said.

"Well?"

"Want something to drink?"

"No thanks."

"Grapefruit juice? Orange juice? Milk? Tea? Coffee? You can choose, I've got them all."

"No, thanks," I said. "I don't want anything to drink."

"If you want to sleep with me, I am not going to."

"Oh," I said. There was a pause. "Why?"

"Don't want to."

She looked at me casually, but there was curiosity hidden behind the look, I thought. I looked down and shrugged.

"Well," I said, "I guess I'll be going."

"But then," she said in her casual, curious manner. "Maybe I was pushing you a bit on that."

I shook my head. "No, not really."

"It was a nice supper."

"I am glad you enjoyed it."

"Yes."

Her eyes wandered behind me, on the wall, above my head. "Sometimes patience helps," she said slowly.

"We don't have much time, nowadays."

She shrugged.

"O.K.," I said. "I'll be going."

"O.K."

I started toward the door, then turned back.

"I am interested," I said. "What did your parents say when you decided to come here or did they just not give a damn?"

The curiosity went out of her eyes. They were just cold. I was instantly sorry about what I had just said.

"Maybe they didn't."

She picked up a newspaper from the table in front of her and looked at it.

I hesitated for a moment, and then I said, "I think I hurt your feelings."

"That's right," she agreed, her voice like the sound of ice cubes rocking in an empty glass. "But you don't have to feel sorry about it. You probably wouldn't anyway."

She turned a page.

I put my hand up to my forehead and rubbed it, then I put it down on the doorknob and pushed.

"The joke is," I said, "that I really am sorry."

Going at forty miles an hour through some of the narrower streets in town, it was hard keeping the car on the road, but I managed it. Beautifully handled evening, I thought, mentally patting myself on the back. Almost no mistake omitted. Beautifully done.

From the radio, a soft mellow voice blurred out sentimentally.

> Once I had a pretty girl
> I loved her as my wife
> I put my hands around her neck
> And choked away her life.

The audience burst out laughing. It was a recording of a live show.

I turned the radio off.

I drove home.

Chapter Eight

IN the next few weeks I busied myself writing my novel, studying as little as possible, and cutting my social life to nothing at all.

I wrote nearly a hundred pages, typed in the best English I could master, and then I sat one evening and read the entire thing. I panicked. It didn't seem right. For the first time, the possibility occurred to me that there might be more to it than hammering with my two forefingers on the keys. I couldn't rely on my judgment but I knew of no one I would like to have read it. Except Joy, to whom I couldn't give it. I ended up by locking the pages in a drawer, and pulling my Hebrew typewriter out of the cupboard.

I typed an eighteen-page short story. It took me eight hours. The sun was rising when I was through. I was tired and fed up, unable to force myself to read what I had just written. I placed the pages in a large envelope and went to the post office to mail it. I sent it to the editor of the one literary monthly magazine I knew of. I asked him to drop me a note if it would be published. Then I drove back home and went to bed, telling the ever critical voice in my head to shut up and do the same. The hero of the story, whom I named Evyatar, was a young man studying to be a physician and about to be married to his high school girl friend. Then, one morning, bright and clear, taking a hard look at his future, Evyatar concludes that he doesn't want any of it.

He doesn't leave it at that. He quits the university, calls off the wedding and leaves his wealthy home. He rents a small, dirty room in one of the poorer quarters and finds himself a job in a garage. He waits for his boredom to pass away and for enthusiasm and new interest to take over.

But nothing happens. Instead he grows more and more apathetic. His life falls into a monotonous routine, and stays in it. Evyatar does not feel like a new man, as he thought he would after the change in his life. He feels like the same man he was before, only a lot older. Life is not interesting, he thinks. You can't do what you can't do, and what you can do has been done before. Any effort is just a waste of energy. It can't get you anywhere new. One rainy day, a young American girl knocks on his door. She has nowhere to go, and is looking for a room. It is raining very hard. Evyatar can't be bothered to kick her out so he puts her up, and tells her to be quiet, because he needs silence in order to think. Evyatar is good at thinking, but it never gets him anywhere, it only helps him find more flaws in things.

The girl, Angela, who is beautiful and all heart, stays in his room for one week—long enough for her to fall in love with him. He is so indifferent that this is inevitable. But the guy is not the cooperative type. He won't even sleep with her when she tries to seduce him one night, despite the fact that she is rather sexy. By that time, Evyatar realizes that all he wants from this world is to go to hell, and he tells the girl that she can go to the same place, in so many words. Afterward, satisfied that he has expressed himself clearly, he goes to sleep on the floor, since his bed is still occupied, and he dozes off immediately. He is not awakened once by her sobs the whole night.

He realizes, of course, that Angela is by far the best thing that ever happened to him but he ignores her because he doesn't think he really cares. The only reason he lets her stay is that she is paying twenty pounds per week, all she can afford.

After four days he has to leave for a week's training in the army. Coming back he finds the room empty and the bird gone.

This is a surprise to him, because he is not used to having girls leave him in spite of the way he treats them. Sitting in his room, that evening, he decides that he really doesn't give a damn. Evyatar signs up as a career officer in the army, thinking that since he doesn't care about anyone, he might just as well. It takes him two months to receive his first decoration for bravery. Fortunately, by that time, he has already been dead seven weeks.

After I woke up, late that afternoon, I called my father in his office. His secretary told me to hold on. After a few minutes I heard his voice over the line.

"Hello."

"I'm game for anything," I said. "You just name it."

There was a short pause.

"All right," the clear, calculating voice said finally. "I will let you know."

He hung up.

Later on that week, I found myself sitting in the party secretary's office, reading through a huge heap of uninteresting papers about this and that, and nothing in particular.

I reminded myself that my father had never said the work would be exciting, he just said it would be useful.

My working hours were from eight till two-thirty, but it was made clear that I could leave during that period if lectures in the university and other such urgent matters demanded it. My job was not clearly defined. I was to assist the party secretary, Mr. Barak, in any manner he found helpful. It wasn't a very complicated task, but I didn't like it. I didn't like the party secretary either. He was a Russian-type Jew, who liked to talk slowly, at length, and about little. I got no kick out of my job. By the end of the first week, I was ready to leave, but I thought it would be unwise, so I stayed.

A few days later I received a long letter from the monthly's editor. It surprised me. It said that he, as well as his colleagues, thought the story was rather good and that it would be published in the next issue of their magazine. It said I should keep writing. I had a future (so it said).

I was a bit disturbed by their enthusiasm because I didn't sincerely think the story was any good, but I told myself that one cannot expect things to be perfect.

Many of my evenings were occupied with meetings, in which the party secretary and other party workers and political figures made speeches. Watching them and their audiences, I came to the conclusion that politics wasn't promising for people who weren't either forty-five or former members of the Haganah, which amounted to the same thing.

The reasonable way to get into politics for a person like me, if at all, is from the outside. Not by starting from the bottom in the party, and climbing slowly up, waiting my turn, but by making a name and a career in another field, and then joining in, already at the top. Otherwise, your best years will also be the most boring ones, and that is no way to handle life.

I decided to keep the job for one month and then quit.

I thought of Joy often.

I didn't go to see her. I regarded that as an achievement. One had to know one's priorities.

Never get hooked.

But a guy did get lonely. One evening I found myself driving to Ruthi's place on the outskirts of town with the sole intention of making her.

It was around ten when I arrived there, wondering if she would be home, and if her roommate would be out. Both possibilities seemed highly unlikely, especially as a combination.

As it turned out, Ruthi opened the door and she was all alone. She didn't look very happy; she just looked tired.

Ruthi had on a robe, which was buttoned only halfway up, revealing a piece of tanned skin and a white bra. Her hair was untidy and her eyes a bit wild, which led me to the conclusion that she had been sleeping.

"Hello," she said.

I stepped inside and closed the door behind me.

"I am surprised at you," I said disapprovingly, sitting on her bed. "Napping at such an hour of the day."

She came over and sat on the bed near me, very wearily.

"I wasn't napping."

"You look a bit like a dead banana, for an unnapping broad," I said.

"You missed the nine o'clock edition of the news," she said drily. "It's rather inefficient of you. I'm surprised."

"O.K. So who got killed?"

"Remember Amnon?" she asked, a slight edge to her voice.

"From our company? You mean the redheaded one?"

"That's the man."

I shook my head slowly.

"Well, what do you know. Wasn't a friend of mine though. Was he a friend of yours?"

"No. I knew him though."

"Yes."

I was wondering, far away in the back of my mind, if this was going to mess up my seduction plan. That would be just too much.

"How did it happen?" I asked, not really wanting to know. "Come on, tell me."

"Oh," she said, "chasing some Fatah someplace. One was left alive when they thought they had them all. Half dead, actually, but he had his Kalashnikov by him, so he took a few shots when they were advancing. It was a damned lucky thing he didn't kill more. Yoav got him."

Yoav, the company commander.

"How do you know all that?"

"I spoke to Yoav over the phone," she said wearily.

"I called the camp after I heard the news. I still remember the number. He was in the mess hall, but they sent for him and he came to the company's office and we talked. He had been hit himself in the left arm, but he says it's only a scratch. There weren't any other casualties."

"Just Amnon."

"Just Amnon."

"Wasn't in my platoon," I said apologetically. "I almost didn't know him."

"They had been after them for seven hours," she said. "Yoav said it had been very tiring. He said he was going right to bed, after he had his coffee."

I leaned my chin on my hands and looked gloomily at the floor.

"Is Yoav a special friend of yours?"

"What? No, no."

She seemed a little surprised.

"Not especially," she added, lighting a cigarette absent-mindedly. "I was in the company for five months, that's all."

"Where's your roommate?"

"In Tel Aviv. Miss her?"

"Not at all. I had been hoping she would be out."

She looked at me speculatively, dropping a small roll of gray ash on the floor.

"Oh, really?"

"Sure."

She shrugged and went on smoking, staring at me with no particular expression.

I was looking up at her, my face still resting in my palms, and thinking how pretty she was. There was a hardness in her features I had never been aware of before, but she really was a pleasant sight. Her figure was slim and curved and the best parts of it emerged, somewhat exposed, from the loose robe she had on. Her face was flawless, except for the lack of tenderness in her expression. The untidy flow of her hair made her look younger.

I leaned closer and put my arm around her, and started kissing her the best I knew how. She sat motionless for a moment, her warm lips pressed drily on my mouth. Then she sighed quietly, and I felt her dropping the cigarette on the floor and stepping on it. She put her arms around my neck, nestling in my grip, and drew me down to her. Her tongue rubbed gently against my teeth, and wriggled through, deep into my mouth. I found the ribbon that tied her robe and pulled. The softness of her body pressed hotly against my chest.

"I thought you were going to ask me to the movies first," she said huskily.

"Noooo," I said softly, pushing her down on the bed.

She rolled on her stomach and wriggled away from underneath me.

"There might be visitors coming," she said. She went to the door and turned the key in the lock. I started peeling my clothes off, folding them primly and laying them neatly on a chair, a thing I never did at home. She turned and stood leaning on the door, watching me curiously.

"Self-confident, today," she said, but not disapprovingly.

I kicked off my shoes.

"Easy come, easy go."

She laughed thickly, then, putting one hand behind her, she loosened her bra.

It dropped on the floor in front of her.

"Any more proverbs for the occasion?"

"Yeah," I said. "I heard it in a movie actually. Goes like this: 'If you gotta shoot, don't talk, shoot'."

"Yes," she said, indistinctly. "Yes, why not?"

She moved slowly forward and sat next to me on the bed. She put her arms around me again, and closed her eyes. I gently put my hands on her small, firm breasts. Her breath came hastily, deeply. Her breasts moved delicately against my fingers, and sent a quiver through my arms. I moved one of my hands to her thighs and we sank down on the mattress. Her eyes opened briefly.

"I hope you like me," she said coyly.

I buried my face in her perfumed hair and pulled her fiercely to me.

"Yes," I said. "Yes."

"Actually," she said about half an hour later when we were lying quietly in bed, "I don't know why I did it."

She looked at me from above her newly lit cigarette.

"Wasn't it romantic enough?" I asked.

She laughed. "Well."

"Yeah," I said. "Life is a bit mechanical, nowadays."
She laughed again.
"Bastard."
"But I did enjoy it."
She nodded her head.
"Thank you."
"Being romantic isn't so practical any more," I said. "What with life getting shorter all the time, for young people."
"You're telling me."
"On the other hand," I meditated, "for the older generation, life is getting longer."
"What a miscalculation on God's part."
"The average remains the same, though. In this world, it's the average that counts."
"Yes. The world belongs to the average."
She puffed small rings of smoke and watched them dreamily.
"You are a lovely girl."
She turned two green eyes on me. Small bits of mascara were smeared on her cheeks.
"I think I will turn off the light," she said, "or would you like to go home?"
"No," I said, moving closer to her, "not right now."

Chapter Nine

"WHAT the hell is this?"

The voice that woke me had an impatient, rigorous impact that didn't go well with my dream. In the dream no one had been impatient or vigorous. It was a pleasant dream; I hated to let it sneak away. I opened one eye and cast it wearily on the alarm clock. The hands indicated that it was just six-thirty. I closed my eyes and sank back into my pillow.

"I haven't got all day," my father said, and slapped me disrespectfully on my cheek with something he held in his hand. I gave up snoring and opened both eyes to look at the something that slapped me. My father was wearing an expensive gray suit, a colorful silk tie and a stiff-collared white shirt. He had his black brief case with him, and I realized he was already late for work.

Usually, his day started a six in the morning and ended around midnight, after he had exhausted his workers and assistants. Since I seemed to be the cause of his delay, I thought I might just as well be polite.

"Morning," I said.

In his right hand he held a thick magazine. He waved it in front of my eyes.

"Yes," he said. "What is this story business here? Come on, tell me all about it."

I sat up and took a look.

"Well," I said, "it's a short story I wrote. They published it. I haven't seen it yet."

"Yes," he said, his eyes unamused. "Forgot to mention it to your beloved parents and they sort of wonder why."

"Wanted to surprise them."

"Ahha."

He went over to my desk and put his case on it, then he sat down on the chair. I glanced again at the clock. He was really full of surprises this morning.

"Your mother is quite upset," he went on, staring at the ceiling. "She seems to have taken the description of the parents in the story a bit personally."

"Oh, come on now."

"I know, but she thinks so, and she is hurt because you didn't tell her about it. She regards it as a slap in the face."

"Oh God."

"There is some similarity in the background."

"Then be glad I didn't try a murder story. I did consider it."

He stared at me.

"This wasn't supposed to be an autobiography," I said lightly. "It's just a story, you know."

"Maybe it expresses an attitude that isn't very desirable," he said. Then he shrugged. "I really don't care. I am probably not such a good father, it doesn't matter. But your mother is more sensitive and she's seen such hard times in her life. She is a very good woman."

"Yes," I said.

He finally looked at his watch.

"Well, I have to go."

He stood up and took his briefcase.

"It must be terrible for you."

"What?"

"You have wasted almost half an hour."

I got out of bed, and stepped into my pants. He had stopped by the door where he stood watching me. The face was

composed as usual, but behind it the little wheels in his brain
were hard at work. I could almost hear them click. I couldn't
guess what he was thinking.

"Actually," he said, "I think it's a pretty good story you
wrote."

He was out of the room before I could catch my breath.

The short story, as it turned out (quite unexpectedly, as
far as I was concerned) got some attention, and what criticism
there was was most complimentary. It seemed, however, that
many readers came to the conclusion that one of the writer's
aims had been to sneer at the Israeli army, the Israeli spirit,
and the Israeli youth. They found the attitude expressed a
cynical and unhealthy one. I decided to ignore their reaction.

People close to my family would say to me, "We enjoyed
reading your short story," or a similar phrase which amounted
roughly to, "We don't approve, but we have to say something."

I bumped into a neighbor in the grocery and I heard her
saying as I walked out, "Things come too easy to this boy. He
has no appreciation and no gratitude."

I ignored that, too.

Publication did give me enough confidence to feel ready
to go on with that novel, and the sooner the better. I didn't
care about the rest.

One morning, my mother said, "Assaf, it makes me sad to
get the feeling that you don't really care about people around
you. I don't know why you are like that. Did anyone ever do
you any wrong?"

"No," I said, "but I am not doing anyone any wrong, either.
Maybe, I am just not as considerate as I could be."

"You are so self-centerd," she said in the same quiet, sad
way that used to make me feel like climbing up to the roof
and taking a shortcut down. "I don't think you have any
friends, or social life. That is unhealthy, and not right."

"I am O.K.," I said. "I am fine."

"People should care for other people," she said. "The world
will crumble when people stop caring."

"It's crumbling anyway, and it's not up to me, Mom."
She just shook her head.

I went back to writing my novel. Short stories were fine, I thought, but they couldn't make you. Two hundred pages of a book in English might do the trick.

But, I thought a few days later, maybe my mother did have a point. It did seem a unhealthy way of life, to spend the evenings with a typewriter. Ruthi was a possibility, but once I let my mind wander in that direction, I knew it was not her I wanted. If you have to do it, I thought, let's have it right for a change; let's have the real stuff, once.

On Thursday morning, armed with this decision, I stepped into the TWA office, with my mind made up to play it cool.

"Hello," I said to Joy, parking myself in the chair in front of her desk.

She looked up at me and raised an eyebrow. She didn't seem surprised or happy to see me. She didn't seem unhappy either. She just sat there.

"Long time no see," she commented from behind a pack of papers.

I leaned forward.

"Say, listen."

"Yes?"

"I want to go and spend the weekend in Caesarea. We have a summerhouse there. It's quite nice, by the beach."

At least she was listening, because she stopped writing and put her pen down. I couldn't see her eyes because there were eyelashes in the way, so I continued, just the same, though my self-confidence was fast disappearing.

"I thought maybe you'd like to join me."

She just looked at me. I tried to force a smile that probably didn't even reach my mouth. She burst out laughing.

"Why do you smile so unnaturally? You'll ruin your face!"

I didn't think it was entirely to the point, so I let it ride.

Her face turned serious again and her eyebrows went up.

"Problem is, I was already planning to go some place this weekend."

Not a good enough approach, I thought.

"Well, that is too bad," I said.

"Life is too crowded nowadays," she offered sympathetically.

I pushed my chair back and stook up. I took a slow look around the room. It was a pleasant little office with lots of colorful advertisements of beachy countries.

O.K., I thought, say good-bye nicely and run along.

"I wish you would come though," I heard my voice saying.

She looked surprised.

"Well."

"That's as romantic as I get," I said, embarrassed.

She considered that for a moment.

"Then, maybe I should come, in that case."

"Please."

"O.K."

"I'll pick you up around noon?"

"O.K."

"Tomorrow."

"Yes."

She scratched her nose and smiled at me brightly, as though she had expected me to visit her all along. I looked at her and shook my head. I was hooked.

"See you then."

"Yes."

The summerhouse had two small bedrooms, a living room, a bathroom, and a kitchen. It stood behind a small hill that protected it from the view of other houses. On the other side, the waves almost reaching the stony wall, was the sea.

When you were inside, all you could see through the windows was the sky and the water and the sand. People rarely walked around there and the illusion of utter solitude was seldom disturbed.

I loved the house. I always regarded it as my place. I used to think of it as a castle. When I was alone there, sitting with my feet dangling in the water, the rest of the world quietly took off.

That was why I didn't go there too often. I feared that staying there too frequently would break the spell and make it common, just a house on the shore. I hadn't been there in the last few months and neither had my parents. They had had no time.

We arrived there after sunset. It was an unusually stormy evening and the rain poured ceaselessly. I set up the fire in the living room while Joy took a shower and changed. Then I went to the kitchen and prepared salad, sandwiches, and eggs. I brought the food and some plates into the living room and arranged it all on the floor.

I picked up the guitar that was hanging on the wall and sat down by the fireplace. I started playing softly. It wasn't too good to begin with, and I was out of practice. She came into the living room, wearing blue jeans and a red blouse, with her hair up. The bright flames from the fire twinkled in her eyes as she came and stood close by, stretching her arms to me.

"Can you really play that thing?"

"I'm not very good," I said.

She pulled up a chair and sat near me, smiling into my eyes.

"Sing," she said coquettishly. "Please sing me a song."

"What song?"

"A love song," she said dreamily, closing her eyes, still wearing that faint smile. "Yes, I would like that," she added softly.

She leaned her head on the back of the chair and the leaping flames threw an occasional glow on her profile.

I sat close to her feet, watching her, plucking the strings uncertainly. Then I started quietly crooning, a few lines that found their way into my mind.

Oh baby baby baby,
It isn't easy at all
For a doll is so soft in her heart and her brain,
She will go on sighing and crying in vain,
Even though all has been washed by the rain,
And the rain long ago stopped to fall.

And baby baby baby
It isn't easy at all,
If you want to be strong there is just one way,
To have walls round your heart and be sure that they stay.
And don't let a doll come and push them away.
For when they crumble you fall.

But baby baby baby
It doesn't matter at all
For sitting down here and gazing at you,
And hoping that some day you might love me too,
Makes this the best night I ever knew,
The most beautiful of them all.

I got quite carried away while I was singing, but I was glad when I finished. My voice had been pitched too high, and the tune didn't strike me as particularly good. I put the guitar down on the floor.

"Not bad, for the spur of the moment," she said in a voice so low it almost escaped me.

"I do better when I have time to think."

"Do you?"

"I am writing a novel or two at the moment. Maybe you can read some of it, sometime, somewhere."

Her mouth curled slightly.

"Maybe."

I picked up one of the plates and shoved it toward her.

"Eat and be happy."

"Yes, be beautiful and shut up," she said.

We ate, looking through the french windows at the sea and the rain and the black sky. The waves were high and foamy and threatening as they broke thunderously on the shore.

"This is enchanting," she said. "The sea."

I went to the kitchen and made two cups of coffee. I brought them to the room. We drank in silence.

"The food was good," Joy said, putting her cup down. "And so was the coffee. Really."

"One has to do something right."

"Is it some kind of a biography?"

"What?"

"This novel or two you're writing."

"Yes. No. I don't know," I said uneasily.

She was sitting with her feet close to the fire, moving her toes in and out near the flames.

"What is really the matter?" she asked.

I shrugged. I was doing a lot of that, that evening.

"When I was small," I said, "I was going to grow up to be brave and handsome and clever and generous. I was going to pick out my friends only from among people who were also like that. Then, one day, I was going to marry a beautiful, kind-hearted, sweet girl, with blond hair and blue eyes. It was all going to be great."

I felt stupid about the whole story, but I went on anyway.

"She might have looked a lot like you."

"Then what happened?"

I drew back a bit, and smiled at her.

"Nothing. Children are not very practical."

She was still rather near me. Her face was flushed. I stood up and walked to the other side of the room.

"You see," I said uncertainly, digging my nails into the wall and scratching pieces of white paint, "I get a funny feeling a lot of the time. Everybody tells me how fantastic my father is, what a terrific time I have, and how grateful I should be to be me. I have the notion that I am expected to be somebody, to achieve something, and yet, at the same time, I think it isn't really me who is expected to do all that. It is just my role. I am not a person. I am a part that has to be played. And then, when I do try to play that part, and be special, because that is what it demands, not to be common, then people say, 'Ah, he thinks he can do anything just because his father is rich and influential. He thinks that this makes him so bloody original and gives him all the right in the world.' "

"Well?"

"Well," I said, and walked a bit around the room, "if every-body feels compelled to say that everything always comes my

way, then I'm damn well going to make it come my way.
That's the only way that's left to me. Can't you see? I've got to
be rough and not give a damn about anything or anybody in
order to get away with it. Because I don't really have it made.
People just act as though I do. It isn't me who has it made.
But I do have to do something about it, fast. Otherwise,
it will hurt too much, when I'm finally left in the lurch. I am
not trained to be happy just being anybody. I am not equipped
for it."

"How do you know if you never tried?" Joy asked.

"I cannot try."

She played with a long, yellow curl that fell down on her
neck, rolling it around her thumb and undoing it again.

She stood up and stretched her body, her face still hot, and
her eyes sparkling. She raised one hand and removed the pin
that held her hair up. It fell down to her shoulders; she had
long hair,

"How does Ram fit into the picture?"

"Ram was O.K.," I said, "while he lasted. That is probably
why he didn't last long. So he also let me down."

I laughed.

"I'm such a sad little boy. Everyone fails me."

She came and stood close to me, leaning on the wall by
my side.

"You're so beautiful," I said. "I'd hate to see you fade away.
But you will though, won't you?"

"I don't know."

"I know."

She put her hand on the back of my neck and pulled me to
her. She kissed me on my mouth, sucking my breath, then she
pulled away.

I breathed hard.

"You've got to care for people," she said. "Because only
people count for anything in this world."

Above us, the rain hammered violently on the roof.

"If you want to swim, this is your night," I said.

"Not right now."

I put my hand on her blouse but she backed away, shaking her head.

"No."

I let my hand drop down and waited.

"I won't sleep with you. I won't make love to you."

"Why not?"

"I don't want to." She shrugged. "I had too much of it in the past, I guess."

"Oh."

We stood looking at each other, not moving, but still very close. She seemed to be thinking of something because her eyes got dreamy again. Her hands rested at the sides of her body. I gazed at their long, thin shape. She had no rings. I touched them gently and moved my fingers slowly along her arms and up to her shoulders. She was quiet, breathing softly. Her eyes never left my face. I moved my fingers down and started undoing the buttons of her blouse. She still didn't move. The remote mellow expression on her face did not change. It was all very peculiar. I was not entirely aware of what I was doing. I took off her blouse and unhooked her bra. It slipped over her body and fell slowly to the floor. Her breasts were full and as tanned as the rest of her body. I put out my hand and caressed the smooth skin, very lightly.

She still didn't talk, she just closed her eyes.

My hand moved down her body, slowly, till it reached the thick blue cloth of her pants.

Joy opened her eyes and shook her head. Her face was set and grim, almost unfamiliar.

My hand froze for a moment on the slope of her stomach; then it dropped down. I stooped and picked up her bra, and handed it to her, together with her blouse.

"We should be in the movies," I said. "This would have been one hell of a memorable scene."

She put the bra on and turned for me to hook it.

"I don't know," her back said to me. "Melodramas are not exactly 'in' now."

Hooking her bra didn't improve the situation but there didn't seem to be any other choice, so I did it.

"Thanks."

She turned back to me, starting to put her blouse on. She laughed. It sounded like whiskey on the rocks.

"Our Father who art in Heaven," she said, much amused. "And here you are alone with me and you can't get anything out of it. That must be terribly frustrating."

I decided to shrug again.

"O.K., O.K.," I said. "Let's all get drunk, and then maybe we can sit and chat."

"Got Campari?" she asked, catching her breath with difficulty. "I mean, have you got Campari?"

"No."

She wrinkled her nose at me.

"Gin O.K.?"

"Man's drink."

"He-man's drink."

She made a face. It still didn't make her look bad.

"O.K.," she said. "Let's take a go at it."

She placed the seat of her pants on the floor and the rest of her slumped down with it. She leaned comfortably back on the wall and peered at me expectantly.

I went to the kitchen and brought the ice bucket, along with two glasses and a brand-new bottle. I put all that carefully on the floor near her and sat down.

I poured two glasses full, and gave her one.

"To the Russians," I said, raising my glass. "South of the border."

She shook her head in dismay.

"No, I won't drink to that."

"O.K. To our brave soldiers. I hope that will do."

"That's better," she said solemnly and gulped a good mouthful. It didn't have any effect that could be seen. I wasn't sure I could take alcohol that easily.

"What do you actually think will happen with all those

Russians and things?" she asked soberly. "You are losing ten soldiers a week, aren't you?"

"Probably."

She watched me closely.

"Let's not be too superior and indifferent again," she said.

I swallowed some gin. It burned its way pleasantly down my throat.

"As a matter of fact, I do care," I said. "But I do not know what will happen. Furthermore, I wish to state that my father, the man himself, says he doesn't know, and that is something."

She played with the glass and frowned.

"But what do you think will happen?" she asked doggedly.

I gave up.

"I don't think they will ever take us. Anyway, they will never take us alive."

She raised her eyebrows and took another swig.

"No, I guess not."

I didn't like the subject, so I took the bottle in one hand and the glass in the other and gave it a substantial treatment. Within the next ten minutes, I drank about a third of the bottle and commenced to feel warm and homey. I even began to relax.

"Tell me a little about yourself," I said to Joy. "Tell me the story of your life. Tell me your problems. Tell me anything."

"O.K.," she said. "Why not? But I'll just help myself to another tiny one, if you don't mind."

I put the bottle in her lap. She opened it, took a gulp that would have killed a sailor and screwed the top back on. She placed the half-empty bottle carefully on the floor within reach. Then she turned to me.

"I was born," Joy said, "in a little town in the state of Washington, called Greenwood. It is such a small town that it is almost a village. And there is nothing there except a whole lot of woods. It is a very quiet place, very conservative, and very provincial, but it is not so bad, if you go for that type of thing."

As she talked her gaze wandered over to the french windows and then returned to me to see how I was taking it. I was taking it rather well and she shifted her eyes back to the sea and went on talking.

"My father was a lawyer. I mean, he still is a lawyer. And he wasn't doing badly, but there wasn't a lot for him to do. You can't imagine how quiet those places can be. He was also conservative, but, of course, not as backward as many people there. Anyway, one day he decided to pack up his family and belongings and move to New York. He had a brother there, who was also a lawyer and they decided to form a team. So, when I was fourteen, we all moved to the big city, my father, my mother, my sister, and me.

"I was," she said solemnly to the windows, "a pretty smart girl. I was a good student and I was well liked. I was awfully happy when we left Greenwood because I felt I was buried alive there. I wanted to be modern and sophisticated and up-to-date and in the center of action and God knows what. I had finished school at the head of my class and I was also the first girl to try marijuana."

She looked at me and smiled without happiness.

"Of course, smoking then wasn't what it is today. It was quite something, especially for girls. I was against all the well-established traditions of the older generation. I loathed them."

She laughed.

"That's a pretty good word, 'loathed'."

"Not bad," I said.

I couldn't make out if she was drunk, but she seemed to be losing her good spirits.

"Anyway, I loathed religion, money, and virginity. When I was seventeen I jumped into bed with a Negro boy who hung around in the neighborhood, a relatively nice guy, incidentally; but that hadn't been important. I was having a pretty good time, feeling grown up and experienced and all that. But it wasn't as good as I had expected it to be."

"No meaning," I said through the bottle.

"Yeah, that's it," she said. "The point was—one of the points was—that my parents wouldn't stand for my attitude. To my father I had become worse than a slut. He wouldn't stand any wild behavior and I was quite wild at that time. They grow some rather conservative people in Greenwood, Washington, and they are stubborn ones. Probably they know that if they adopt a new outlook, the logic and understanding of their world will be ruined. They will lose their ability to enjoy it in their own way. They will have to change their views, standards, and way of comprehending. It's not easy for people who are not young, who don't grow into it. My mother took his side. She was too weak not to take his side, in anything. She utterly depended on him. It used to outrage me. And the upshot was that I left home slamming the door behind me."

I poured another shot and offered it to her, but she shook her head, so I took it myself. I was dizzy and swimming in slow circles over the room. I thought of Joy, all alone, leaving her home on a cold rainy day, and the thought filled me with sadness. I put my head in her lap. I wanted to say something suitable and comforting, but I couldn't find the words.

"Then what did you do?"

"I went to Berkeley and studied psychology for three years. The first summer I was away, my sister went to England on vacation. I think she was fed up with home herself. Anyway, she met an Englishman and married him and settled there. She lived happily ever after."

"What is her name?"

"Lynn," she said. "Or rather Lynda. Her husband is a medical student. They live in London."

"And what became of Joy?" I asked, feeling sweet melancholy taking over. "Whatever happened to Joy?"

She straightened her legs out under me, banging her knees against my back.

"I was coming to that," she said.

I turned my face to her blouse and closed my eyes.

"Joy stayed in Berkeley for three years, leading a wild, crazy life," she said softly. "I had what you might call a 'self-actualization mania.' That's a term they use a lot in those books. I had to do everything and understand everything. That is, about myself. I was afraid to miss something. It never quite left me, but it changed its form. I started disliking the modern sophisticated America as much as I resented the rigid old one. They are forming the two extremes now. You can either be for law and order, against Negroes and any liberal cause or general freedom, or you can be with the new left and for socialism and bringing down everything that exists, the good, together with the bad. Some believe in just being against everything, and not contributing anything, anywhere. I was getting to be really sad. People are going wild because they don't know what to do and that makes even less sense.

"I used to be quite loose during those years, going out a lot with different guys and sleeping with most of them, because I used to think that it was artificial to be strict. After all, what's wrong with having fun? But, I was also getting sad about the emptiness of everything, feeling that it all was going to the dogs. So, probably as a reaction, I was getting romantic and concerned. Deep inside, I thought there just had to be more to life and I knew I had to try and find it."

She stopped. "Does it often storm like this?" she asked suddenly.

"No. This is quite unusual."

My head was filled with an alcoholic version of America reforming the world, attaching labels of meaning to each of its items, instead of prices. For some reason it made me think of religion.

"Probably Jesus was born on a night like this," I said.

"Your knowledge of the New Testament . . ."

"My opinion is as good as anyone's, especially now, when I have vision. But you were saying?"

She placed her arms on my chest, her hands resting lightly on my sleeve.

"After I had finished my third year, I went back to New York. Not visiting my family there, and without much of a plan. One day I was riding on a bus, somewhere near Harlem, looking around in the streets and getting depressed. There were three young Negroes in the backseat behind me. They were making all kinds of dirty remarks about me, which I ignored. One of them kept repeating, 'Milking white cow, milking white cow,' and I thought he was probably retarded. When I finally got off the bus, they got off too, and followed me, still making their remarks, and not in a low voice, either. I thought they might try something, but I didn't give much of a damn. I was walking slowly, taking a good look at the small, filthy streets. I wanted to get a better understanding. See what I mean?"

"Yes."

"Then, maybe after ten minutes or so, the three of them caught up with me. They grabbed me and dragged me to a yard at the back of a house, and raped me. Maybe rape isn't such a good term. I didn't offer any resistance. Being on the pill, I didn't see much point in putting up a fight, and they did seem surprised at that. I almost went as far as telling them it didn't matter to me, just in and out, that's all. When they had finished, they cursed me some more, and the one that had been saying 'milking white cow,' when he had had his turn, slapped me in the face, and kicked my dress over my head while I was lying on the ground. He called me a whore and a slut and a fake, and then they left. I went back to my room and washed and changed and put fresh make-up on my face, and told myself there was nothing more to it. I said to myself that it didn't matter at all. But a bit later I felt disgusted with myself, and I thought to myself that these things have to be important. If parts of my life are not important, then all of it is not important. Life is all I have got. It cannot be worthless."

She looked abruptly down at me and then turned away. I stared at the glittering glass which framed the sea and through the haze I could see very clearly Joy lying on the ground with her white dress over her face and her legs kicking helplessly at nothing. Then the figure blurred away into the waves but it was still somehow there, lying motionless in the french window, and it was not the same. It was Ram sprawled

on his back in the sand with the blood running all over his
chest making everything red except his face. His face was untouched.

"I am glad he didn't get it in the face," I murmured. "He
had such a beautiful face."

"You see," Joy said indistinctly, from above the fog, "at
least to some extent one must be able to determine his own
life."

"What does a man profit, if by gaining the world, he loses
his own soul?"

"No," she said, "that is not what I'm talking about."

I buried my face deeper in her blouse, and the bottom
button opened. I pressed my lips to her stomach. She didn't
move.

"I went to England," she continued, "because I needed a
change and because, having a sister there, it seemed the most
reasonable place to go. I liked it there, so I stayed for a few
months, but it wasn't what I was looking for. I needed a
more extreme change. Somewhere younger and with more
enthusiasm, where things were created, not destroyed. So that's
how I finally ended up here."

She stopped talking. I didn't say a word. I lay dizzily, my
face buried in the warm safety of her lap. I didn't want to
move.

"Well," she said after a while, "that is the entire story."

I opened my eyes and looked up.

"It is all wrong," I told her brown skin and her red blouse.
"It is all wrong."

"What?"

"For you to be stuck here with me, you being enthusiastic
about building a brave new country, and looking for ideals
and meaning with all that energy. You may very well be the
right girl, but I am definitely the wrong guy. It is a pity,
though, because I am quite drunk now and apt to feel sad and
pathetic about things I would generally not even notice. It is
a shame, it is all wrong."

"You just talk," she said, touching my mouth with her

fingers. "You like feeling cynical and original. It feeds your need for superiority. It makes you feel older."

"I am twenty-two."

"That makes two of us."

She pulled her hands to her hot face, and pushed her hair behind her ears.

I picked myself up and dropped into the easy chair at the corner of the room. I couldn't figure out where the hell all this was leading to.

"I want to swim," she said suddenly.

"Well, what's stopping you?"

She got up.

"Coming?"

"No."

"O.K.," she said, "I'd like to use one of your towels, if it's all right with you."

"Sure," I said, "go right ahead."

I shut my eyes and drifted gratefully into a haze.

When you are small you want to be great you want to be greater than your small friends and you want to show them that you are superior and that you can make it where they failed and sometimes this may drive you real hard but even then by the time you have made it and are great some maybe twenty years later there is no one to show because all those that mattered have been killed and buried a long time ago so what is the use of all the efforts people don't last anyhow there is no point in caring about them one day they are here the next they are gone inanimate objects are more reliable at least you can lock them up in a safe.

The door slammed and I heard her retreating footsteps.

Is it my fault that this stupid idiot Ram goes and gets himself shot clean in the heart when there is the whole goddam platoon standing around him and nobody else ever gets so much as scratched and it is just stupidity itself to go and risk things you don't want to lose and then say oh yeah mother I'm really sorry I lost them they were so beautiful but they went away and what am I gonna do now when there aren't any of them left that is why you either don't like things or else don't risk losing them just because this is the fashion and goes well with society's taste how many lives do you think you live I don't want to fall in love with this girl that isn't what I want just to screw her I don't want this blond face to haunt me I don't need faces to see in nightmares. I didn't ever see such white high waves as these screaming so loud and this yelling wind where did this girl say she was going oh you have to be crazy to go swimming on such a night and you can't go very far or very long not against those waves you can't really you had too much to drink can't even move my legs properly never expected it to be so hard to walk a few dozen feet.

I stumbled heavily to the water line, shivering as the cold water swept over my feet. I couldn't see anything at all. The sky was masked with heavy clouds that hid the moon and the stars. It was dark and wet and the constant blowing of the wind was the only sound. I started yelling her name and my voice hardly reached my ears. Well, I thought to myself, this is what you get, goddammit. I turned my back to the water. Then I saw a remote faint orange light coming from the end of her cigarette. It threw a dim, obscure light on her face. As I walked toward her, I wondered how she had ever gotten it lit in that wind.

"The water is terribly cold," her voice said, "but most refreshing. It makes you feel like new."

"Oh," I said.

Coming close, I saw her sitting on the sand with the towel wrapped around her. Her hair hung, wet and dark, on her shoulders.

"It's so beautiful," she said, looking over my head as I knelt and sat down beside her, "and I am freezing."

Chapter Ten

"I HEAR you got yourself a girl friend," Gad said.

We were sitting in his room, smoking two big Havana cigars I had taken from my father's house.

"Say," I said, "do you think the Russians are going to fight us?"

"Fight us?" he laughed. "What the hell for? They'll just tell us what they want done, very peacefully. They won't have to threaten. We'll do it anyway."

"No need to exaggerate."

"Come on," he said, "America couldn't lift a finger for us even if she wanted to. They are out of the game, and we can't handle the Russians. With the way the morale in the army is going, we soon won't even be able to handle the Egyptians."

"So what's left are the Chinese."

"Yes, but we should have thought of that before, not when they are already on the other side and liking it. How is she?"

"Who?"

"The American girl."

"All right."

"Going to convert her?"

"Stick around and I'll let you know."

"You know, Nixon's a bastard. It shines on his face so you can see it for ten miles," he said. "He had always been anti-Israel anyway. I just hope our government knows it, too."

"Yes. It is a pity, actually, that Ted Kennedy had to go for a swim. We might have been better off otherwise."

"Don't worry. By '72 it won't matter any more."

"Listen," I said, putting my cigar in the ashtray, "what I actually wanted from you were your economics papers from last year, all you've got. I don't want to be writing a lot of papers this term."

He laughed softly.

"I'll have to see if there are any of them left," he said, brushing his curly black hair with his fingers. "People have asked for them before."

"Come on," I said sweetly. "I'm sure you haven't been that generous."

He laughed again.

"Some of them have been young, attractive females," he said. "I was tempted to bribe them."

"Oh, you don't need that, Gaddi. You could just talk them into it."

"Without a white sports car? Could you?"

"I haven't got your personality."

He inhaled luxuriously from his cigar and did not speak.

"Try and take a look in that cupboard," I said indulgently. "You never know what surprises can come out of cupboards."

"It's only in the movies that they're already undressed and willing," he said. But he got up reluctantly and walked to the other side of the room and pulled out the drawer. I came after him.

"There are two here," he said. "See if they can be of any use."

"They'll be fine."

I folded the papers carefully and put them in my breast pocket. Gad was a good student; he got all A's.

"Thanks."

"You're welcome. Maybe you'll invite me for a cup of coffee some evening. I'd like to see the girl. What's her name?"

"Joy," I said, walking with him to the door. "I don't know. You see, she isn't really my girl friend."

He smiled.

"Then it would be even better," he said.

My relationship with Joy was something I found hard to define to myself. I saw her quite often and we had a good time together. But the platonic nature of it had disturbed me. I used to pick her up at her house and go to a movie, or for a drink, or to swim at the beach. We had long talks and she often kissed me, wrapping her arms around me and pulling me close to her, but it never got further than that. I didn't know what to do about it. Occasionally, I planned to call it quits, but I didn't.

When I had told my father, toward the end of one month of work that I was dumping the job, he didn't offer any objections. He said that that was O.K. with him but suggested I get more involved in the activities of the young group in the party. This, he thought, was more practical and involved less effort. I accepted the idea.

I started giving writing more time, and toward the end of another month, had finished a detailed outline that ran over a hundred pages. It was, in fact, a lot more than an outline. The whole book was not planned to have more than two hundred pages.

I passed the exams of the first semester with good marks, and my mother sighed with relief. She believed that the only things you know are those you learn which is, of course, true, except that, for her, learning could be done only within the walls of an institution especially established for that purpose.

Even my social life became more active. It was linked to the increasing number of dead soldiers per week. There were often gatherings of our graduating class in the beautiful cemetery on the hill. They became occasions for hearing and telling the latest jokes about the "situation." We felt awkward standing solemnly, looking at the new tombstones instead of lying inside the coffins. There wasn't anything suitable to do, except say our apologies and smile stupidly at one another.

One afternoon, shortly after the beginning of the second semester, there was a funeral for a classmate named Mickey who had been killed the day before. I came late and because of gym, missed the ceremony. Gym was the only class I couldn't miss, because one absence was sufficient to add another semester of it to my studies. I didn't want anything added, so I didn't miss a class.

As I came hurriedly through the stone gate of the cemetery, I saw Eitan walking idly toward me.

He was of medium height with sandy hair and eyes. His mouth was constantly curled up higher on the right side than on the left, which gave the impression that he was always smiling. It also made his right eye narrower than his left one. He insisted that it made him look like a movie star.

"Over already?"

"No," he yawned. "It's getting too long for me. There is a shortage of girls this time and those present are no good."

"Yes, Mickey was no lady-killer."

"You're telling me. It's just no fun."

"You shouldn't leave, though. I heard that after the ceremony we stay to pick our own plots."

"Oh yeah?" he asked lazily. "In that case I'd better stay; the competition being what it is. I thought of taking one overlooking the city."

"There were six this week, weren't there?" I asked. "That almost beats the road accident score."

"One Egyptian soldier was wounded though, and I wonder who did it."

"I hear they changed the proverb 'Generations come, generations go' to 'Generations go, generations go'."

"Ho, ho."

"At least our planes are still attacking. That's something."

"Yes, but they are attacking our posts now. That's why there are so few shot down. It's a brilliant idea—eliminates casualties and sustains activity."

"I don't know."

"I saw a couple of Russians at the movies the other day. They assured me they want no violence."

"Didn't know they were actually here."

"Yeah," he said. "That's sort of un-nice."

"I do have lots of relatives abroad. I am not worried. I could always visit them if things got bad."

"Been a nice twenty-two years, though. It was an experience."

"Listen," I said, "I think I'll go in. Are you coming?"

"No. I guess I'll drift home."

"See you next time then."

I walked in and joined the line passing by the newly dug grave, each person in his turn shaking hands with the family. The parents stood with their three other sons and muttered their thanks to the embarrassed offerings of condolence. I shook their hands and walked away without saying a word. I didn't know them.

I was glad to be back in my sports car. Passing a red light at full speed, nearly running over a woman and her baby, brought back to me the feeling of life.

Ruthi had drifted out of my mind. In fact, she had never really been there. She was a nice girl but I did not especially like her. Despite her good looks, she was too tough for me. After I had made love to her once, the attraction was gone. I felt no desire to experience it again. We did remain on friendly terms, though. She was not the type to be heartbroken. It did not take her long to acquire a new boy friend, a good-looking captain in the tank corps. She liked professional soldiers, and they seemed to like her. I had no objection.

Sitting in my room one evening, I went through the hundred typed pages of my novel and decided it was time to have an objective opinion. I packed it carefully into a plastic case and drove over to Joy's house. I found her sitting in her living room, wrapped in her red robe, and having Turkish coffee with Muhammed.

"Hello," she said, as I closed the door behind me. "Come and join in. We are talking about the Palestinian nation and whether it exists or not. It's very interesting."

I remained standing with the plastic case in my hand.

"Some other time," I said, controlling my irritation. "I meant to take you for a ride."

She was silent for a moment.

"Sit down," she said finally. "Where are your manners? Don't you see I have a guest?"

"I wanted to talk with you," I said dully.

"Sit down and behave. We will talk."

"No, this won't do," I said belligerently. "Are you coming or not?"

She looked at me curiously, and in her eyes, glowed anger. Muhammed looked neutrally into his cup.

"What is the matter?" she asked tensely.

"Nothing. I want to go, that's all."

"Maybe I should leave," Muhammed said gently.

"No, please don't," she said.

Then she turned to me. "You'd better sit down and cool off."

I looked at her helplessly, and the need to take her in my arms and squeeze her and suck her breath with my mouth was almost too strong for me to bear.

"No," I said. "I don't want to. Are you coming or not?"

"No."

"O.K. Good-bye then."

I turned and walked out, closing the door behind me.

I drove around town, cursing aloud, trying to hit the sidewalk when taking the curves and violating each and every traffic regulation. But there were no policemen around and the pavements did not curse back. I had a bad headache, my usual sympton of a bad mood, when I finally stopped by Ruthi's house.

I did not really want her, but I needed a girl and there was no one else I could think of. The fact she now had a boy friend added some interest to it all. The hell with him, I thought, climbing the stairs violently. I'll screw her just the same.

Cursing Joy and her robe, I pushed the buzzer and stuck my hands in my pockets.

Her roommate opened the door.

"Oh, hello. Good evening," she said.

"Hello. Is Ruthi in?"

"No."

"Where is she?"

"She went to her home in Tel Aviv," the roommate said, embarrassed. "These are the holidays, you know, and her father has not been too well."

I considered her for a moment, but she was fat and ugly. Her eyes shied away from me. I called myself a few nasty names and then I called God a few more of the same.

"Thanks," I said. "Good night."

I went back to my car. I turned on the radio loud and pulled away from the curb. I made Tel Aviv in thirty-five minutes and enjoyed the reckless drive.

When I reached town, I realized I had forgotten to ask for Ruthi's address. I stopped for a hamburger in a small restaurant and looked her up in the phone book. A quarter of an hour later, I was there. It was almost eleven when I parked the car near the small house. It was on an alley that had no street lamps or lights of any kind. I went through the gate and up the short path and looked at the name on the door. It was the right one. I went into the garden and walked around the house. It was all dark except for one window which was dimly lit. I tiptoed up to it and listened. There was quiet popular music coming softly from within, and there was no other sound to be heard.

She must be alone, I thought, not really caring but nevertheless remembering that her boy friend was serving far south in the desert. Highly unlikely that he is here now. And girl, I thought, you'd better not be difficult, because that would really make me mad.

The window was half-open and only the curtain was in the way. I put my hand on the sill and slipped one foot over and then the other and landed in the room. I hit a small night table with a flower vase on it, which was standing beneath the window. It went with me to the floor, making an unpleasant smashing sound. I cursed and got to my feet. Someone gasped and then the lights went on. I took a look around, blinking my eyes at the sudden flash of light. Then I caught my breath. It wasn't Ruthi who was standing by the door. It was her father.

We looked at each other, and neither of us moved. His face was very red and his eyes stared at me, large and white. His breath came heavily and with effort.

Hell, I thought, all of a sudden, this guy has really gotten a scare. His face was rapidly turning deep purple and his breathing came harder than before. I licked my dry lips with my tongue and opened my mouth to speak. I couldn't think of anything suitable to say. Suddenly his feet gave way and he started going down. I took a few quick steps and caught him before he hit the floor. He was not heavy, just limp. My heart stopped for a second and then started beating again, faster.

I dragged him to the bed and lifted him onto it. He felt cold and clammy. He was a thin elderly man with graying hair, and he was wearing a robe over his pajamas. His eyes were closed and his mouth opened helplessly, like that of a fish out of water.

This doesn't look good. I though, staring at him, hypnotized. Could be a heart attack. He might be passing away any minute.

I'll have to get a doctor, I thought.

I spun around when I heard the key turn in the lock of the front door. I heard it open and shut softly. I was standing in the center of the room, frozen, when Ruthi walked in.

She was wearing her elegant black dress and looking sweet and cute. For one second my reason for coming flashed back into my mind. Her jaw dropped in surprise when she saw me, and she stopped for a moment, startled. Then her eyes darted to the bed, and her face turned as white as the wall. I moved toward her wondering if she was going to slump down too, but she pushed me aside and ran forward. I backed away and watched her in silence. She knelt by the bed and shook him gently.

"Daddy!"

There was no reaction from the still figure.

"Daddy, are you all right?"

He still didn't move. She jumped to her feet and rushed out of the room. I heard her dialing and talking urgently into the phone. Then the receiver dropped and she came back. She sat down on the floor and looked at the unconscious face. When she turned to me, her face was almost calm.

"What happened?"

"I came through the window," I said, getting my hands out of my pockets and not knowing what to do with them. "I thought it was you, with this radio here. I wanted to surprise you. I surprised him, instead."

She nodded, not speaking.

"How is he?" I asked.

"I think he is dead," she said simply.

"Dead."

"You'd better go," she said quietly. "The doctor will be here soon. Your being here will only complicate matters."

"Dead," I said again, my voice sounding loud and peculiar.

Ruthi reached her hand over to the small radio and switched it off. It was advertising Coca-Cola. The announcer had a deep feminine voice.

"He had already had a bad heart," Ruthi said. "The doctor said he wouldn't live much longer. It was just a matter of days, or weeks at the most. You don't have to blame yourself. It would have happened anyway."

"I thought it was you, because of the music," I said.

"Yes, yes," she said. "I understand, but you'd better go now. The doctor will be here any minute. I will call you to-morrow and tell you how things are. You mustn't stay now."

"I'll go," I said, still not grasping it all, and thinking to myself that this girl really had strong nerves. "I will, unless you don't want me to."

"You should go," she said. "There is nothing you can do."

"All right, I'll go then."

"Yes."

"Good-bye."

"Good-bye," she said.

She walked me to the door, as if to make sure I wouldn't take the window again.

I waited till I was back in the car, and then I wiped my face. I started the motor and drove slowly away, wondering why nothing ever worked out right.

"You're better off with Coca-Cola," the announcer said in her deep, sexy voice. "Ice cold."

As I drove by, people were getting out of the second show at the cinema and going home. I watched the girls, freezing in their short dresses and thought that, if there was anything worth feeling in life except instinct, it was unknown to me.

Passing through one of the streets close to the shore, I spotted a girl with dyed hair, leaning on a lamppost, winking at me. I pressed on the brakes and backed up to her.

"Come in, doll."

She half-leaned toward me, not moving from the lamp.

"It's twenty pounds."

So why not? I thought. Whatever you lack, it's not money. But then, taking another look at the ugly, dumb expression on her face made me feel sick. Why are professionals so ugly?

I drove away and headed for the main road back to Jerusalem. I kept the accelerator down to the floor the whole time. There was almost no traffic. I passed three cars on my way back. They were the only ones on the road. I had passed the third one on a sharp curve when I saw two lights coming toward me. They were very near and I spun the wheel violently to the right and missed them by inches. I went clean off the road. It was a moderate slope of sand and stones, and I kept going down, slamming on the brakes and turning the wheel to the left. The car bumped and bounced and jolted, but it did not turn over. And then, I was back on the road again. Behind me, a horn was blowing frantically and I looked in the mirror and saw the car I had passed parked in the side of the road with its headlights going on and off. I stepped on the gas and shot forward again. There didn't seem to be any serious damage to my car. It picked up speed, and smoothly and quickly I drove on.

I fell asleep the moment I got into bed that night.

I was walking through a large field surrounded by mountains. It was a dark night and the air was fresh and cool and soothing. I was on a narrow sandy pathway and I couldn't make out where it was but it looked familiar and I knew I had been there before, and wanted to be there again. I advanced slowly, not hurrying at all because I had all the time in the world and then I saw him lying across the path with the blood all over his shirt but the helmet was not on his head and I could see his face and it was not the face of a dead man because it was laughing and I thought yes he was just that type of guy to pretend to be dead while all that time he was actually alive and having a better time than all of us here and I wanted to join in his laugh but I couldn't it just wouldn't come and I realized the joke was on me and I started backing away carefully and then he pulled the trigger and I felt the pain burning in my side but I thought to myself no I won't fall no but I just couldn't hold on and I dropped to my knees and I was sweating coldly and I said damn his soul if he would just stop laughing but as if he could see through me his laughter became louder and louder and I realized I could no longer stand and I was sagging down and there was nothing in the world I could do to stop the fall.

"You have a phone call."

I had a hard time waking up. Sleep didn't want to let me out of her arms, but my mother's voice repeated the message again, louder.

"You have a phone call."

I opened my eyes and shook myself out of bed. I was wearing all my clothes and they were moist and wrinkled.

"What time is it?"

"Eleven-thirty."

I rubbed my eyes vigorously with my palms.

"Don't rub them out," my mother said.

"For you, anything, Mom," I said weakly, leaving them in their sockets. I got unsteadily to my feet.

"You look terrible," she said. "Where have you been?"

"Out."

I walked into the hall and picked up the receiver.

"Hello?"

"It's me," Ruthi's voice said on the other end of the line.

"Yes?"

"Well. He is dead and it was a stroke. The doctor said he had expected it. He wasn't surprised. You know, he hadn't been working for the last two months. He had been in and out of the hospital.

"Well," the cool voice continued, "I have to be going back. The house is full of people. They are expecting me."

"When is . . ."

"Twelve o'clock, but please don't come. There would really be no point."

"I'd like to."

"Please."

"All right." I said, resting my head heavily on my arm. "I would like to come and visit you, though."

"I will see you at the university in a week or so," the voice said.

"All right," I said wearily.

"So long."

"Yes, take care."

She hung up.

Forget it, I thought, going downstairs. The guy wants to have a heart attack, let him. Easy come, easy go.

I had my breakfast of orange juice and three aspirins, and then I went out to look at the car. It had a small bump in the front, and had lost some paint, but that was all.

Around noon, the mailman brought me a letter from the connection officer of my reserve unit. It was an order to report to camp in a week's time for a maximum of three days, for parachuting practice. It was the first time I had heard from the army since my discharge.

God wishes to punish you, my boy, by preventing your parachute from opening. You'll make a deep hole in the ground.

The idea appealed to me. Yes, I thought, if God exists and he is angry, he can punish me now. This is his big chance.

Throughout the week I spent a great deal of time reading detective stories. I did a little bit of studying. I didn't write, and I didn't see Joy.

When the parachuting day finally came, I found that I was nervous. I sat in the Nord with thirty other civilians in uniform, and wanted it to be over with. Most of the men were older than I and married with children and permanent jobs. There were a few familiar faces. When the bell rang, we stood up and folded our seats back, then we checked the parachutes. I glanced at the open door in front of me and grimaced disapprovingly. It seemed like a long way down.

"I don't think your parachute is right," I said acidly to the man in front of me. "The strings seem loose."

"You can make those stupid jokes," he said angrily. "You have no kids."

"O.K. Don't say I didn't tell you."

Where did you get that hilarious sense of humor, Assaf, I thought. You should be in show business.

The green light came on and we started moving toward the door. I dove out improperly with my head forward and my arms spread wide. The earth came rapidly toward me in wild circles, and then the harness pulled hard on my ribs and I stopped in midair. I gave God a wink and went slowly toward the ground. Landing, I rolled very correctly on my side and got up to my feet, shaking the sand from my face. I folded the parachute and thrust it into the bag, and started walking toward the gathering place. After a few yards, I bumped into a man lying behind a bush holding his foot and cursing violently. I went closer and took a better look. I recognized the guy who had stood in front of me in the plane.

"What's the idea?" I asked him.

"I broke my goddam ankle," he said, staring at me with impotent fury.

"I'll get the medic," I said.

I turned away, remembering his kids. I could sense his mean look following me as I retreated slowly. I guessed he probably thought it was my fault.

I came home late that afternoon, took a hot shower, had a hot meal, and went to bed. My mother woke me about an hour later, with a loud knock on the door.

I peeked at the clock. It was a few minutes after seven.

"I'm sleeping," I yelled back. "I'm sleeping, O.K.?"

She opened the door.

"You have a visitor."

"Tell him or her or it to come some other time," I said venomously. "I've been up since five this morning. I'm tired."

"It's Udi," she said.

I went into the bathroom and shoved my face under a stream of cold water. I wiped it fiercely with a towel.

"O.K.," I said, stepping back into the room. "O.K., send him in, and please"—I patted her cheek—"be an angel and send us up two cups of tea, sweetheart."

"All right," she said, smiling against her will, "but you behave."

"Sure. Thanks, Mom."

I put on a shirt and ran a brush through my hair. It was quite long already. I had not had it cut since the army. I'll have to cut it myself, I thought. It is getting too long.

Udi knocked on the half-open door.

"Yeah."

He came in. I had not seen him for over three months and his likeness to his brother shocked me. He was as tall as I and strong and slim. He is probably another one of those guys, I thought, who'll be an officer in the paratroopers and get to be a dead hero.

"Hi," he said, a bit timidly. "Am I interrupting you?"

"No," I said, buttoning my shirt. "Take a seat and make yourself at home."

"Thanks."

He sat down on my chair and looked at me awkwardly.

"You invited me once, remember? So I came. I wasn't sure if you meant it, though."

"Sure," I said. "I said I could beat you in chess. Would you like to play chess?"

"I don't know," he smiled. "No, I think not."

"We'll be getting tea and biscuits in a minute. Guests don't get chocolate here. I use it all up myself."

"I read your short story. I think it's great."

I studied his face. He looked as though he meant it.

"I'm glad then."

"Are you writing anything else?"

I moved uncomfortably on the floor.

"I am trying a novel," I said, "but it will take time."

The maid knocked on the door and came in with a tray. She put it on the table and left.

"Help yourself."

"Thanks," he said, taking a biscuit. "What is it about?"

I gestured meaninglessly with my hand.

"I don't know exactly. A 'fictional autobiography' you might call it."

"Yes, that's what I thought."

I got up and helped myself to a cup of tea. I put in two spoonfuls of sugar and sat down again.

"I would like to read it. It will be interesting."

I gazed at him above the cup.

"You seem to think I'm going to be some big author, some day," I said.

"You'll do all right."

"How do you know?"

"I'm sure. Also, Ram used to say that."

"O.K. Well, in that case."

I emptied my cup briskly and put it on the floor.

"You just watch me and see what a smashing career I'm going to have."

"Yes, I will," he said quietly, and drank from his cup.

"I don't understand. What is it to you?"

"I would like to do the same thing myself, one day," he said.

I sat down again, wearily.

"How's your mother?"

"Like always. Ram was her favorite."

"He was one hell of a guy."

"I know."

I drew a circle with my toe on the floor.

"He was one person who shouldn't have died. Want more tea?"

"No thanks. I guess I'll be going."

He got up. "I'll be seeing you," he said.

"Yeah."

He went out, leaving me with a peculiar feeling. I walked to my desk and sat down. I took out all the pages of the book I had typed and leafed through them briefly. It seemed like an anti-everything book: lots of words *against*. I didn't want to write a protest work, rebellion for rebellion's sake. I wanted it to have some beauty. There has to be beauty in things; that's what makes them worth while.

Two female hands suddenly cupped themselves tightly over my eyes. I smelled the light perfume and recognized her, and it was a surprise. But I thought, O.K., if she wants to play, let's play.

"Oh, Mother," I said, "what's come over you?"

Her hot lips pressed on mine and shut my mouth, and as she was leaning over me, I caught her by her wrists and turned her around and pushed her down. I pinned her arms to the sides of her body, and then sat comfortably on her stomach.

"Let me go!" Joy said, breathing hard.

"Like hell."

"That's no way to treat guests."

She made a sudden effort to wriggle herself free, but I was not that weak.

"The guests were asking for it."

"I'll hit you," she threatened.

"With what?"

She made a face.

"What are you going to do? Sit on me for hours like that?"

"No. I'll rape you. What did you think I was going to do?"

"I'll get angry."

"All right."

"Let me go," she gasped, "or I'll yell for your goddam mother."

"O.K.," I said, "if you really don't want me."

I got off her, and stood up. She rose slowly to her feet, fixing her clothes and catching her breath. She was wearing blue jeans and a yellow blouse that matched her hair. Her face was flushed.

I went to the other side of the room and sat on my bed.

"Well," I said, "if you didn't come here to seduce me, what did you come for?"

"I moved."

"What?"

"I moved to another flat," she said, pacing around looking the room over, "partly because of you, in fact. Your being so worried about my living among the enemy. Anyway, I moved."

"Where the hell to?"

"Meah Shearim," she said airily. "You know."

I thought of the fanatically religious people and their women with shaved heads, and I didn't even laugh.

"Oh my God."

"Well, aren't you happy?" she asked anxiously.

"I guess if you survive that, you'll survive anything; but will you survive it?"

"Don't be stupid," she brushed me off carelessly, finally landing on my bed. "They are cute, with those long beards and black hats. I like them, even if they pretend not to like women."

"Ahha."

"It's a nice room you've got. Untidy, but nice."

I coughed dryly.

"Well," she said impatiently, "don't you want to come and see my new palace?"

"Sure. Why not?"

I went over to my desk and collected the pile of papers.

"Listen," I said, "will you do me a favor?"

"Anything for you."

"Read these in your spare time and give me a nice, objective opinion. There are only a hundred of them."

She took the sheets and glanced at the top one.

"Be glad to, but I am not so sure about my objectivity."

I opened the door for her and we went out.

"Your mother looked me over quite thoroughly," she told me when we were in the car, "as though I was one of the first young girls she has seen in ages."

"I do not have many female guests."

"Why not?"

"Lucky in cards, unlucky in love."

We got to a section where the streets were almost too narrow for the car to pass. Joy pointed out a small yard.

"Park here. "We'll only have to walk a little bit."

We got out of the car and started climbing a line of narrow steps leading to a cluster of old, yellow houses. The place was crowded with people, especially young children with long side curls and small caps.

No wonder anti-semitism exists, I thought, looking at them in dismay.

The area was dirty and had a bad smell. On some of the walls there were posters and proclamations against the state and the government, warning the people not to conform to its corrupted rules.

We passed through a bunch of young men coming out of a synagogue. They stood in the middle of the stairway, staring at us with open mouths. I pushed two of them to the side to make way for us to pass. They cursed, but backed away.

"You've got yourself one hell of a neighborhood," I said acidly. "Would have been better off stuck with the Arabs."

"Why are you so much against religious people?" she asked. "They live according to their faith and beliefs. I think that's wonderful, especially nowadays, when nobody believes in anything any more."

"They make me feel inferior for being Jewish."

"Then you're an idiot."

"Maybe."

We climbed the rest of the way in silence.

"There it is," she said, pointing to one of the old buildings.

It had a big yard where chickens were running around. A woman in a long dress and a turban-like scarf was chasing them, cursing under her breath.

Someone tapped me lightly on the shoulder, and I turned around. It was a small, ancient man with a long white beard and thick glasses. He had a Bible under his arm.

"Please," he said.

"What?"

"Please," he repeated again meekly, "tell the young lady not to walk in this neighborhood wearing pants. It's against our tradition."

I shook my head in wonder.

"You want her to walk around without pants?" I exclaimed. "Man, you're way ahead of me."

He stared at me with a shocked expression, and then murmured a prayer and hurried out of sight.

"You shouldn't have said that," Joy said irritably. "I understood."

"Oh, screw him if he can't take a joke."

The apartment itself was not as bad as I had expected. It had two small rooms plus a kitchen and a bath, and it was very clean inside.

We had coffee and talked for a while. She told me she was having trouble getting a work permit, since she had tourist status and was non-Jewish. I told her the Ministry of Interior was in the hands of the religious party, because that's how democracy works in Israel. Only the religious have their way.

"If you really want to hang around here," I told her, "you might as well convert."

"There's no need to exaggerate," Joy said, "it will probably work out in the end."

I laughed.

"I would hate to see you convert."

"I'll let you know in time, then."

"If you really have trouble, let me know. I can probably have something done about it."

Joy shook her head.

"No," she said. "I'll have to do it on my own, or not at all."

Chapter Eleven

THE following morning was one of the rare occasions I went to the university for a lecture. Or rather, it wasn't for the lecture I went. I was hoping to see Ruthi.

I stepped into the hall a few minutes after the bell rang. I closed the doors behind me and looked around. I saw her almost at once. She was sitting on one of the back benches, smartly dressed and well made-up. Her hair was done in an elegant style. She was diligently writing in her notebook.

I walked in and sat on the vacant bench beside her.

"Hello," I said.

"Good morning."

She looked at me and smiled briefly; then she went on writing.

"Let's go and sit on the lawn," I said to her when the bell rang again forty minutes later.

"All right."

We settled ourselves on the stone bench by the strange, gray statue by Henry Moore. Ruthi didn't want to mess up her dress sitting on the grass. It was the best one she had with her in Jerusalem.

"It's getting hot again," she said, looking up at the sky.

"Yes, it'll soon be March."

"I love the spring."

"How are you getting along?" I asked.

"I'm O.K."

After a while her mouth twisted with slight bitterness and she said, "With so many young men I know dying, somehow my father's death doesn't affect me as much."

She took a pair of dark glasses out of her bag and put them on.

"I know it sounds horrid, but it's true."

"What will you be living on?"

Through the dark glasses I couldn't see her eyes.

"That is not a problem."

"Please, tell me."

"My father was a civil servant," she said. "I have his pension, and I have a job now, here at the university."

"Your mother is dead?"

She shook her head.

"No. They were divorced, years ago, and she married again."

"You see her?"

She shrugged.

"Sometimes. I visit, sometimes, not too often. I don't like her husband."

"Look," I said, cutting a few grass leaves with my nails and dropping them through my fingers, "if there is anything I can do, I'd like to do it."

A smile crept over her lips.

"Thank you," she said, "but there is really nothing. Anyway, I will probably be getting married soon, so in any case, that should settle me."

She looked up to the sky again.

"That captain?"

"Yes. Of course."

"O.K.," I said. "It's O.K. then."

"I guess I've gotten used to professional patriots," she said. "I do like you quite a lot," she added, "but we don't have much in common. It's a lucky thing, probably, that we didn't get closer."

"O.K.," I repeated, "but send me an invitation."

She took her glasses off.

"I will."

Farther away, a bell started ringing.

"Well, I have to go."

She got up and arranged her dress properly on her hips.

"Good luck," I said, remaining seated. "See you around."

"So long."

I looked after her as she walked away and then got up and went to the car, relieved. I drove home, planning to start writing the full version of the book.

When I entered the house, closing the door quietly behind me, my mother appeared in the hall, coming from the kitchen.

"Assaf," she said, "who was that girl who came here last night?"

"A friend."

"American?"

"Yes."

"She seemed nice," she said cautiously. "Very pretty."

"That's right."

I started for the stairs.

"O.K., Mom."

"Why don't you ask her over for dinner on Friday?"

"Don't want to," I said over my shoulder.

"Assaf!"

She didn't raise her voice, but it was edgy and tense. I turned and looked back. Her face was sad and upset. An uneasy feeling came over me. I hesitated, then started climbing the stairs again.

"Yes?"

"You live in this house," she said, her large brown eyes peering at me from a pale face. "You can't just ignore us any time you want to."

"For heaven's sake, what's that got to do with the girl? I don't know what you want."

"I'd like to know the people you associate with," she said. "You are so closed, so far away, I never know what you do or think."

I shut my eyes and opened them again.

"I'm just hanging around. It's not that interesting."

"That's all you ever say," she said softly, and then to my astonishment, she added, "like father, like son, they think they don't owe anyone except themselves anything."

I leaned on the railing and gazed at her. She looked down at the floor and raised her hand automatically to smooth her graying hair. I saw the small blue number on her arm and sudden nausea came over me. I leaned more heavily forward and took a deep breath. Suddenly I couldn't stand the sadness in the dark eyes. I knew I didn't understand it, but I wished it would go away. It had always been there and I didn't know what I could do about it and I looked past her into the wide, empty hall.

"All right," I heard myself saying, "Friday night, then. I hope she will come."

I didn't want to bring Joy there. I wanted to have her for myself. I didn't want to share her.

My mother looked at me and smiled.

"I'll have something good cooked," she said almost vivaciously. "It will be nice having a young girl over."

"Yes," I said uncertainly.

I turned and continued up the stairs.

I brought Joy home around eight o'clock on Friday night.

I extended the invitation with a remarkable lack of enthusiasm, but she was rather pleased.

"I am eager to meet your parents," she said happily. "I think it's charming of your mother to invite me."

"She is just curious to see what evil I'm up to," I said irritably. "There is nothing charming about it. In fact, charm has nothing to do with it."

"Don't be like that," she said airily. "It's a pleasant thing for a young, lonely girl like me to have somebody take an interest in her. You wouldn't understand."

"I do. I'm just not sure that I approve."

"So who cares? And I am anxious to meet your father. I've heard a lot about him. He must be interesting."

"Yes. He's great."

"You're dumb," she said joyfully, tying a blue ribbon in her blond hair and looking at herself critically in the mirror, "but I don't care."

When we arrived, I led her to the living room and introduced her to my parents. My mother smiled at her warmheartedly and said how pleased she was to have her there and Joy said something similar, though in a more reserved manner.

My father said, "Hello," and went on reading his paper and it was one of the rare times I stopped to notice how indifferent he was to people. I was so used to it I hardly ever noticed any more, but I went cold with fury, seeing Joy's face growing red with insult as she took a chair opposite him and directed her gaze toward her long, polished fingernails. She was wearing one of her white dresses again and looked very beautiful, especially when she blushed. I cursed myself for bringing her home.

My mother stood hesitantly at the door, staring at the three of us, and then she said the food would be ready in a few minutes and she excused herself. We remained sitting there, each in his big chair, no one saying a word.

After a few moments of silence, my mother came in with trays and dishes and asked us to come eat.

Joy got up and walked to the table, and stood looking at the candles with a blank expression. I went over and stood close to her, rubbing the skin of my lips against my teeth. We waited for a few minutes till my father finished reading his article and joined us at the head of the table. Then my mother lit the candles and we all sat down. We started eating. When she had said she was going to give us a good meal my mother was telling no lie. Joy sat quietly and ate with elegant table manners while my father and I stuffed in the food like two starved wolves.

My mother ate slowly, looking at Joy for a long time, and smiling at her over her plate.

"Have you been here long?" she asked her.

"Almost six months."

"Like it?"

"Yes, this is a good country," Joy said.

"Your family did not come?"

"No."

"Prefer the States?" my mother offered, smiling with under-standing.

"Yes. They are Americans."

My father swallowed a mouthful of wine, paying no visible attention.

"Yes, of course," my mother said uncertainly.

"They like their country," Joy said.

"Yes," my mother said slowly. "But it's really a question of where one feels one belongs."

Then my mother caught herself and paused.

"I'm sorry," she said, "I did not mean to offend you."

"You didn't. It's perfectly all right."

There was a short silence and they both ate. My father had finished long before.

My mother put her fork and knife neatly on the side of her empty plate and looked up again.

"So you are a new immigrant?" my mother continued.

"Don't let it upset you," I said to Joy. "This is part of the show, but the food is reasonable."

My father smiled at his glass.

"It's O.K.," Joy told me, and turning back to my mother, she said: "No, I'm a tourist."

Mother touched her cheek absent-mindedly with the tip of her finger.

"But you will settle, I guess."

"I don't know," Joy said patiently. "You see, I am not Jewish."

I put my hand on the neck of the bottle and poured some wine into my glass. My mother was silent for a moment. Look-ing at her, I thought, What the hell is going on here? She can't be that stupid. My father was watching the two women with interest, his pale blue eyes moving slowly from one to the other.

"This is what they call a tense moment in the cinema," I commented drily.

My mother blushed.

"Excuse me," she said to Joy sincerely. "I was just a little bit surprised, that's all."

"I am sorry if I upset you," Joy said calmly, never moving her eyes from the older woman's face.

"Nonsense," my father said, and drank some more.

"I'll bring the dessert," my mother said, smiling hollowly. She got up and walked out of the room. My father looked at Joy curiously. Their eyes met and held, and a light charming smile appeared on his face. Joy did not smile back, she just looked at him, thoughtfully.

"I wonder what brought you here?" he said finally.

"Probably you could call it curiosity, or hope," she said.

My mother came in and put the small plates with the neatly sliced pieces of melon in front of each of us, then she sat down.

"And," my father said, slowly raising the small fork to his mouth, "was this hope fulfilled?"

Joy was still looking at him, remote and far away.

"I don't know."

"Probably life here seems hard for someone who comes from a rich country like America," my mother said. "It is pretty tough sometimes, even to us, but when you have no alternative, you cling to what you have. For people who went through hell not having a country of their own, even suffering in a place where they belong, where they are home is true salvation."

She paused and I saw Joy looking at the number tattooed on my mother's arm.

"I don't know if it's easy for everyone to understand all that."

Joy didn't say anything more.

"Everything is relative," I told my mother drily. "Your generation still sees this country as a miracle. To those of us who were born when it was already here and made, it doesn't

look so fantastic. We can even see things that could have been
better."

"Yes," my father said. "You cannot appreciate anything, you
just think you deserve everything."

"Well," said my mother, rising, "shall we sit on the terrace?
It's very hot tonight."

"I think I have to go," Joy said, "if you'll excuse me."

"Already?" my father asked.

"Yes. You have been most kind. I am grateful."

"Can't you stay a bit longer?" my mother asked.

"I really have to go."

Both my parents looked at me. I said nothing.

"Well, good night," Joy said, offering her hand to my mother
who took it uncertainly. She nodded politely at my father.
"Thank you, good-bye."

I walked with her through the long corridor to the front
door. We went out into the garden and to the street.

I had reached the car and put the key in the door, when I
noticed she wasn't by my side, and I looked around. She was
walking slowly away, on the pavement.

"Hey."

She turned and stood motionless.

"Where are you going?"

"Home."

I left the car and reached her with a few quick steps. I
looked at her face, and thought I could detect a thin, bitter
smile.

"What's the matter?"

"Nothing," she said. "I'm just quitting, lollipop."

"Didn't like the food?"

She smiled. It was quite a broad smile this time, almost a
grin, but it still didn't reach her eyes, and it still was bitter.

"The food was O.K.," she said. "I just don't like pushing
myself on people. I just didn't get the feeling I belong. I don't
think your parents think I belong. They are probably right. I
don't think I'd have fun in their company, so I'm quitting."

"Lollipop," I repeated.

"That's that, I guess," she said.

"O.K., so what are you going to do?"

"I want to be on my own until I can make up my mind, that's all."

"All right."

Her blue eyes gleamed in the dark, steady, and unblinking. Something heavy took a seat in my chest and stayed there.

"I'll drive you home."

"No. I'll be on my way," she said. "Good night."

"I wish you wouldn't go," I said softly.

I thought she hesitated for a moment, then she shook her head.

"I'd better," she said and started walking away.

I looked after her. She suddenly stopped and turned back.

"Oh," she said. "I'll send you your novel outline with my remarks. I think it's pretty good."

I looked after her retreating figure and she suddenly seemed small and frail, like a little girl. Her high-heeled shoes clip-clopped away until their sound faded into the silence of the night. I walked back into the house.

As I passed by the living room I heard the rattling of a paper and my father's assertive voice came through the half-opened door.

"Assaf."

I walked into the room and sat on the sofa. I leaned back and watched him.

"Has she gone?"

I nodded.

He sat facing me in his big armchair, his chin leaning on his fist. He did not talk, so I sat silently too. I picked up a few almonds from a small glass plate that stood on the table in front of him and started flipping them in the air and catching them in my mouth.

"Do you like her very much?"

I made a meaningless face and stooped to pick up an almond from the carpet.

"It's nothing to be ashamed of."

I grimaced.

"I am not in the least against it."

I just looked at him.

"I wouldn't be particularly for your getting married," he said. "You are much too young and it would only cause complications. But otherwise . . ."

His eyebrows rose thoughtfully.

"Anyway, I don't think you want to get married."

I chewed and then spat the almond into the ashtray. It was a bitter one.

"Maybe your mother has a somewhat different attitude than I," he said. "She had a different background and is altogether a bit more . . ." He paused briefly. "Conservative."

He hesitated, playing with the newspaper.

"She did go through a most horrible time during the war, and everything here means more to her, or in a different way, than to many other people."

I rubbed my face with the palm of my hand.

He put the paper back on the table.

"What does the young group in the party think?" he asked. "Do they oppose the majority on any big issue?"

"No," I said. "This young group has not much to say as far as I can see. They just sit and wait their turn. They have a long time to wait."

"Yes," he said. "It is strange that there are no new shining stars in politics in this country."

He paused.

"You wouldn't have a hard time making it, if you wanted to."

"Maybe."

"You're writing a book?"

"Yes."

"And then you'll try to make a movie out of it if it goes?"

Not bad, I thought.

"Maybe."

"That will take a lot of money."

"Should be about half a million."

"Possibly," he said. Then he added, "Nothing comes free in this world. You play along with me, I'll play along with you."

"We'll see about that."

A significant part of sexual attraction, I thought, is rooted in a feeling of inferiority. That is why Christian girls seem to be so sexy. I remembered how we had learned in school about the anti-semitism in Europe and how Jews were being treated by the Christians like dogs. In my phantasies it was always the sneering Gentile girls that were so attractive. I wanted to do it to all of them. There must be something psychological to it. Maybe intercourse is really like conquering, and it has to be the conquering of something superior in a way, in order to make it really worth while. It is probably for the same reason that so many Christian girls come here and jump into bed with everyone they meet. Christians must feel inferior to Jews because of the reputation Jews have for their intellect.

The attraction, I thought, comes from the fact that it is taboo. I never felt attracted to Arab girls. Israelis don't feel inferior to Arabs.

"Think about it," my father said.

"I will."

I got up and yawned.

"I'll go to bed, if that's O.K. with you."

"Sure," he said. "I'll be going to bed myself soon."

You play it his way, sure, I thought, climbing up to my room. Half a million for a movie could make it worth while. You've just got to get started, I told myself, then you've got it made. It's the beginning that's hard.

That lousy broad.

Chapter Twelve

FOUR days later I got a large envelope through the mail. It contained my papers and Joy's notes. They were mostly corrections of grammar, spelling mistakes, and style. There were also a few remarks about the plot and the development of the stories. Reading it all, I realized she had done a rather thorough job. I accepted most of her comments and suggestions; they made good sense to me. On the last page I found a short line: *Don't rush it too much, this could be good.*

I hoped she would call or show up, but as the days passed there was no sign of life from her.

For four weeks I locked myself up in my room and wrote, typing frantically with two aching fingers. At the end of that time I was through with the book.

I thought it was pretty good.

It was told in the first person and was the story of a disaffected young man. He is so disaffected that he is able to climb straight to the top and become an extremely successful businessman. He had a talent for exploiting people and making use of every situation, and he doesn't mind doing either. His decline begins when he stops caring about his success too, and finds that he has nothing to long for, because he has it all anyway. In the last scene he dies in the Six Day War during a private attack on an enemy post that will probably earn him a handful of decorations. He is twenty-eight at the time and he is bitter because he doesn't think he's the type to sacrifice his life.

In its final form, the story was a hundred and eighty-two pages. It was a bit less than I had expected, but I couldn't force myself to work on it any more, so I hoped it would do.

I sent two copies to two different publishing houses in America, and decided to wait for a while and see what happened.

That same evening I went over to Joy's place, thinking that this was a sufficient excuse to celebrate, but the windows were dark, and she wasn't there. I sat out in the car for over an hour and waited, wondering how she would look, but no one showed up.

At home I found a group of people, all connected in one way or another to the military industry, who had come for an after-supper drink and talk.

The Defense Minister was there.

Seeing him, I went into the living room. The man had always fascinated me. He was not as boring and crisp and flat as most other politicians, he had charm. A rough, brutal kind of charm. He was good looking in a strange way, but his chief appeal to me lay in his direct, quick, I-don't-give-a-damn manner. He was known to join patrols on the Suez Canal, and ambush squads in the Jordan Valley. His face and hands were tanned and bruised, but that was one of the sources of his popularity. With him, soldiers didn't get the feeling they were the only ones who had to risk their lives.

My father, who was standing with him at a corner of the room, waved to me to join them. I picked up my glass and walked over.

"Good evening," I said to the massive, tough-looking man.

He nodded and flashed his magnetic smile.

"How is the youth doing?" he asked, stuffing some peanuts into his mouth.

"How do you mean?"

"How is the morale among the students?"

"It's all right," I said, "still."

His face showed curiosity.

"Still?"

"As long as they don't start seriously doubting the government's policy."

"I wonder," he said, looking at my father and then at me, "if there is a chance of this new left catching on with students here."

He paused.

"We don't need student riots here," he added.

"Students don't have time for riots," I said. "When they are not in the reserves, they are busy catching up with the exams they missed."

"Yeah, well," he said, "maybe we'll have to add some more annual days of reserve duty anyway." He winked boyishly.

"Better not," I said.

"Oh," he said, amused.

"If students do start rioting, you'll have a tough case on your hands, the toughest yet."

"I am trying to persuade this boy to go into politics," my father said mildly. "Young blood is needed there."

"That is so," the minister said, watching me with his hawk-like stare.

Eating peanuts didn't go well with his image.

"He is not excited about it."

"He is right. It is not a job for human beings."

"Thanks," I said.

"It's going to be a hard summer," the Minister of Defense said to my father. "We have to increase missile production. It will be vital."

I moved away, draining my glass, and put it on a table near a fat American millionaire. He looked up at me and smiled absent-mindedly. I smiled back at him and wandered out of the room. I heard my father saying something about building a new factory for aircraft engines, and I closed the door behind me.

I walked into the kitchen and took a Coke bottle out of the refrigerator. I wondered when he would get the Israel Prize again; it would probably take some time. This year an honorary doctorate from the university would have to do.

I went up to my room and took a look at the list of my exams for the second semester. I threw the empty bottle at the wastebasket at the other side of the room and missed. It shattered on the floor into small, glittering pieces. I turned off the light and went to bed.

The following morning, around eight, my mother woke me up, saying I had a phone call. I jumped out of bed and landed on a few dozen splinters of glass. My mother opened big horrified eyes and raised a hand to her mouth. Cursing profoundly, I went to the phone, leaving a faint trail of red behind me.

"Hullo."

"Know what today is?"

"It isn't my day," I said, thinking the opposite.

"O.K., but other than that," Joy insisted.

"Friday, I guess."

"Good Friday," she said patiently. "The processions start at ten-thirty. Would be good for your education."

"I'll be over at ten."

"Fine."

The line went dead.

"This time I get you and keep you," I told the receiver, and sat down for my mother to wrap my foot with the white bandage she had brought.

"You've probably never watched these ceremonies," Joy remarked to me as we walked toward the Via Dolorosa. "It should be most interesting to see it carried out here in Jerusalem."

"It will be wasted on me; I have no stomach for religion."

"Who's religious? It's just beautiful."

The place was swarming with people, from all countries and of all religions. The Arab shopkeepers were lying on the side of the way, smoking their nargiles, and watching the passers-by with a faraway look.

Even as we were advancing, elbowing our way through the
sweating crowd of people, there was a long procession parading
toward us. It was an American group and there were a few
good-looking, miniskirted girls among them. In the lead were a
priest and two elderly women carrying a wooden cross.

We stopped walking and pressed ourselves to the wall,
watching the advancing procession.

"Isn't it impressive?" Joy asked. "All those different people,
united in their faith?"

"Hey, Margie!" one of the fat, elderly women carrying a
cross whispered to the other ecstatically.

"What?"

"This is where Charlton Heston was kept prisoner in *Ben-
Hur*," she whispered like thunder, pointing to the Antonia
Fortress. "Right Here!"

"Oh, really, Sally?" the other said glowingly, looking hard
over her shoulder, through her gold-rimmed glasses and stumbling against a small stone. She let out a high-pitched shriek
but managed to steady herself and continue on her way.

A few middle-aged Negro women brought up the rear,
singing "Jesus' Blood Makes Us White as Snow," smiling
sheepishly at heaven.

"I don't know," I told Joy after they had all passed. "I
don't know about that."

"Let's go and see the fortress," she suggested. "It's an interesting building."

Inside it was cool and pleasant. A few nuns strolled around,
smiling politely at the visitors. We went through a hall built
of huge stones which had a low ceiling and a slippery floor.

"Here Christ was given the cross," Joy told me, "and from
here they marched him through the Via Dolorosa to Golgotha,
where he was crucified."

There were some other visitors in the place besides us.
There were a few hippies and a few young religious Jews.
With their beards and long hair they all reminded me of
Jesus. I was getting to feeling holy.

We walked slowly out and came to the Expresso machines near the exit.

"Those technical miracles in the heart of history," I said. "That is impressive."

"Shshshsh."

"That's where he stopped for coffee?"

"Shshshsh."

We went out.

"What now?" I asked, yawning.

"Let's walk a bit. Don't you want to walk a bit?"

"Anything with you."

When we approached the Wailing Wall we could see the two groups by it, the men and women, doing their daily mourning.

"All those goddam people, standing by some goddam wall, crying for a goddam building that maybe stood here a goddam thousand years ago, when we don't even get those dozen goddam Phantoms," I said for conversation's sake. "I just don't believe it. Tell me it's not true. I just don't believe it."

"You don't understand."

"No. I don't approve. Why do they keep praying to Jesus or Moses when they've got much more contemporary folk singers?"

She was not impressed.

"This kind of faith," she said, pointing to the Wall, "kept these people strong and united as a nation through only God knows what, and that's a bloody miracle."

"Oh, for Christ's sake."

We stood watching in silence. A few small Arab children came to us offering small wooden camels for sale. I waved them aside but they kept pushing against us saying "buy," "beautiful camels," and other such slogans they had mastered in English. There was no way of getting rid of them. They made their living like that. There was nothing else for them to do. Finally, I kicked one of them lightly in the behind. That made them leave.

Joy eyed me warily.

A group of tourists approached us, led by a guide. He was explaining to them in English the history and the meaning of the places around them. They came to a halt next to us. Joy removed her irritated gaze from me and placed it peacefully on the guide. She stepped forward and joined the group. I walked after her.

My eyes fell on a tall girl who was standing a bit outside of the group. She was wearing a light, revealing dress. She was dark haired and rather pretty. Our eyes met and a brief smile appeared on her lips.

"You must tell me someday how you do it," Joy said venomously.

"Someday," I said darkly.

The girl suddenly winked at me, mischievously, and then shifted her eyes away.

"Holy places always make girls look sexy," I said to Joy. "Maybe because they are usually hot and the girls don't wear much."

"Maybe."

"I finished the novel," I said dully.

"Gorgeous."

"How are you getting along with your job?"

"Great."

I shrugged and looked back at the dark-haired girl. She was only half-listening to the guide, fixing the strap of her bra lazily. Our eyes met again, and again the sly smile appeared and played on her mouth.

I smiled back at her.

"So, will I start seeing you again now?" I asked.

"Why don't you go over to her?" Joy asked drily. "You seem to get along quite well."

"It's you I want," I said, still smiling.

"But that's probably harder. I hate to think what you're missing."

"Jealous?"

She laughed abruptly.

The group started moving away.

"Maybe you'd better give it a try, because I tend to stay on my own."

"Look," I said, "let's cut this out."

Joy started walking quickly, going to join the group. I slowed down, watching her.

"Hey!" I said.

But she didn't stop.

"A little family strife?" The new voice was deep, with a heavy French accent. The perfume, I thought, was French, too.

"I thought you were American," I said to the tall, dark-haired girl.

"No I am French."

"What's your name?"

"Veronique."

"I am Assaf. How do you do?

"How do you do? You want to shake hands?" she asked sardonically.

"No. Not the hands."

She laughed profoundly.

I stopped walking.

"Well?"

She shook her head, grinning.

"I am with the group," she said pointing forward with a long finger carrying a long lilac nail. "Aren't you coming too?"

"No, I have seen it before."

"That is a pity," she said coquettishly. *"Au revoir."*

She squeezed my arm gently and walked after the group. I turned and started going in the other direction, back to the car. As I passed by the Jewish quarter I thought I might as well take a walk and look around while I was there. It was not hard to distinguish the Jewish quarter from the other parts of the Old City, because it was the only area completely in ruins.

Hell, I thought, walking between the remains of two synagogues which had only a few stones to them. And they are complaining that we mistreat them. They say we oppress them. That's really a laugh. With all their mosques and shops and houses untouched, and their getting all the water and electricity and things they never had before. After they had put their sheep and donkeys in those old synagogues and used the tombstones from the Jewish cemetery to build their houses.

There was a little boy with side curls and a small cap, sitting on the ground throwing stones at a wild bush a few feet away from him. He was good-looking and I stood on the side watching him silently. When he saw me he dropped the stone he was holding and looked at me suspiciously. I smiled at him.

"Why do you miss all the time?" I asked.

"I don't," he protested, frowning.

He picked up the stone and threw it, hitting the bush square in the middle.

"You see?" he said, smiling at me triumphantly.

"Absolutely great," I said, shaking my head. "Now I can go home and rest in peace."

When I reached the car, I found a group of Arab kids standing around it. I got the key out of my pocket and opened the door.

"We guard the car. We guard the car."

I pushed them aside with one impatient gesture of my hand and got inside. They stood by me, knocking on the door with their small fists and repeating their demand in an endless stream of protest. I started the engine.

A tall dark man appeared at my side and put his hand on the door handle.

"They guard the car," he said in English, with a heavy Arabic accent. I clamped my hand on his wrist and pushed it away. I was beginning to get annoyed.

"Get lost," I said to him. "Make it snappy."

He kept standing there, leaning on the door. The blood came to his face, making it darker.

I stopped the engine.

"They guard the car," he said again.

I moved to the other seat and climbed out through the door. He watched me coming and straightened up. I walked over to him and hit him in the face as hard as I could. He stumbled back and I kicked him viciously in the stomach. Around us the small boys were screaming at the top of their voices.

A whistle blew not far from my ear and then a man in dark uniform stepped between me and the tall Arab who was again leaning on the door of the car, his face navy blue.

I took a step back and looked at the policeman. He was dark and thin and I thought he was an Arab too, but I wasn't sure. They are hard to distinguish from the darker Israelis.

"What's habbening here?" he demanded in a voice that seemed bigger than he was; "habbening" made him an Arab.

The small kids were jumping around excitedly, yelling: "We guard the car" and "He not pay." The policeman blew his whistle once more to silence them. He pushed them aside, bawling in Arabic. The tall Arab stopped leaning on the car and stood up. His face had regained its normal color. He didn't speak.

"What habbened?" The policeman turned to me.

"He didn't let me get out of here," I said, motioning with my head toward the car and the tall man, "so I pushed him."

The Arab said something in Arabic I did not understand. I saw his mouth was bleeding but his face was composed and blank.

"Give me your identity card," the policeman told me.

I drew it out of my pocket and gave it to him.

He looked at my card. Then he gave me a quick glance, and looked briefly at the car. I saw that he recognized the name and it irritated me. I looked over his shoulder.

"O.K., sir," he said to me, giving me back the identity card. "You may go now. I hope nothing like this habbens again."

"Thanks."

I climbed back into the car and started the motor again. The policeman walked slowly away. The tall Arab stood lean-

ing on a nearby car rubbing his chin. He didn't look at me.
The small children were beginning to gather around me again,
but they were more careful.

"What a lovely car."

I looked up. Veronique's handsome face smiled at me, her
perfume was still as good and strong as before.

"I have to get moving," I said. "Can I give you a lift?"

"Please."

I opened the door for her, as she got in. The small kids
started closing in on us again.

"Rooch!" I said threateningly. It was one of the few Arabic
words I knew. It means, "go away."

I pulled away from the curb.

"Where do you have to go?" I asked the girl beside me.

"To the youth hostel, it's . . ."

"I know where it is," I cut in. "Do you live there?"

"Yes, for one more night."

"And what then?"

"I am flying back to Paris tomorrow morning."

"Oh, I see. Do you like the youth hostel?"

"Well, it is not very elegant, but it is cheap."

She took a small mirror out of her bag, and looked at her
reflection.

"Oh, I look terrible," she said.

"I'll put you up for the night, if you want."

She turned to me and crossed her legs, smiling knowingly.

"What will your wife say?"

"It's my mother," I said dully. "She'll be furious, but she
won't say anything."

She laughed.

"You live in a big house."

"You'd fit."

She put a cold, bony hand briefly on my shoulder.

"I would be charmed," she said.

"Good."

"But, my room in the youth hostel . . ."

"We're on our way there," I said, "to get your suitcase."

"I have three," she said, her deep laughter rang in my ears. "I bring many dresses when I travel."

"We'll take the three of them, then."

"And in the evening you take me out for supper?"

"Perhaps."

After we had supper in the Italian restaurant called La Gondola, we went to The Khan night club. It was an old building that had once been a caravansary, and was turned into a small theater and a night club. I was having a good time that evening, drinking wine and dancing. I did not find it difficult to dance when Veronique was my partner, because she clung very close, pressing against me with the whole length of her body. It would have been hard to make technical mistakes. She was enjoying herself, too. I imagined she was the type who probably always did, especially in night clubs.

"It is beautiful music," she said breathing hotly in my ear. "I love beautiful music."

My mouth was occupied with her dark hair. I did not offer any comment. I kissed her.

"Ahh," she said softly, when I wriggled my lips free in order to breathe. "Not so fast."

It was after two when we came home. We tiptoed up the stairs, both a little drunk and not steady on our feet. Veronique was given a small room next to mine which was occupied by only two Chagall lithographs and a small bed. My mother had registered a displeased question mark when I had carried the three suitcases up the stairs, followed by the smiling young lady, but I told her Veronique was the fiancée of an old friend from the army. My mother had to accept that explanation, even if she didn't believe it.

"Well?" Veronique said, at her door. "Good night. I will see you, no?"

"My room," I said, trying to shake the wine out of my head, "is more comfortable."

"All right," she said, and walked into her room.

I sat down at my desk and got rid of my shoes and socks. I took a pen and a piece of paper and started drawing a face. It came out remarkably beautiful. I tore it up. The door opened and Veronique peeped in. She wrinkled her brow wonderingly and then stepped in, closing the door behind her. She walked around the desk and stood behind me, peering down over my shoulder. She wore a transparent, light blue nightgown.

"What are you doing?" she asked hoarsely, looking at the torn pieces of paper.

I caught hold of her hips and pulled her down on to my knees.

"Nothing."

"Not so fast," she laughed huskily. "There is this." She pointed to the bed.

She freed herself from my arms and jumped into the bed, covering herself with the blanket.

"Oh," she cooed. "This is so warm."

I walked after her and sat on the edge of the bed.

"Do you like me?" she asked slyly.

"You are very attractive," I said.

She extended her hand foppishly.

"Come," she said like some mock-French queen, inviting her favorite knight for the night.

She removed the blanket and I knelt and kissed her neck and sank down by her. She wriggled herself out of the nightgown and put her hands on my chest. Her fingers began unbuttoning my shirt, and then pulled it off me.

"You are strong," she whispered in my shoulder.

My lips moved on the smooth chambers of her body from the thin chestbone to the dark, erect nipples. I sunk my teeth in the soft skin, feeling her hand digging under my pants. Then she pushed me aside and sat up, supporting herself with her elbows. Her small breasts rubbed delicately against my face. I closed my eyes.

"You lie on your back," she said thickly, drawing me down on the mattress, "and I will make you happy."

I felt her smooth, flat belly against my cheek as she kneeled over me.

"Girl," I said quietly to myself, "you are what I have been looking for for a long time."

I put my arm over my eyes, shaking, when I felt the touch of her lips.

Chapter Thirteen

A FEW weeks later, I had a letter from one of the publishing houses to which I had sent the book. My heart skipped a few beats when I read it, and I considered patting myself on the shoulder, when I was through. They said they would publish it. There would have to be a few changes, the letter went on, but it would definitely be published. I should write to their office and a contract would be drawn up.

I was feeling down at the time and I welcomed the letter. I had not seen Joy since Passover. The few times I went to her house she was not there. There was only one conclusion that seemed plausible. I was out and someone else was in. I could not find any other reasonable explanation.

Late that evening I went into my father's office. He sat by his desk, a burnt-out cigar in his hand, napping over a pile of his never-ending papers.

I sat down on a chair and thumped both feet heavily on the floor. The noise woke him up with a start.

"You should be in bed," I told him.

He rubbed his eyes with the back of his hand.

"Probably," he agreed, lighting his cigar and shaking his head, "but since I am awake now . . ."

I shrugged.

"Well?" he said.

I scratched my cheek with my forefinger and waited. His eyes narrowed.

"I was wondering," I said finally. "If you could lend me your lawyer one of these days, to help me with something."

He was fully awake now and his eyes shifted to his wrist watch, but only for a fraction of a second.

"What for?"

"There's a contract I need to discuss," I said mildly. "I was hoping he could help with it."

"What contract?"

"I can sell a book I wrote, a short novel. I'll need a lawyer."

He looked down at the table.

All right, I thought, come on, ask already, you bastard. You must want to know something about it.

He raised his eyes to my face.

"O.K.," he said. "I'll talk with him. Let me know when you need him."

Sure, what did you expect? I thought, trying to conceal my disappointment. People are what they are, so who cares?

"Thanks, that would be fine."

He was looking back at his papers. I got up.

"Oh, by the way."

I stopped at the door.

"Yes?"

"I heard you ran into some policeman, a few weeks ago, on the other side of town."

"You must be confusing me with someone else," I said.

"No, no. It was you. Had something to do with a young man who spoke to you, in the parking lot. You hit him."

"Oh yes, I remember. What about it?"

"It is undesirable."

"Oh, well."

I stepped out and closed the door softly behind me.

The next evening I went to Joy's apartment again but she was not there. It was around nine. After waiting for a few minutes, hoping for some miracle to happen, I drove to the center of town, and walked into the first cinema I found which was showing an Italian Western. Seeing everyone get shot except the hero and the girl made me feel good again, so after the movie was over I went home and sat in my room for two hours drinking Coke and listening to a dozen Sinatra records.

After one, I went to look for Joy again, but the place was dark and my constant knocking on the door brought no one out but the cats. My good mood faded away again in no time at all.

I went to sleep angry.

The next morning I went there again and after finding that she still wasn't there, I dug the landlady out of her bed. She was a fat, old religious woman, who, I could see immediately, did not approve of my existence. Her eyes went over my long hair and red shirt with naked disgust.

"Good morning," I told her.

"What do you want?"

"The American girl downstairs, do you know where she is?"

"What do you want from her?"

It was obvious that whatever she thought I might have wanted wouldn't be something she would approve of, but I ignored that.

"I am an old friend of hers. I've got a message for her, from relatives in the States."

She stared at me for a moment.

"She is not here any more," she said finally.

I shifted my weight from one leg to the other.

"You mean she checked out?"

"Yes."

"When?"

She sighed and looked up to heaven, significantly. When she came back I was still there.

"Two days ago."

"Left any messages?"

She shook her head.

"Where did she go?"

She shook her head again.

"O.K., thanks."

The goddam bitch, I thought.

I went to the TWA office and asked the new girl who was sitting at the desk what happened to her predecessor. She said Joy had had to quit because of troubles with her work permit. She had no idea where she had gone. She had hardly known Joy at all.

The goddam bitch, I thought.

When I came home I went to the kitchen and joined my mother who was having a late breakfast.

I buttered my toast silently, eating the dry skin off my lips.

"Whatever happened to that American girl?" she asked. "Joy, was it? I haven't seen her since."

"She vanished."

She looked thoughtfully at the splinters of the plate I had dropped on the floor with the butter.

"Yes, well I could have told you. Girls like that don't stay in one place long."

"Oh, you could have told me, could you?"

"They have no roots."

"No, they don't, do they?"

I swept the splinters and butter into my hand and dumped them into the garbage can.

"So who cares?" I asked, walking out. "I've still got you, Mother."

At noon I found a letter addressed to me in the mailbox, but the sender was not a blond female. It was the army. I looked through it briefly: thirty-four days, bring all your military equipment, your boots, warm clothes, etc. Report at camp on May 30. At least someone wanted me.

I worked the paper into a small, shrunken ball and tossed it at the wastebasket at the other side of the room. I missed. I walked over there, picked it up, opened it and smoothed it carefully, and then put it in a drawer in my desk.

Till July 2, I thought. That's actually well timed.

The academic year ended on the twenty-eighth of June, my first exam was on the fifth of July. But still, who the hell needs the bloody army?

A few days later I signed a contract with the publishing house. I was going to get an advance of a thousand dollars, and fifty cents for each copy sold. I thought it was a good deal.

But it was going to take months before it would be out on the market and, meanwhile, life had to go on.

I started going to party meetings, young group and old group. Anything.

Another thing I started doing was speaking at those meetings. I thought, if I bother at all I might as well bother all the way, and being any duller than the rest of the speakers would have been hard. The problem was that everything had already been said thousands of times about the peace talks and the occupied territories and the Palestinian problem, and it never helped any. I didn't care for repeating those old chewed and predigested ideas. I didn't care to say anything at all.

I did pick myself a line, because if you want to make an impression you need some line, although it does not matter very much which one. I spoke for returning everything except Jerusalem and the Golan Heights in exchange for a peace treaty.

I spoke twice before small meetings of the younger group. I did it in an aggressive, mocking manner, suggesting rather clearly, that anyone who didn't agree with me just had to be awfully innocent or terribly stupid. It got to the stage where I almost enjoyed my performances. I was surprised to see that my speeches caused quite a lot of debate, and after the second one, there was even a review in the daily paper run by the party that referred to a "promising, new personality."

I didn't think I would go far because I limited my activity to evening meetings. I couldn't take it in larger doses. In broad daylight it just looked too stupid.

My father, on the other hand, meeting me for lunch on a Friday, expressed his satisfaction with my conduct and suggested that I increase my participation. I told him there was no use in pushing. Young people were not taken seriously in politics. Maybe student riots would get some attention, but in this country, students couldn't afford them. Once people started revolting, the country couldn't hold on the way it had to. That was one thing I was sure of, and that was one reason why politics didn't appeal to me. What we actually needed, what I would have actually liked, was to change the system and rid it of the monopoly of the older generation. But we just couldn't afford it in this country. It would amount to supporting the enemy, so I didn't want to be bothered.

I was becoming fed up.

Then, one day, I got a letter from Joy.

Dear Assaf,
I have moved to the biggest town in Israel. I needed the cnange.
The address is 7 Horkanos Street. Drop by if you ever feel like it.
Sincerely,
Joy

I drove around Tel Aviv for nearly an hour trying to find the damned street, when finally a motorized policeman hunted me down for speeding.

"Are you mad, sir?" he asked me, breathing with effort. "Do you know that there are human beings living in this town and even walking in its streets?"

I turned the radio off.

"As a matter of fact," I said, "I am looking for one of them, she lives in Horkanos Street. Would you know where that is?"

But his face was blank.

"Give me your identity card, driving license, and registration. I shall have to give you a ticket."

That brought me back to reality.

"I did tell her we were through," I said grimly, putting my hand in my pocket. "Still, sleeping pills are no solution. But I guess in a few minutes it will be over anyway."

"What did you say?"

"She'll be better off that way, won't she?" I asked him

anxiously. "I mean she never got much of a kick out of life, poor thing."

"Man do you realize . . ."

"Do you know where it is?"

"Follow me," he said, breathing hard again.

He mounted his motorcycle, and roared away.

After ten minutes of speed violation, we were there. I told him I would rather keep it inside the family if nothing had happened yet, and finally convinced him to wait outside. He told me he had enough troubles with his girl friend himself, but they were going to be married next month, thank heavens. I nodded my approval.

"If I'm not down within ten minutes forget about it," I said, "and thanks."

It was a large seven-story building of gray concrete, like the ones all over Tel Aviv. These buildings do not add to the beauty of the city, in my opinion.

I started climbing up the stairs, looking at the names on the doors and seeing nothing familiar. I reached the seventh floor and stopped for breath, wondering vaguely when they were ever going to put elevators in these funny buildings. I looked around. There were not many alternatives left. There was really only one, the emergency exit to the roof, so I climbed up there.

Outside, on the roof, there was a small cabin with a gray, peeling door. There was a white sheet of paper on it, bearing the name Joy in large, careless ink letters.

I knocked on the door. It was late afternoon and the sun was setting on the sea behind the huge cluster of gray buildings. I looked at the city with dismay. I thought it had no beauty at all.

Nothing happened. No one came to open the door and there was no sound except the noise of the traffic below, I knocked again, louder, saying to myself, "Don't push me, God. I've warned you once, I won't warn you twice."

Again nothing happened. I leaned on the handle and shoved the door and it opened, creaking like an old window.

I stepped in, closing it behind me and looked around suspiciously. The room was rather dark and for the first few seconds I couldn't see anything at all. Then my eyes got used to the gloom and I saw that there was a dim light coming from a small window that threw a soft glow on the bed at the corner of the room. Upon it, fast asleep, crumbled in a woolen blanket, lay Joy.

I walked slowly around the room. It took me three steps to get from one end to the other, and they were rather small steps. She did not stir.

Her breathing came quietly and regularly. I was wondering how long I could contain myself when I stumbled into a small stool that had been hiding in the corner. It turned over and hit the floor like a cannon shell. Joy sat up with a jerk.

"What is it?" she asked with a weak voice that was out of tune. She was trying to see through the dark.

"It's O.K.," I said, pulling the stool up and sitting on it. "It's O.K."

She focused her eyes on me with an effort. They were large and searching and, along with her disorderly long hair, made her look helpless and young like a small, frightened child.

She turned on a small lamp that stood on the floor by her side. She smiled and leaned her head back on the pillow.

"Hello."

"How are you feeling?" I asked.

The corners of her mouth curled up a little bit.

"Fine."

I got up and paced the room some more. There wasn't much space left around the bed. By it stood a wooden chair and on that was a white dress. There was a small cupboard with a heavy suitcase on it in the corner. That was about it.

"I was glad to hear from you," I said cautiously, "after you had disappeared."

She stood up and let the blanket drop to the floor shaking her hair from her face. Except for her panties and bra, she had nothing on but smooth, sun-tanned skin. I moved to the other side of the room and bumped into the peeling gray door.

"I'll make some coffee," she said, "O.K.?"

"Yeah. Anything you say."

She dug a finger into a blue eye and rubbed some sleepiness out. Then she smiled.

"Won't be a minute."

She retreated into a narrow gap in the wall that was so small I had missed it before. I assumed it led to an ultra-modern vast electric kitchen. I sat on the stool and waited. She came back after a moment, placed herself on the bed, crossed her legs and looked at me innocently. I picked up the white dress that was draped over the chair, and tossed it to her.

"You are tempting me, plus you might catch a cold."

She put it obediently over her head and slipped it on.

"One or the other," she said with a muffled voice, through the thin cloth. "The other is more likely."

Her face appeared from under the white curtain. "I am happy to see you," she said.

"Why did you disappear?"

"I'm sometimes impulsive."

"No, I really want to know."

"I was angry with you, then I lost my job. That made me a lot angrier. Why do you have to be Jewish to have any rights in this country?"

She gestured emptily with her hand.

"Anyway," she continued, "I just felt like getting away from everything. I was practically on my way to London, then I thought better of it. I moved here."

"At least it's nearer to the airport," I commented.

I moved on my stool; it creaked in agony.

"Not so fancy here, is it?" she said and got up. "I'll get the coffee."

She brought the two cups and placed them carefully between us, on the floor.

"The sugar is already in."

"So now you're hunting for a job?" I asked carefully.

"I've got one already. Can you guess what it is?"

"I don't know. What is it, TWA?"

"Egyptian Airlines . . ."

"Oh."

"No hijacking or anything."

I tried the coffee.

"No," she said. "It's a small bookshop. They needed an English-speaking girl. It's not fantastic, but for the time being . . ." She made a meaningless gesture with her hand. "It will have to do."

I put my empty cup on the floor.

"Come back to Jerusalem," I said. "I'll get you another job, a better one, any job."

She looked at me.

"No problem?" she asked, smiling into my unhappy face.

"No . . ."

The smile broadened a bit, then disappeared.

She shook her head.

"No. If I stay, I have to be able to make it on my own. I have been sorry about that Good Friday," she said. "I was rude."

"That's all right."

"What did you think of that tall girl, remember her?" she asked me. "I thought she was very sexy."

I nodded.

"Yes, so did I. She was quite dumb though, but then they usually are."

She seemed surprised.

"You spoke to her?"

"Yes."

Her eyes watched me closely. The amusement was still there but, behind it, I thought there were signs of tension.

"And what happened then?"

"I put her up for the night. She had to leave the following morning, for Paris."

"Was she another hard case?" she asked thoughtfully, wrinkling her brow. "No, I guess not," she added after a pause. "I don't think she was."

"She was easy," I said, thinking, so the hell with all of it.

"She was the easiest one I have ever come across, but, then, I haven't had a lot of experience."

"Oh, I see," she said.

Raising her cup to her lips, she took a few sips.

"Was she good?"

"I don't know. All right."

"Well. At least there is that."

I licked my teeth with my tongue.

"It's you I want though," I said. "I told you that already. I wish you would come back."

"I have to stay here."

I climbed slowly to my feet and walked to the other side of the room.

"Assaf?"

I looked down at the floor where some small, black ants were emerging from underneath the door.

"Yes."

Then, I heard her light footsteps behind me and her arms tied themselves around my neck. I felt her quick, hot breathing on my cheek. She kissed me with a low moaning sigh, and I kissed her back and I heard her sigh again and I put my arms around her and pulled her fiercely to me and we were stumbling backward until we sat on the bed and her eyes were closed and her mouth was hot and dry on mine and her arms were pulling me down on top of her. And my hands wandered over the smoothness of her skin until they came to the hook in the back of her dress and I stopped hesitating and I undid her white virgin-like dress and then she kicked the dress away and it fell on the floor and her long thin fingers unbuttoned my shirt and touched my chest and she sighed again, and I pulled off her remaining clothes and I was never sure until the last minute if she was really going to, but she drew me to her and her eyes were like clouds so close and her body was soft and I felt her legs around me and I never stopped wondering and I thought to myself maybe it isn't what it always seems and then at that moment I didn't feel sad any more.

Afterward, when we were lying on our backs in the narrow

bed, she looked at me, like a small girl trying to find something lost. I was trying to figure out what she was thinking, and after we lay there for quite a while in silence, she leaned over and kissed me, and her lips were dry and caressing, and then she smiled at me and there was no melancholy in it.

"Well?"

"You are beautiful."

"Is that all?"

"No. That's a lot, but that's not all."

Her face flushed.

"Kiss me once again," she said, "and I'll go and make some more coffee."

I pulled her to me and kissed her. She clung for a long moment. Then she sat up, suddenly energetic.

"O.K.," she said, "coffee."

She slipped into her white dress.

"Mustn't catch a cold," she said coyly and went to the kitchen.

"Listen," I said to her, when we were drinking the coffee, "won't you come back?"

"I shouldn't," she said, clutching my arm with her hand. "I have to be sure, I need some time, can't you see?"

"O.K., then let's not talk about it any more."

"Don't be cross," she said softly. "I don't want to quarrel any more."

"I am not cross."

"Then, it's all right."

"I sold the bloody book," I said.

Chapter Fourteen

"WHERE did you spend last night?" my father asked me the following evening when we ran into each other in the hall.

"I visited Joy in Tel Aviv. Why?"

He looked at me thoughtfully.

"Drop in to my study some time later, will you?"

"Sure."

I went to the kitchen and snatched a bottle of Coke. My mother looked at me silently.

When I entered my father's study holding the bottle loosely in my hand he wasn't looking at his papers. He was sitting at his desk staring straight ahead of him. I sat down on the sofa and took a drink.

"I hear you are speaking on Monday night," he said after a while, "in the party delegates' meeting." He raised an eyebrow. "That is quite something. What are you going to say?"

I shrugged.

"Nothing much. Mostly my view about the government's 'so-called policy' on the Arab question. Mostly that."

"Yes," he said darkly. "And what are you going to say about your view of the government's 'so-called policy' on the Arab question?"

"Well," I said, "I'm going to say, first of all, that there is no policy to speak of and, secondly, whatever policy there is is not one which initiates peaceful solution. If we want peace, we've got to tell them exactly what we are willing to give back for it, and it will have to be most of what we have taken. That is the only practical solution, and no one ever articulates it."

His pale eyes narrowed just a bit.

"That's no good," he said.

"That is what I am going to say."

"Better not."

I licked the mouth of the bottle.

"Don't be a fool," he said suddenly. "We'll give it all back and they'll try to wipe us all out, three months later. There is no other safe way, except being strong."

"Lately I don't feel so safe," I said flatly.

"That is no good," he repeated. "You shouldn't go against the official line of the party, not when you are just a beginner, not when you've just started establishing yourself. You speak well. Argue for the majority opinion and you'll rise quickly. Maybe afterward you can afford to change your opinions."

"That isn't the way I want to do it."

"What good does it do you?" he said, not raising his voice. "You can't influence anything, one way or another, before you are important, and if you say what you want to, you won't ever be powerful."

I licked my lips, my mouth felt dry. I wished I had another bottle.

"I never did want to go into politics," I told him.

"It would be worth your while," he said.

"I don't know."

"Think it over," he said. "I hope you take it easy with that American girl."

"Her name is Joy."

"Yes," he said. "I hope you are not going to behave stupidly over her. At your age it's easy to make mistakes and hard to pay for them."

I got up.

"Thanks for the tip."

"You think over what I've said."

It sounded a bit like a threat.

"Sure," I said, walking out. "Sure."

He still looked at me like he was working out all the possibilities in his head in order to decide on the best one.

It was going to be harder from now on, I thought. The atmosphere in the house was becoming more tense. I wasn't sure how to handle my attitude toward politics. The most reasonable thing seemed to be to follow my father's line. He was certainly no fool.

After having a bad night's sleep, I called Eitan the following morning. I felt like having a long sarcastic chat. Eitan liked talking about politics which he felt made no sense at all, and about the approaching hot summer. Since the Six Day War, every summer was described as hot, because of the constant firing on the Canal.

Despite his frequent laughter at the world, Eitan was no less patriotic than anyone else.

His mother answered the phone.

"Is Eitan there?"

"Who is it?"

"Assaf."

"You're sure calling at the last minute. He's already got his pack on his back. Hold on a moment; I'll call him."

After a few seconds he got on the line.

"Hullo?"

"Where the hell are you going?" I asked.

"Three guesses."

"Well, I'll be damned."

"Yeah, they really like me lately, second time this year. I think I'm going to join the peace movement."

"The Canal?"

"Yeah."

"How many days?"

"Forty."

"That's a pity, I wanted to talk to you."

"Looks like you've missed your chance."

"You are missing my brilliant speech next Monday," I said, "before a full house of excited delegates. You could have chosen a better time to walk out on me."

"What are you going to say, anyway?"

"I had been depending on you for that."

"Oh, I see. Well, I'm really awfully sorry."

"That's all right."

"I have to go now," he said. "I've got a bloody long way to go."

He paused.

"See that I get a plot overlooking the city."

"Anything for a friend," I said. "I'll be there with a bouquet of roses."

"See you, then."

"Yeah," I said, "in one of the other worlds."

I hung up.

That weekend I went to Eilat with Joy. I picked her up in the early afternoon and we sped south.

It was slow and lazy and dreamlike in Eilat. The last time I had been there was five years before. I had come with Ram then, a short while before he was drafted into the army. We had spent our time swimming and listening to the stories and songs of the hippies who had been camping there. It had seemed like a new world. I had been fascinated at that time by their careless, timeless, purposeless way of life. Ram had been more reserved.

I didn't go looking for the hippies on my trip with Joy. We spent all our time by ourselves on the beach, and we also slept there. I was happy then. It seemed like a part of a novel I had read a long time before, then given up and forgotten.

Joy was all smiles and vivaciousness. I enjoyed just watching her, splashing in the water like a child who'd found a new toy.

Sitting by a small fire that Friday night, I decided that this was probably the charm of beautiful things. You knew they wouldn't last, and that knowledge was what made them seem so complete. Joy was telling me about her early childhood in the state of Washington, and how she used to go camping with her family. It all of a sudden seemed like I had missed a wonderful thing by never having gone camping with my family. I think my father would have had a stroke if someone had as much as mentioned such an idea. I couldn't picture him sitting on a beach in bathing trunks wearing a straw hat. He had to work for fun.

Lying in the one sleeping bag we brought, which meant no sleeping, I felt warm and satisfied. Joy was moving around restlessly, giggling each time she stuck her elbow in my stomach and saying sorry sorry sorry. She also told me that once, before she had started studying psychology, she had considered becoming an actress. She said she had never quite given up the idea, but had decided that she would rather make herself more intellectual first, because once you start with a mania like acting, you don't have time for much else. I told her not to worry, I would still make a star out of her one day, when I really got going in the movies. Sure, Joy said, that was what she was counting on. Her only fear was that she would grow old while I was getting started.

The next day we started driving slowly back. We passed through the old Herodian fortress Masada, where the Hebrew zealots had killed themselves during their war against the Romans rather than surrender. Nowadays, I told Joy, the young tank corps recruits were sworn in, on the top of the rock, in the night, with the words "Masada shall not fall again" burning above their heads.

Her face was anxious, as we stood upon the rock, looking at the hard wild desert below us.

"No, it can't fall again," she said anxiously. "This country has so much going for it. It can't fall."

As we were climbing down I tried to explain to her that we had only two alternatives, holding, or being pushed to the sea. As the latter was really no alternative at all, we had to hold, so we would. It was as simple as that.

We reached Tel Aviv after dark and went to have pizza in Dizengoff, the so-called Fifth Avenue of the city. We walked for a while in the street, biting wolfishly at the food we had in our hands. There were many soldiers wandering around with their machine guns hanging at their sides, looking for girls to take to the beach, which was only two blocks away. There were many soldier-girls too and they would also go down to the beach, because, besides being soldiers, they were also girls. Joy watched all of it with wide curious eyes, clinging to my arm as we passed through the masses of hurrying people.

"It's fascinating," she said. "It is so lively and free. No one seems to be scared or worried, just as if there weren't any Arab countries around at all."

"What is there to be worried about?"

The next morning I struggled to write an outline for my speech. I reminded myself that it should follow party policy as my father had advised, but when I tried to put it on paper, it didn't come out right. It finally occurred to me that I could talk about a subject on which I would not clash with the majority of the party and still say things I believed to be true. I decided to speak about the tasks of the younger generation in the party. Having made up my mind about it, I felt a lot better and managed to put it out of my mind.

I started thinking about movies. With my book coming out in nine months and hopefully becoming a reasonable success, I could easily develop it into a script and perhaps get money to produce it. Joy, I thought, could play one of the main parts.

If worst comes to worst, I thought, I could probably get some money from my father. After all, I had pretty much been going his way.

That afternoon, I took myself to a movie. When I came back, I sat down and wrote the outline for my speech in a few moments. After supper, I went happily to bed with a thriller I had taken from my father's study. I read it passionately till two o'clock in the morning and then had a bar of chocolate and a Coke and went to sleep.

I woke up late in the morning and strolled lazily down to the kitchen. I made myself breakfast and turned on the radio

for the twelve o'clock news. The announcer was reading out
the names of the three soldiers killed in action the previous
night on the Canal, but I was not listening to him. I was
chewing my buttered toast noisily, trying to figure out how
much a low-budget hour-and-a-half movie would have to cost.
I couldn't make up my mind if it was absolutely necessary for
it to be in color. I was inclined to think so.

It was only after he had read the weather forecast that the
announcer read out the names again, and this time I did not
miss them. It still took me a few seconds to figure out who
Eitan Sharon, aged twenty-two from Jerusalem, could be. But
I managed it. I switched the radio off and walked up to my
room, still biting on my last piece of toast. I lay down on my
bed, putting the thriller carefully on the floor. I tried to
go back to sleep, but I was not tired, so after a while I got
up and took a cold shower and got dressed.

A bit later my mother called me down for lunch. Surpris-
ingly, my father was also there. Such occasions were rare.

"Hi," he said to me. "All ready for tonight?"

"Yes."

"Good."

He stuffed the food into his mouth, satisfied, "We'll see how
it turns out."

"Assaf," my mother said, "why don't you finish your meat?"

"Not hungry."

"Why?"

"Had a late breakfast."

"Should go quite well, this evening," my father said, chewing. "The Prime Minister will be there and most of the party's
ministers. You should make a good impression. It's tricky—
nothing provocative, but somehow original—you understand?"

"Mmmm."

"Think you can do that?"

"I don't know."

"Don't you like the potatoes, Assaf?"

I stood up.

"Where are you going, Assaf?"

"Out."

"You didn't finish eating yet."

"I just did."

"You . . ."

"Leave him be," my father cut in. "So he is not hungry. Just don't work yourself up," he said to me. "You shouldn't be tired tonight."

I stood politely until he finished speaking and then I walked out.

I went upstairs and got my driver's license and a few pounds and shoved them in my pockets. I went down to the car, and pulled quickly away from the curb heading for the main road. On the way I passed my father's car, but he did not see me. He was absorbed in his newspaper. The driver nodded to me.

Like hell I'm going to speak tonight, I thought.

Fifty minutes later, I parked in the lot by Joy's house. It was two-thirty.

I climbed up the stairs and knocked on her door. Waiting there it occurred to me for the first time that she had a job and wouldn't be in. I tried the door, but it was locked and I smashed my shoe into it. It only knocked some paint off.

I drove back into the center of town and found a movie. It was a stupid American sex comedy, but I thought I might as well be there as sitting in the car. After it was over, I had some coffee in a small place near Joy's house. It was after seven when I paid my bill and walked out into the cold evening air.

When I approached the door, I could hear voices coming from inside. I waited for a second and then knocked.

Joy, with her hair up, wearing a black leather dress, opened the door. She had on heavy make-up and small silver earrings. Her eyebrows arched in surprise.

"Hullo," she said brightly.

Over her shoulder I saw a bearded young man and a plain-looking girl, sitting on her bed.

"Well," Joy said brightly, "come in, won't you? It's a lucky thing you showed up, because we were going to go out and I would have had no date."

She walked into the room and I followed her, grimacing.

"Glad to meet you," the plain girl said plainly, and smiled up at me.

"Hi!" The bearded one's name was Jim.

"Sit down," Joy said. "We'll be leaving in a minute. This is Jim's birthday so we're celebrating. Would you believe he is twenty-six?"

"No . . ."

"But he is," she said happily, putting on two silver high-heeled shoes. "They are old friends, from Berkeley. Anyway," she added, "first we'll go and have a good meal and then, a night club or something."

"I won't be joining you," I said, "if you'll excuse me."

"I certainly will not."

"Come on," Jim said, "be my guest."

"Thank you," I said, "but I think I'll be leaving."

Joy's eyes were cold with anger.

"What are you doing," she said, "spoiling the evening for me?"

I did not answer.

She was puzzled. The other two were becoming embarrassed.

Joy walked out the door, and I followed her.

"What is it?" she asked me warily, turning to face me, once we were out on the roof.

"I wanted to see you alone," I said. "I wanted to see you alone, that is all."

She shifted her weight from one leg to the other impatiently.

"Well, I am not alone, you can see that."

"You could get rid of them."

"Get rid of them? I see. Just like that. Do you know that these are almost the only American friends I have seen since I came to this damned country, and they'll be leaving in a few days."

She paused. "But then, what would you care about that?" She almost spat the words.

"All right," I said, "let's not get upset. I'll be leaving. I shouldn't have been here tonight, anyway."

"Assaf, your behavior is insulting."

"I am sorry," I said, "I won't stay."

"Why?"

"I came to see you. I don't want to be with them, not tonight."

Her eyes were gleaming in the dark.

"Sometimes," she said, "I get the feeling that all you want to do with me is sleep with me."

I was silent for a moment.

"Well—" I said.

I turned and went through the emergency exit into the building and down the stairs. I got into the car and drove back to Jerusalem. I arrived at the concert hall where the meeting was taking place, shortly after eight-thirty.

It was supposed to have started at eight.

The hall was crowded and hot and filled with smoke. The chairman of the committee was speaking when I arrived. He saw me and winked, and I walked through the long passage between the two blocks of benches and sat down in one of the front rows. I felt strangely calm and comfortable and remote and far away. The crowd around me seemed like an empty space; it didn't mean a thing.

The audience clapped in mild enthusiasm, and I realized the speaker was finishing his speech.

I leaned backward in my chair and closed my eyes.

"I will now let," the chairman was saying, "a younger and probably more promising person than myself"—he paused, waiting for applause for that gallant gesture of modesty; he got some, and then went on—"say what he has to say. And I am sure he has things to say. Assaf Ryke."

I went up to the stage and shook the chairman's hand.

"You get a funny impression from following the news in this

country. We have all been raised, at least my generation has, that more than anything else we want peace. Yet, from following the statements of ministers and government officials one gets the impression that they are afraid of peace. Whenever anyone makes any suggestions for a solution, our leaders point to the Arab or Russian interest behind it, and turn it down. One gets the feeling that our leaders, deep in their hearts, do not believe in the possibility of peace. They believe that the Jews' fate is to fight for their right to exist from generation to generation. History seems to support this feeling. We don't believe in the possibility of peace any more and therefore we are not willing to give up anything we have accomplished as a necessary step toward achieving it. I think this is where we go wrong."

I paused. In the first row I saw a few disapproving faces. I went on.

"I am not an optimist and I think that the Russian and Arab leaders will try to prevent any solution for quite a while anyway. But if we want peace, ever, we should be willing to make the first steps. Our status as victors permits and suggests that we should be the ones to initiate it. We have to make it harder for the Arabs to maintain their hostility. We have to get world opinion on our side.

"A peaceful solution will necessarily require our giving up land. Let us realize that and form a policy in accordance with that realization. Our government has no clear line on the boundary question. It is a mass of contradictory opinions.

"I want to make absolutely clear that there is no political group I resent more than those who deny our right to this country. I do not question that right. But I believe that we also have to be practical.

"My proposal is simply this: that we express our willingness to give back the West Bank and Sinai if that will make it possible for us to reach an agreement for peace. Let's give it a chance. By demonstrating our willingness to meet the Arabs halfway, we have nothing to lose. If they reject our offer they will have a harder time with world opinion and also among themselves. If they accept, it could at least be the beginning of a solution. Should there be peace we would not need all that land with its Arab population. We want this to be an Israeli country.

"That is, if we want peace at any cost.

"I know there are many people who believe the present situation is safer than a doubtful peace within narrower borders. After all, the number of people getting killed in the fighting, scarcely reaches a third of those killed in road accidents, only they're younger. So maybe we could just keep it as it is.

"But for how long?

"The younger generation in this country does not believe in the eternal Jewish fate of suffering. They don't want just to fight all the time, they want to live, too. In the long run, young people may start doubting if it is really an absolute necessity that they carry arms all the time. They might come to the conclusion, right or wrong, that they should rebel and try to change the way things are handled.

"We have to avoid this. We cannot afford doubts, let alone revolutions. We have been strong because we have been immune to both these things.

"The government must begin to take the younger generation into consideration. This country, which depends so much on its young people, has too little place for them in the political arena. This is wrong. Why aren't there more young people in the government and the Knesset? Why does one have to be middle-aged in order to have a say on the national affairs and actions of Israel?

"We have to make any possible effort toward peace. The government has to give the young people the feeling that it's doing everything it can to end the fighting. Maybe those efforts will even see results, who knows? But let us not lose any more time."

I caught sight of my father's face for the first time. He was sitting in the third row looking at me. His face showed no expression, but it was very pale.

I talked for another ten minutes and, when I was through, there was a weak round of applause. I went to my seat, sullen and dissatisfied. I remained there for the following half hour until my successor had finished his speech and gotten noisy applause. I went out before the next one started talking.

The cool breeze hit my face as I stepped out of the building and walked to the car, but it didn't do me any good. I drove home and found it dark and deserted, except for the maid. I wondered if my mother had been there as well to watch the show. I had not seen her. I paced the halls trying to invent some way of occupying myself but I didn't come up with anything reasonable. I didn't come up with anything at all.

Finally I went to my room and took out my paints and canvas. I started drawing with no knowledge of what I wanted to draw. I drew automatically, not because I felt like doing it, but because I remembered it used to help me relax.

Out of habit I drew a face, but it wasn't until much later that I noticed the close resemblance it had to Ram. It was a strong, handsome profile, and I went on working on it, becoming more and more absorbed in the face. When I finished the sketch, over an hour later, I decided that it was the best I had ever done. It was vital. I was impatient to see it painted and completed.

I set the board with the canvas on my chair and put the oil colors on the pallet. I had scarcely started painting when my father walked into the room. Only then did it occur to me that I had forgotten to lock the door, but it was too late.

He stood looking down at me with his impassive cold stare. It irritated me immensely, and I stared stubbornly at the canvas hoping he would go away, and knowing he wouldn't.

Up on the cupboard, the clock struck twelve. I looked at my watch and back at the canvas.

"So you really had to mess things up, didn't you?"

The voice was calm, but there was an edge to it.

"You just had to go and ruin everything you've gained till now in one stupid quarter of an hour." I heard him walking slowly toward me and his footsteps sounded dim and flat. "Why did you do it?"

"I said what I thought I should." I answered curtly, hoping he would go. I didn't look at him.

"I think there is a fact you have overlooked," the voice said coldly, "as long as you live in this house and on our account, you have obligations to more than one person. You can't just do what you want."

I tried to concentrate on the picture, mixing the red and yellow and white for the face and knowing that this time it was not going to work.

"You know," I said, matter-of-factly, carefully putting some paint on the brush, "I never wanted anything to do with politics. I'll tell you why. First, I don't like doing things in which in order to succeed I have to flatter people and run after them and wait patiently for my turn. Secondly, because I knew that I wouldn't be able to do what I really want to." I carefully painted the line of the brow and put the brush down, I looked up at him. "I just don't want any part of all that."

"The trouble with you," he said scornfully, "is that you are getting too big for your britches."

I picked the brush up again and looked at the silent face on the canvas.

"The trouble with you," I said quietly, "is that you are too full of the idea that you are so bloody important. Do you really think that I'm impressed."

"Maybe not. That's your misfortune."

"Looks like it."

He didn't react for a moment. I was moving the brush caressingly over the neck when he suddenly leaned forward, and slammed the canvas board face down on the seat of the chair I had it propped up on.

"Look at me when I'm talking to you, goddammit."

I put the painting back up. The little amount of paint on the screen was smeared to a shapeless stain, covering the thin, drawn lines of the eyes and the neck. I stared at it wordlessly.

"Damn you!" he shouted. "Put that stupid thing away."

I picked up the board.

"Go to hell," I said.

Chapter Fifteen

I FOUND a room the following day. It was in Baka, which is one of the older quarters of the new city. It was a small room, with no furniture except one bed, but it was the first one I found. It had a small toilet connected to it and a door opening into the yard. It cost thirty-five pounds a week. I found it suitable.

In the afternoon I went to Eitan's funeral. There was a large crowd of people gathered in the cemetery, and among them were a few officers from his company.

Eitan had been killed by a shell when he was climbing out of his tank. It had cut his head off.

He was buried in a plot on the eastern side of the hill, overlooking the city.

I promised him I would bring a bouquet of roses, I thought, smiling grimly as I stood with my hands in my pockets on the rim of the crowd. Can't even keep a bloody promise.

"May he rest in peace," the cantor sang, "as his family and all the people gathered here pray for him . . ."

I saw Gad approaching me. He was wearing a white shirt and the expression on his face was obscure.

"May his soul be bound in the bond of life, Amen."

"Lousy situation." Gad said quietly, stopping close to me.

"Yes."

He smiled.

"I hear you made yourself unpopular last night."

"So?"

"Nothing."

"What's this white shirt doing on you?"

"Oh that," he said vaguely, "I have to be going to a wedding afterward."

"Whose? Yours?"

"No, just a second cousin," he grimaced, "it's going to be a tiring day. I still haven't met your American girl friend," he said quietly, "I'm getting impatient."

"Looks like you've missed your chance."

"Oh, I'm sorry."

"Don't be."

"Who do you think is going to be next?" he said, pondering. "There are not so many left."

"In that case," I said, "it had better be you."

I found myself work as a supervisor of some construction being done in the Old City. I worked from seven till two-thirty in the afternoon and I liked it. I knew it was senseless but I enjoyed it. I was satisfied with the fact that it made no sense. I lived like this for three weeks, being disturbed by no one and talking to no one except the other workers and my landlord. I used to come to my room every afternoon feeling pleasantly tired and go to sleep until the evening. Then I would fix myself a few sandwiches, salad and coffee and sit and read a book or sometimes go to a movie. My parents didn't know where I was and I had no visitors. I knew that they would find out soon enough and then there would be a scene. My mother never would accept a son of hers leaving like that. It would imply that he was dissatisfied with something about his home.

But I was not worried about my parents finding me. I didn't have much time anyway, the thirtieth of the month was approaching.

It would have been flawless, except for Joy. My thoughts about her became increasingly disturbing. I welcomed the approaching month of reserves. At least it would leave no place for conflicts. My parents, I recalled, did not know I had to go. I had never gotten around to mentioning it to them. I was glad of that, too.

After three weeks I checked out. I had one suitcase of personal belongings and I took it with me to the camp. I told my landlord he needn't keep the room for me. If I wanted it again I'd know where to look. He said O.K. I paid him a hundred and five pounds out of the four hundred I had made, and stuffed the rest in my breast pocket. Then I said good-bye and left.

On the first day we received all our supplies, clothes and weapons, and got organized. Then a few busses transported us east, to the Jordan Valley. It was familiar scenery and in the beginning I thought this was going to be the same thing all over again. Only, this time there was no Ram, and there wasn't even Ruthi. But then, the reserves wasn't exactly the same as the kind of army I had gotten used to for three years. The atmosphere was free and informal, and the topics of conversation were usually concerned with civilian, not military life. The soldiers did not necessarily shave every day, some grew long hair, and some were bald. Most of them had golden wedding rings on their fingers and they were fond of showing snapshots of their wives and children to one another.

There, I thought to myself, looking at the picture of a fat, naked two month's old monkey: Babies, that's all you need. That is what happens when you get stuck on a broad. No more freedom to do what you want, just a plain, stupid, good-for-nothing family man.

But it was no good. I didn't need more than three days to realize it was not going to work.

During the long hot days and endless nights on the post I came to the conclusion that I was hooked. I had time enough to work it all out cautiously and with great care and the conclusion remained the same. What is more, I thought grimly, even if you'd had a reasonable chance, you've messed it up in the last few weeks playing games. And now, the army.

I finally made up my mind to write her a long letter, and try to explain (I wasn't sure what). It took me almost a week and gave me something to do in my free time. I didn't have many friends in my company, I needed a lot more than thirty-four days to make friends. The letter was six long pages, when I was finally through writing it, and I felt satisfied. This had to work on her, I thought. If anything could do it, this was it. I read it with growing confidence and then gave it to the company clerk, who was in charge of handling the mail. I wrote the address of my military post inside and on the envelope and calculated that I should get an answer within six days. It gave me something to look forward to.

One evening in the second week of my reserve duty, two soldiers were wounded by a bazooka shell during a terrorists' attack. There was a lot of firing and noise for about an hour without anyone's knowing too well what was actually going on. In the morning a single deserted body was found not far from the post and there were signs that the other side had had more casualties than that. We had two wounded and they were both transferred to a hospital on the same night. One of them had only been scratched and he was back two days later but the other I never saw again. His friend, returning from the hospital, said they had to cut his leg off, above the knee. It would be harder for him, therefore, to use an artificial leg and it would take more time for him to learn how. He didn't know any more details.

It seemed strange to me, unnatural. It was all right for soldiers in the regular army to get wounded, but it was inappropriate for the reserves. They were civilians. They had just taken a month off from their work. They weren't playing it for real, were they? Don't ever get wounded, I told myself, get killed if you want to, but don't get wounded.

As the third week went by I was getting restless because there was no letter from Joy. I seemed to be the only guy in the company who received no mail. It didn't make sense to me. Joy wouldn't be the type not to answer. Even if she were really irritated, she would still bother to write a few lines.

But then, maybe she is sick, or dead, or married, I thought, how should I know?

Finally I decided to ask for a twenty-four-hour leave on the next weekend, if I had had no mail by then. I didn't have the patience of the older people around me. I felt a stranger, out of place among these peaceful good-tempered men.

They were mostly kibbutz members and they were always as patient and self-content as elephants.

On Thursday morning, instead of going to arrange my twenty-four-hour leave, I went with the rest of the company on a chase. It was, of course, something that could not have been foreseen, and had to be dealt with, fast. There seemed to have been a penetration by eight to ten people in the night. Their tracks had been found on the sand path along the river. We did not use helicopters but were driven as far as our vehicles could go and then started closing in on foot, on a crest of hills. It was an ambiguous business and likely to take a lot of time. I was still preoccupied with Joy, but gradually my thoughts shifted to the rocks and bushes around us. The general atmosphere got to me too. The general atmosphere was one of tense alertness.

It occurred to me slowly that people were actually expecting trouble here. Their faces were set, and flushed from effort. I had a superstitious disbelief in the possibility of anything's happening to me. I was due back home in two weeks. Who would shoot at me?

We climbed a steep hill, walking in threes, quite far from each other. We had a good part of the small crest covered in a wide half-circle. There were two more groups searching, because there were two more crests with caves. They had to be somewhere within the three crests but we had no idea in which.

I could feel the tension growing as we were coming to the top. The caves were still a few hundred feet away, on the very top, and it was going to be there or not at all, I could hear the quietness grow.

The burst of fire came almost at the instant when we finally saw the caves. They were about a hundred yards away and a little bit above our level.

I took a few running steps and threw myself on the ground behind a small mound of sand. I peered carefully from behind it, but the fire did not come near me. It was not directed at my area at all. They were aiming somewhere far to my left, and it was easy to locate where they were shooting from. Looking carefully I decided that all the firing came from a single cave, the one closest to us. I figured that there weren't more than four automatic weapons in operation there all together.

I heard someone call my name and I looked back. I saw the bowed figure of my platoon commander, a twenty-five-year-old tall, thin boy with strawlike hair and a freckled face. He waved for me to come down to him; there were a few more figures lying there. I lay on my side, holding the submachine gun pressed to my chest and rolled down to them.

"O.K.," the lieutenant said, as I came to a halt by his side, breathing quickly, "that makes enough of us." He had to shout because both sides were doing a full-time job shooting, not bothering to be quiet about it. "We'll outflank from there," he continued, waving to our right, where it was hardest to approach because the slope was steepest, but where it was also well concealed from the caves. "We'll get heavy cover," he said, a boyish smile popping on his face and disappearing just as fast, "and they won't ever see us, so don't get nervous."

Looking at him I found it hard to believe that he was already out of high school but I brushed that thought aside.

"O.K.," the lieutenant shouted, staring ahead of him. "Let's go."

The six of us descended a few yards and then started a wide U-turn that brought us to the foot of the hill, on the other side. We climbed up in a row, with the lieutenant first and me last, until we were close to the top. That brought us about sixty meters to the right side of the caves, at approximately the same height. We stopped for a moment to catch our breath. There was a loud, intensive humming of automatic weapons from the other side, where our soldiers were lying, and no reply from the caves.

We waited there for a few seconds, kneeling close together. Then the lieutenant raised his hand and waved.

"O.K.," he said again, more as if to himself, "let's go."

We started moving in the same order as before.

"The first is the one we want," he said.

There were no signs of life from the cave as we came near it. The lieutenant got behind the rock that marked the entrance and threw a grenade in. He reminded me of a high school boy throwing a tennis ball. He was very calm. He waited for the explosion and then passed quickly to the other side. The next two soldiers did the same, then the three of us left on the other side dove into the cave pouring bullets all over. It was carried out just like an exercise and it felt like an exercise, smooth and automatic. There were six figures pressed to the walls of the cave and none of them had the time to move. By the time my eyes got used to the semi-darkness inside they were all sprawled lifelessly on the ground and my magazine was empty of bullets. I put it in the pouch and stuffed in another. It was totally impersonal, I didn't even get a good glimpse at the faces.

"It is possible not all of them are here," the freckled thin boy said, as if to himself, brushing back a wet yellow curl that sneaked from his helmet and fell on his brow. He took a grenade out of his kit. "We'll have to take a look in the other two." He looked around at us. "O.K."

We went into both caves, following our grenades and bullets, breathing hard and looking hard, but there was no one there.

Outside, the shooting had ceased completely and when our submachine guns stopped operating, unnatural silence prevailed.

We stood in the third cave, which was also the smallest, with our ears still ringing from the shooting and our faces shining with sweat. The lieutenant paced around, bowing his head because the cave was so low, and looking aimlessly at the walls.

"Looks like that's about all, huh?"

His voice sounded strangely loud, after the short silence.

No one answered.

He hung his weapon on his shoulder and shrugged.

I turned and walked slowly out, idly removing the second empty magazine from my submachine gun. The sun hit me in the eyes as I popped my head out of the cave and straightened my body in the fresh air.

I closed my eyes and stepped to the side, turning my head away from the blinding light and leaning with my shoulder on the warm rocky wall. I scratched my back with the empty magazine and opened my eyes.

My first reaction was to close them again in disbelief, but this reaction didn't hold.

Right in front of me, about ten yards away, kneeling between two big pieces of rock was the small figure of a man. His face was dark in contrast with the khaki clothes and his black eyes were fixed on me in a stiff stare. His rifle rested in his hands, leaning on his bended knees with the barrel pointing downward.

I stared back at him and in some separate part of my brain I was calling myself all the dirty names I could think of. I dropped the empty magazine on the ground and reached to the pouch for a new one, still cursing myself and never moving my eyes from his face.

He seemed to be moving extremely slowly, raising his rifle and aiming it at me, and I jammed the magazine in, starting to fire almost at the same instant and still knowing remotely that it wouldn't do.

His finger crawled slowly to the trigger and pulled and then his face became a mask of blood and the eyes disappeared, but he was still kneeling there like before, with the rifle squeezed in his hands. I felt a sharp, cutting pain at my side and I staggered slowly down with my limbs going numb. I was still shooting aimlessly when I hit the ground.

Part Three

JOY

Chapter Sixteen

EVERYONE was wearing white. The color was ubiquitous. Only the people's faces that floated in it, vague and far away, were different. Pretty girls came in and out, carrying different objects, and they never said a word. Sometimes I tried to move because I wanted to get up and take a look at the place but my muscles wouldn't obey me. And after a while, everything would fade away and then I didn't feel anything at all.

Something was coming back to me slowly making its way into the back of my head as if it was in no hurry to put in an appearance. I opened my eyes with an effort and stared straight ahead of me.

"Assaf?"

It took me a few seconds to focus my eyes on the figure towering about me. Then she became clear.

"Asaaf," my mother said again, leaning forward anxiously in her chair and staring at my face with her quiet, sad eyes.

"What?"

The word didn't come out because there seemed to be nothing but dryness in my mouth. I wet my lips with my tongue and swallowed hard and then I said the word again. This time even I could hear it.

"What?"

"How do you feel? she asked anxiously.

"O.K."

"You're fine. The doctor said you're fine."

I raised my eyebrows, wetting my lips again.

"You were operated on this morning," she said distinctly, leaning a bit closer. "There were no complications at all."

She smiled at me reassuringly.

"What?" I said, feeling very dizzy, closing my eyes for a moment. "What?"

"You were hit in your left side," she said, "near the stomach, but it didn't hurt anything vital. That was lucky."

I closed my eyes again, feeling helplessly tired. The world was coming to me in small red points out of a black space.

"You rest now," a voice said somewhere in the dark. "Take it easy, there is nothing to worry about."

The next time I woke up it was evening, and it was different. I didn't feel so utterly weak and I knew where I was. My mother was still sitting in the same place in her chair, looking at me with her sad quiet eyes.

"Hey," she said looking away at someone who wasn't me, "he's awake."

I made an effort to move my head in the direction of her gaze but it was not necessary. My father, in a black evening suit and wearing a light blue silken tie that matched the color of his eyes, got up and moved urgently to the foot of my bed. The hand holding the newspaper dropped to his side.

I was surprised to see him stare at me with the same anxious look I had seen on my mother's face. It was the first time that I found any similarity between the two of them. It bewildered me.

"Well," my father said. He cleared his throat. "How do you feel?"

"Fine," I said, my voice coming more smoothly, "thanks."

He licked his lips.

"Well," he said again and smiled, a bit nervously, "I am glad to hear that."

I wanted to say I was sorry if I had kept him from something important but I didn't. Instead, I felt my mouth twisting in the beginnings of a smile.

"Thanks," I said again.

"You were pretty lucky, it seems," he said. "I hear it was a pretty close thing."

He loosened his tie and opened the top button of his white shirt.

"Bloody hot in here, isn't it?" he said.

"Sure," my mother said, smiling pleasantly, "it is summer."

They looked at me with their plastered, uncertain, expressions. I drew my hand carefully from underneath the sheet and touched my forehead. It wasn't difficult at all.

Then a young nurse came in. She had short blond hair and painted green eyes. She was very pretty. She carried a small tray with a glass of water and three colorful pills.

"So, he is finally up," she said deeply, as if addressing an audience from a stage. "You sure can sleep."

"Sure," I said.

"Well," she said, looking from me to my parents and back, "this will help you sleep some more. Here." She hooked her body over me, nearly touching my face with her heavy bosom, and offered the pills and water to my mouth. "Take these like a good boy."

I took them like a good boy, and leaned back on my pillows. All three of them grinned happily at me.

"How long is it going to take." I asked the pretty nurse.

"What?"

"How long do I have to stay here?"

"Oh"—she waved her hand, dismissing my question—"probably three weeks or so, you'll be out before you know it."

"And I'll be perfectly all right?" I asked.

"Sure," she said, "you'll be perfectly all right, probably even better than before." She laughed lightly and went on, "Of course you'll have a souvenir, a scar, but I guess you won't mind that."

I felt the sweat running in a cold thin stream on my warm back, and on the palms of my hands.

"How big?" I asked her."

"What? The scar?"

"Yes."

"I don't know," she said. Then she held up her hand. "Something like this, maybe."

I looked at her hand. It was thin, pale, and delicately shaped. It seemed monstrous to me.

I closed my eyes and had an exaggerated nightmare vision of a permanently gaping wound. I felt sick. I felt like vomiting! I wanted to wake up from a dream and find myself somewhere else. Me with a scar. A defect, like a cripple. I hated cripples.

"There is nothing wrong with a scar," the pretty nurse was saying. I opened my eyes. "There is nothing wrong with it."

I thought she had winked at me, but I was not sure.

"Actually, they say it's very sexy."

My mother cleared her throat. We all looked at her. She seemed slightly embarrassed.

"Lots of people have asked me to give you their regards," she said cheerfully. "I don't think you want me to mention all of them."

"No. Tell them thanks."

"There's a radio here," she said. "You can listen to it any time you want since there is no one else in the room, and here are a few books we have collected."

She pointed to the night table.

"I brought you the new Alistair MacLean," my father said. "It just came out. It's very good."

"Well, I'll be damned."

Our eyes met and locked. He still had that anxious searching look and for a moment I forgot the scar and I just felt good.

"It will be the first thriller I've read in hard cover," I said.

"I'll be seeing you," the pretty nurse said and walked out of the room.

"Thank you," my mother said quietly to the retreating figure.

"This is Tel Hashomer Hospital, isn't it?" I asked.

"Yes," my mother said.

"So I'm in Tel Aviv," I said.

"It seemed to be less crowded here right now," my mother said. "That's why."

"I guess we could get you transferred to Jerusalem," my father said. "I guess it could be arranged."

"No, no, what for?"

"Well," my mother said, "I think we should let you rest a bit, so unless there is something you want . . ."

They both looked at me expectantly.

"I am fine, thanks."

"I'll come back tomorrow morning," my mother said.

"There is really no need to . . ." I started, knowing it was pointless.

"Don't be stupid."

"Well," my father said, "take it easy."

"Thanks."

"Take care," my mother said.

"Sure."

They walked to the door.

"Well, so long."

"Yeah."

When they were out, I pulled the sheet off and took a look. There wasn't much to see. I was covered with thick, white bandages from my hip to my chest. I didn't feel anything.

I put the sheet down and pulled it up to my chin.

Three weeks, I thought, in this hospital in Tel Aviv.

Then I thought of Joy.

I read a lot of books. There wasn't much else to do. I was not allowed to get out of bed. My mother came to visit a lot. In the beginning she came every day, until I managed to persuade her that it wasn't necessary. Finally she agreed to come only every two or three days, but she seemed hurt. I was sorry about it, I didn't want to hurt her. Almost nobody else came to visit me and it occurred to me suddenly that I had hardly any friends. Gad came twice, but that was all.

On Friday, seven days after my operation, I had a new visitor. Quite late in the morning a tall, lean, dirty figure in uniform walked into my room carrying a big candy box. The straw-haired lieutenant with his boyish face and freckles tossed the box carefully over to my bed and sat comfortably on the chair beside me, stretching out his legs with childish delight.

"That's from the platoon," he said, referring to the chocolates.

"The money was especially collected. I had to look high and low for a candy store. They all seem to have disappeared."

"I am sorry about that, Lieutenant," I said.

"At ease," he said with some amusement. "You don't have to be formal with me, Sergeant, now that we are on leave."

I opened the box and picked out a piece of chocolate.

"Help yourself," I said, placing it in my mouth.

"Sure."

He leaned forward and took one, and then stretched comfortably again. He looked around the room.

"Looks like you're not doing so bad here."

"Yeah."

"You have regards from everybody. They all had to stay. On duty, that is," he grinned, "except me. That's why nobody else came."

I couldn't think of anyone whom I would have expected to come, but it sounded nice just the same.

"Was there any mail for me?"

"No."

"Are you sure?"

"Yeah," he said after a thought, "I would have known if there would have been anything. Definitely."

"All right."

The pretty nurse came into the room. She held a thermometer in her hand.

"Good morning," she said. "How are you feeling?"

"Fine, thanks."

She passed by the lieutenant and walked over to me. She leaned over and put the thermometer into my mouth and took my wrist in her pale, delicate hand. As she passed him, the lieutenant pulled back his feet and stiffened in his chair. The pretty nurse looked at her watch.

"Maybe you want to take my pulse rate too," the lieutenant said.

"I am sure there is no need to," she told him.

"How has it been since I left?" I asked the lieutenant.

"Nothing," he said. "There's been nothing going on since you've left. Not a thing. Been real quiet."

"So you're through in a week?" I asked.

"Yes," he said.

"What do you do then? Go back to your wife and kids?"

He threw his head back and laughed.

"No," he said, "only to my mother."

"Oh, really?"

"Yes," he said, "my mother likes me."

"But where are you from?"

"Tel Aviv."

"I'll be damned," I said. "Just don't say you're studying political science in the University of Tel Aviv."

He looked a bit surprised.

"Actually, that's almost accurate," he said apologetically, "but I don't take it so seriously, just drive there for a couple of hours a day or so. I'm quite lazy."

"You have a car?"

He nodded.

"Listen," I said, looking at him carefully, "Do you think you could come here with your car next Friday, after you're through, sometime in the evening, and bring me my uniform? I'd like to pay a call on someone."

The lieutenant scratched his chin.

"Yes," he said, "I guess so."

"I'd appreciate it."

"Don't mention it," he said. "When are you supposed to check out?"

"More than two weeks."

"I see," he said.

I took another candy from the box. He got to his feet.

"So, I'll be going. See you around eight in a week."

"Thanks. Don't you dare get shot before then. Don't even think about it."

"I wouldn't let a friend down," he said. He picked a few candies from the box and walked to the door.

"Hey, did I kill the sonofabitch?"

"Yes," he said, glancing over his shoulder. "He was pretty dead, I'd say."

"See you."

He disappeared behind the door.

During the following week I began to feel a lot better. They removed the huge bandages from my body and left me with a relatively small one just covering the wound.

When they took the bandages off for the first time I saw my scar. I had been afraid to look, and seeing it for the first time nauseated me.

It seemed huge, and disgustingly red.

The doctor saw the expression on my face. He was a short powerful man in his late forties and rather quick and gentle for someone of his physique.

"It won't always look like that." he said to me. "The color will go and it will show much less, but it will take time."

I managed to stop staring at the long red stain for a moment.

"Yes," I said.

The nurse placed the fresh, white bandage over the wound and carefully attached it to the skin of my stomach with new brown bands of tape.

"There you are," she said happily.

Welcome Quasimodo, I thought to myself when the whole lot of them finally left the room. But then I told myself. "Don't be such a big fat sissy. So what's wrong with a scar, anyway. It doesn't look so nice, that's all.

I was looking forward to Friday evening, wondering if the lieutenant would show up yet never really doubting it.

My father came to visit two more times. The first time he

seemed a bit embarrassed and said he was anxious to hear my opinion about the book he had brought me. I said it was smashing, which it was. That broke the ice.

On Friday afternoon after my mother had gone back to Jerusalem, leaving me with a heap of magazines and a small electric fan, I got carefully out of bed and paced slowly around the room. I felt quite good. I had some pains when I walked or even just stood, but they were bearable. I felt a lot stronger than I had a week before.

After a while I got tired and sat down on the bed. I unbuttoned my shirt and removed the bandage. I looked at the scar. It was still red and ugly. In a way it fascinated me; it had a hypnotic power.

Suddenly I was aware that someone else was in the room and I looked up quickly, letting my shirt fall back over the healing wound.

The pretty nurse stood not far away. She had a peculiar expression on her face. I blushed deeply. I replaced the bandage nervously and buttoned the shirt. She still had the same peculiar expression on her face; I couldn't figure out what it meant, but I didn't like it. I was aware that I still could not control my blushing.

She shook her head slowly. I suddenly realized that the expression on her face might signify pity.

"You are a fool," she said quietly. "If that upsets you so much."

I didn't say anything.

"Look at all the soldiers around here who've lost hands and feet and God knows what. What's so terrible about a scar? Especially, when it's not on your face?"

I still didn't answer. My brain wasn't functioning at all.

She came a step closer, never moving her angel-like blue eyes from my face.

"It shouldn't matter, anyway," she said quietly, but her face flushed a bit, "unless you force it to matter."

I tried to think of something to say to show that I wasn't really that type of a guy, but I couldn't even manage to smile. I just sat like a statue.

Then Udi, Ram's brother, knocked on the half-open door and walked into the room.

"Hullo," he said, looking from one to the other of us. "I hope I am not interrupting you."

"Not at all," I said. "I am glad to see you."

I moved my eyes away from the pretty nurse and gave him a weak smile.

"Take it easy, that's all," she said. She went over to my bed and placed three pills on the night table.

"I am going off duty now," she said. "I hope I can trust you with these."

"Well," I said to Udi, "long time no see."

"I see you are O.K.," he said, in a very grown-up voice. "My mother urged me to visit you. She sends her regards."

"Thanks, sit down."

He did.

"We only heard about it three days ago," he said.

I shrugged.

"Done any writing lately?"

I realized that I hadn't thought about my writing for a long time.

"Yeah," I said. "You'll probably get a chance to see something by this author—there should be a book out pretty soon. Fact is, I clean forgot about it."

"I trust you'll get me an autographed copy?" he asked, lighting a cigarette. That struck me as strange, Ram never smoked.

He stayed an hour and asked a lot of questions and made me talk a lot too, though I didn't have much to tell him. He had a girl friend, he said, and was doing badly at school, but otherwise no news. I said, well, girl friends are always news, is she pretty? So-so he said and laughed, but she's cute. So who cares?

He left after the night nurse had brought my supper tray. He said he didn't go for hospital food.

I didn't stop him; I was getting nervous about my plans for the evening.

When the night nurse came to take the tray I told her that I was tired and was going to go to sleep right away. She said she was sure it would only do me good and turned off the light as she walked out. She was a motherly type.

Half an hour later the lieutenant opened the door and stepped in. He shut it silently behind him and turned on the light. He had had to lie to the guards to get in but we didn't have any trouble getting to his car. As I climbed in I felt a penetrating pain that made me gasp, but it went away.

"You show the way," he said.

"You've got to start the motor in any case."

"That's true."

"O.K., then," I said, pressing my hand firmly on the bandage, "let's go."

It took us twenty minutes to get to Joy's house and by that time I was sweating.

"What floor is it on?" he asked looking up at the building, as he turned the engine off.

"Roof."

He whistled.

"Then I guess I'll be going with you, otherwise you might die on the way."

"Now let's not exagg—"

"No arguments."

We climbed slowly up the stairs, stopping a few times on the way. I felt increasingly tired. The lieutenant looked closely at my wet face from time to time, but he didn't say anything.

When we reached the roof he stopped and yawned. "I guess I'll leave you on your own from here on. Scream if she hits you."

"O.K." I smiled. "I won't be long."

"Don't worry about that," he said. "I've got no one prettier than my mother waiting for me. I'm not holding my breath."

"All right."

When I got to the familiar grey door the piece of paper with her name on it was not there. I knocked and waited.

There was no answer and no sound. I knocked again and

then tried the knob but the door wouldn't open. I stood there leaning heavily on the door and breathing the fresh air into my lungs slowly and deeply. I wondered why the hell I hadn't expected this, why should any girl be home at this hour on a Friday night. No, I thought, if she were out on a date her name would still be on the door. I closed my eyes.

I walked back inside. The lieutenant was sitting on the top stair, in the dark. I could see the end of his cigarette burning.

"That was quick," his voice was low. It barely reached me.

"Well," I said, "let's go."

"Wasn't in?"

"Uh uh."

"Don't want to maybe hang around for a while and wait?" he asked.

"No. What the hell for? Looks like she doesn't live here any more anyway."

"Ah," he said, as if that was what he had expected all along. He showed no signs of moving.

"O.K.," I said angrily, "let's go back."

"Paratroopers never go back," he said solemnly. "Didn't I ever tell you that? I thought you might want to ask the landlord if he knows where she's gone."

I was surprised that the idea hadn't occurred to me. It seemed so obvious.

"I don't know where the landlord lives," I said weakly. It's a big house."

"Oh, don't be stupid," he said with disgust.

He started going down the stairs; I walked after him.

He knocked on the first door we reached. An old man wearing a white shirt and a neatly pressed suit opened the door. He peered at us suspiciously.

"Good evening," my companion said politely. "We're from the army and we're looking for the landlord."

The old man seemed visibly relieved that we were not looking for him and immediately offered his cooperation.

"Next floor down," he said anxiously. "Steiner. But she is a woman."

"Thanks," the lieutenant said.

"You're welcome," the old man said doubtfully, and closed the door. We heard the key turn in the lock.

"Are you feeling O.K.?" the lieutenant asked as we descended to the next floor. "You are quite pale."

"Let's see the landlady," I said.

Mrs. Steiner turned out to be a very nice woman, indeed, and she adored soldiers. What would we all do, she said, if there were no army? We didn't answer that question. We didn't think she was expecting us to answer.

She was probably a widow, in her late sixties. She very sweetly asked us in, saying that there were always candies in her apartment for young boys like ourselves. I was getting impatient, especially since the lieutenant looked like he might not decline.

"We have no time for this," I told him flatly, not looking at the small woman.

"We have to be back." he explained to her. "Special mission. We are looking for the girl who used to live on the roof."

Mrs. Steiner smiled with delight. It made her face look like a moon.

"A very sweet girl," she said.

"That's the one," I put in. "Where has she gone?"

She looked at me sadly.

"She is not here any more."

"Any idea where she is?" I asked, from over the lieutenant's shoulder.

"No." She shook her head mournfully. I suddenly had the terrifying feeling she might produce some large wet tears any moment.

"Thanks," I said, and turned to go.

"But," said the high-pitched voice from behind us, "I believe she said she was leaving the country."

We turned back to her.

"I don't know where she went." She looked at us apologetically.

Chapter Seventeen

WHEN I left the hospital a week later, I went back to my parents' house. There didn't seem to be much choice. The doctor said I still needed supervision and a lot of rest, and my mother wouldn't hear of my going anywhere else. I didn't really mind it.

I stayed there three days, being completely passive and not going out.

I didn't take any exams. I thought I could take them on the second date they were given, two months later, in September, if I wanted to.

My parents never mentioned Joy. They were cautious when they talked to me. They didn't try to push me in any way and they also didn't ask questions. They were patient. They seemed to believe that time was on their side. They just waited.

I didn't think that time was doing me any good but I just waited, too. I still believed Joy would show up or call. The phone made me nervous whenever it rang, but it was never for me.

On my third morning home, having nothing better to do, I sat down and read the first chapter of my book. The similarity between the hero's way of speaking and mine amused me. I hadn't noticed it before. One chapter ended with the remark: "What good is all that crap if you don't do what you want to?"

I stared at it for a few moments.

I went to my desk and started taking out the drawers. In the bottom one I found the small piece of paper:

Lynda Strawson
2, Arkheight Street
(Near Haverstock Hill)
London N.W. 3

Under those four lines there was an addition in a more careless hand writing:
My sister.
I studied it for a few minutes more. Then I started another search for my bank book. It took me half an hour, but I did find it. Four thousand six hundred pounds, it said. What else, I thought, permission from the army? There shouldn't be any trouble about that. Not now, anyway.

So that's that.

I called a travel agency and asked the girl if there would be any problem getting a student flight to London.

She said, no, none at all. I asked her to book one for me.

The next morning I went to my military camp and asked for permission to leave the country. I got it within half an hour. For those times, it was probably a world record.

I came home and found my mother eating lunch. She looked at me worriedly as she put a plate of soup on the table in front of me.

"I hope you are not tiring yourself," she said. "You shouldn't. Not yet."

"I am not doing anything physical," I assured her, "and I feel fine."

"It's for your own good," she said defensively.

"I know."

I started eating.

She stood by the table and watched me.

"Listen, Mom," I said, "I'll be flying to London. I think I could do with a vacation." I smiled pleasantly at her astonished face. "And a change."

"But . . ."

"I'll rest as much as I do here."

She opened her mouth to protest and then shut it again.

She sat down at the table, facing me.

"When do you intend to go?"

"Eight forty-five, tomorrow. It's an El Al flight."

There was no surprise left on her face, just a thin trace of bitterness.

"I think you could have mentioned it before," she said in a restrained voice.

"I just thought of it yesterday," I said truthfully, "and I had to check with the army this morning."

"You've been home four days."

"I need a change," I said placidly.

"All right," she said.

"I won't stay long. A few weeks, not more."

There was something else bothering her. She hesitated a bit before she finally let it out in the form of a question.

"Going with somebody?"

"No," I said. "Who with?"

It didn't hit me until the plane landed in Heathrow Airport.

Driving to Lynda, the country around me had seemed too real and compelling to be disposed of by a $210 ticket. Israel seemed to be the only country in the world. I hadn't been anywhere else for four years. But now as I looked out the window of the red coach riding through the rain to the West London Air Terminal, I realized that there were no soldiers hitchhiking. The people were actually speaking about the weather in their polite, polished English. No one was talking about the shooting in the Jordan Valley. No one was even alluding to the Suez Canal.

Suddenly a pang of excitement rushed through me. Boy, I thought, looking at the traffic in an orderly procession on the left side of the highway, this is England.

My father had raised no objections to my trip. He was rather open-minded about it actually. I had to grant him that. He

said a change could only do me good. He even offered to give
me the addresses of his business friends in London, in case I
should need something.

I had left the Triumph in the parking lot at the airport. I
didn't intend to be away from home long.

When I boarded the plane and the stewardess showed me to
my seat smiling her polite, professional smile, it occurred to
me that this was going to be the first time that I had flown in
four years without having to bail out.

The taxi driver who took me from the Air Terminal to
Hampstead was a sweet old thing.

"A bit rainy today, isn't it, sir?" he asked me joyfully as he
put my suitcase in the back of the cab. His Cockney accent was
refreshing. I found myself smiling broadly back at him.

"Yes," I said, "but I hear it has rained in London before."

"Oh yes," he said, "it has."

The Rolls-Royces, the red buses, the men in frock coats and
Derby hats, the funny policemen, they all seemed excitingly
new. Riding through the busy city, I was very glad I had
come.

At Belsize Park tube station the driver stopped the car and
turned to me. He lowered the glass screen between us.

"You'll have to tell me more precisely where you want to
go, sir," he said, pulling his cap down around his ears. "This
is Haverstock Hill."

I scratched my head.

"Are we close to a street called Arkheight?"

He sniffed.

"It's right there, sir," he said pointing with his finger.

"Is there any small, reasonably cheap hotel around here?"

"There is one around the corner," he said.

"Let's go there."

"Right."

He stopped by a three-story house of red bricks with a red
roof. There wasn't any sign hanging in front.

"This is it," the driver said in his funny accent, taking out
my bags. "It's a pleasant place."

"Thank you."

I gave him his fare plus a two-shilling tip and pushed the gate open. It led through a small green garden to the door. I liked it immediately. An elderly woman at the reception desk smiled at me in a grandmotherly way and said that yes, I was fortunate they still had one vacancy.

She led me up to the second floor and into a large brightly painted room, overlooking the street. I told her that it was fine and that I would let her know the next morning how long I was going to stay.

I decided the best time to find a girl at home would be around seven, before supper. It was a kind of game I was playing with myself, pretending I was sure she would be there, sitting at the table, just about to start eating the fish on her plate. I could see it all quite clearly in my imagination.

I had lunch at a small Swiss restaurant near the tube station and then I went back to the hotel, took a hot bath, and went to sleep. When I woke up it was past seven and I jumped out of bed, afraid that my oversleeping was a bad omen. I dressed quickly and left.

Number 2, Arkheight Street was a five-minute walk from the hotel. There were only four families living in the house, so the name Strawson wasn't hard to locate.

At the second floor I stopped and smoothed down my hair with my wet hand. In God we trust, I told myself soothingly. It has to be true. It's printed on American money.

I rang the bell and waited.

I heard light footsteps. Then the door opened. A tall figure in a flowery bathrobe stood in front of me. The girl's face was familiar but she had short light curly hair and heavy dark eyelashes. There were a few seconds of absolute silence.

"It's you again," Joy said finally. Her blush was unmistakable even under her make-up. "You've probably been counting on getting a good English supper."

I let the air out of my lungs, slowly and quietly, so as not to make my relief roaringly obvious.

"I find London rather damp," I said. "A bit nasty for summer, isn't it?"

"Oh," she said.

Somewhere, inside, a kettle whistled loudly and then stopped.

"Well, come in, won't you?" she said, but she didn't move from the doorway.

"Don't tell me," she said softly, "that you have come all the way to London just to see me."

"Yes, that is exactly what I've come for."

"Well," she said, even more softly, "I'll be goddamned."

She moved away a bit, to let me pass. I took my hands out of my pockets and stepped in.

"Now," the soft voice said, as I brushed by the thin cloth of her bathrobe, "in that case, perhaps a kiss would be in order."

I held her by the shoulders and pulled her to me. Her eyes closed dreamily and her lips opened a bit. Her mouth was warm and sweet. I felt my fingers tightening on her skin, involuntarily.

"Why did you disappear, damn you?" I said hoarsely when she finally pulled back slightly.

"Now what the hell is this?" a new voice said from outer space.

I looked in the direction the voice had come from. A tall blond girl was standing there, in a bathrobe identical to Joy's. She resembled Joy, but was not quite as pretty.

"What's so special about those bathrobes?" I asked a bit sourly.

"They have quality," the new girl said briskly but her eyes stayed on me for a moment saying, and what the hell is so special about you, flatfoot? And then they shifted to Joy repeating the same idea more or less, only more insistently.

"I might as well introduce you two," Joy said, "This is my sister, Lynda, and this is Assaf Ryke, a tourist from Israel."

"Ah, one of those," Lynda said, but she extended her hand and switched on a pleasant smile. "Actually I believe I've heard about you from Joy, but for a moment I thought you were the new milkman."

I weakly pressed her hand.

"Yes," I said, "they keep changing them all the time."

"And with no notice," Lynda added. "But come in. Why are you two standing in the doorway?"

It was a hard question to answer so I closed the door and we moved through a hall into a small, gay living room.

"John!" Lynda hollered at someone who was hiding behind the sports page. "Come and meet your guests."

He jerked abruptly into a standing position and cleared his throat. He was tall and skinny and pale, every inch an Englishman.

"Sorry," he said, putting out his hand, "how do you do?"

"Don't be," I said, taking it. "I am Assaf. Glad to meet you."

"Oh God," Joy said, "I hope you haven't reformed. This isn't quite your style."

I shrugged.

"I hope I have reformed."

"I trust you will join us for supper," John said, folding his newspaper neatly and placing it on his chair. I decided he must be in his middle twenties, but his hair was cut short.

"Thank you."

"We might as well eat, then," Lynda said.

She led the way to the table, which was on the other side of the room, near the kitchen.

After we had finished eating, Joy asked me: "Where are you staying?"

"A nice quiet place," I said, "a few minutes walk from here. It's in Lyndhurst Gardens."

"Oh yes, I know the place." Lynda said.

"Then, maybe," Joy said, tapping with her teaspoon on the tablecloth, "we could take a walk there. It's a pleasant evening."

"That is a good idea," I said.

She got up.

"I'll get dressed," she said. "You stay here and amuse your hosts."

"I'd like to help with the dishes," I said to Lynda.

"Well, well," Joy said nastily and left the room.

"That's sweet of you," Lynda said, "but there's no need."

"How long are you going to stay in London?" John asked.

"I don't know yet. It depends."

"Oh, I see."

Lynda stared at me with open curiosity. I found myself shifting uncomfortably in my chair.

"You are a year older," I said stupidly, "I mean, a year older than Joy."

"Oh heavens, does it show?"

"Of course not."

"How's Israel?" she asked.

"All right, but you should come and see it for yourself."

"Yes," she said seriously, "I want to. It seems quite frightening from here but Joy says that's a wrong impression."

"You won't get shot in Tel Aviv. It's very safe for tourists and civilians. Only soldiers have trouble, but that is pretty far outside the city."

"Like ten miles?" she asked earnestly.

"We use kilometers there, so it comes to more. It is a lot more than that."

"We'll come and visit, maybe next summer, Johnny?"

John smiled and when he did he suddenly looked rather handsome.

"Yes," he said, "I'd like to."

"I am a quick dresser," Joy said, appearing in the hall.

She had put on a black dress that did justice to her shape.

My face must have expressed my thoughts.

"So, let's get going," Joy said.

"Thanks a lot," I said, to the other two.

"Don't mention it," Lynda said brightly. "We'll be seeing you."

Chapter Eighteen

WHEN we were down in the street I said to Joy:

"Really want to go to the hotel?"

"Yes," she said, "hotel rooms are good places to talk."

I nodded.

"But we can take a longer route," she said, "since it is such a pleasant evening."

We walked in silence for a few moments. It was a restful area; even the pubs were quiet.

"Why did you leave like that?" I said. "I wrote you a letter from the reserves, but I never got an answer."

"Was it a nice letter?"

"Yes," I said, almost bitterly, "very."

"I wasn't there any more," she said, leading me into a narrow street.

"I left the country a week after we last met."

I looked at the straight line of street lamps that marked the way ahead of us.

"Why?"

"My visa expired. That wasn't the only reason, of course. I lost my job again. I went to the Ministry of the Interior to ask for an explanation. The man there was fairly polite, much to my surprise. He explained to me that my taking a job might prevent a new Jewish immigrant from getting one. Immigration is an extremely important matter in Israel. It's vital to Israel's existence. He was a nice man. He said I shouldn't give up, but I should appreciate the difficulties involved."

"But you did give up?"

She hesitated for a moment.

"You might say so. I was very low at the time. You came that night. Then I didn't hear a word. I was angry with myself. My self-confidence was badly shaken. So I left."

In the dim lamplight I saw the blood creep into her cheeks.

"I was going to come back."

"Why didn't you ever call?"

"I did," she said quietly, "once. I talked to your mother. She said you had not been home for a few days. She said she didn't know where you were."

"She didn't."

"I was not sure at the time," she said, "but it didn't matter. I knew you could find me if you wanted, so I realized you probably didn't want to."

I was silent.

"Where were you?" she asked.

"I left. I quarreled with my parents.

"Why?"

"I don't know, I was angry."

Three long-haired, flamboyantly dressed people came toward us. They stepped off the curb into the street when we passed them.

"Boys or girls?"

"Girls," Joy said.

"How do you know?"

"Intuition," she said, "and this." She passed her hand along the round lines of her body.

"I don't know," I said. "Trying to pick up girls here could result in some funny situations."

"I believe most men wouldn't mind," she said. "Where did you go when you left home?"

"I found a room."

"And you didn't return home?"

"I went into the reserves three weeks later. I did afterward."

"Oh."

Our eyes met as we passed under one of the street lamps.

"You look different," I said.

"Worse?"

"No. Different."

"What made you come?" she asked.

"I wanted to see you," I said. "It was the only thing I was sure I wanted."

She kept staring at me.

"I hoped you would be here," I said.

"And are you satisfied now?" she asked quietly.

"Are you?" I asked.

She laughed softly.

"This is it," I said, pointing to the red building that was my hotel.

"Let's go in, then," she said.

We passed by the lounge, where a few of the residents were sitting watching the sports news on TV, and we walked up to my room. I put the lights on and closed the door.

"Not bad," she said, and sat in the only chair.

I took off my coat and sat on the floor.

"I'm afraid I can't offer you anything to drink except water."

"You mean you have no Coke around?"

"I'll see to it tomorrow," I said.

"So what are your plans?"

"I don't know."

She got up and walked to the window.

"Are you working?" I asked her.

"No," she said, without turning, "not yet. I might be starting in a week."

"Oh. Listen, I can rent a car. I would like to go somewhere, to travel."

I stopped abruptly. I suddenly felt a pain in my side.

"Yes?"

I put my hand on my stomach, underneath my shirt and moved it slowly over the skin.

She turned from the window and looked down at me.

"I thought maybe you would be willing to come with me," I said lamely.

"Of course," she said.

"You will really? For a few days?"

"Sure."

"That would be beautiful."

She walked over to me.

"It will be beautiful," she said. "Won't it?"

She moved over to the bed and sat down on it.

"I have missed you," she said.

She crossed her legs and leaned back resting her elbows on the mattress.

"I felt awful that evening after you left. Nothing made sense to me."

"A friend of mine was killed the day before."

"You didn't tell me."

"No."

"Don't you want to come here?" she asked quietly.

"Yes."

I got up and walked to her. I sat close to her on the bed and looked down at her legs. I felt dizzy.

"Assaf?"

She was leaning forward, with her face near mine. I felt her warm, scented breath on my cheek and her blue painted eyes seemed to fill my view. I moved closer and pressed my mouth on her lips, closing my eyes.

She sat up gently and put her arms around my neck, kissing me softly. Then she pushed me down on the bed.

"I missed you," she whispered hoarsely in my ear, "I missed you."

I wrapped my arms around her waist, squeezing her fiercely.

"You are not sad," she whispered in my hair, "are you?"

"No," I said.

She pulled back slightly and started unbuttoning my shirt. I lay on my back with my hands clinging to her hips and didn't open my eyes.

"I hope that you would come," she whispered, "but I knew that you wouldn't."

"But I did."

"Yes."

Then I heard her gasp, and her hands froze on my chest. I opened my eyes.

Seeing the startled expression on her face, I knew what she was looking at. I wondered how I had forgotten before. I sat up and pulled my shirt back. I could feel her eyes shifting away from the scar and moving to my face although I wasn't looking at her. I sat staring at my hands and my face was hot with anger.

She put her arm on my shoulder and touched my cheek with her hand. I moved away, unwillingly.

"I am sorry about that," I said hollowly. "I forgot."

"How did it happen?"

"In the reserves." I paused. Her hand was hanging loosely on my shoulder. "We were chasing guerrillas, one of them was hiding outside the cave. So . . ."

"Does it hurt?"

"No."

She moved her hands slowly down my chest and then apprehension crept into her eyes. She reached down with her fingers and pulled gently at my shirt, not moving her eyes from my face. I grimaced.

"Does it bother you?"

"Yes," I said.

"Why?"

"It's ugly," I said, looking down. "It's red and big and ugly."

"Oh."

Then she laughed.

I looked at her, flushing.

"What's so funny?"

"You. I wondered once what kind of things would bring you down, but I never dreamed it would be as stupid as that."

"Yes," I said, "I know all about it. The nurse in the hospital said it was sexy."

"Did she seduce you?"

"No, she wasn't that generous."

"You are missing the main point," she said.

Her breasts heaved at me under the thin cloth of her dress. I wanted to touch them but I didn't.

"What?"

"That it *is* sexy. That's all there is to it."

She stared at me and somehow I knew she meant it.

"You think I'm lying?"

"No," I said, "no."

"Then, it's all right?"

"Yes."

I put out my hand and touched her warm, silky knee.

"Is there anything else?" she asked softly.

"Yes."

"What is it?"

I stared at my hand until it disappeared underneath her dress. I felt her quiver, and raised my eyes to her face. Her cheeks reddened a bit, and she looked at me almost coyly.

"Make love to me," I said. "Please."

"I think I won't refuse this time," she said, and gently pushed me down again.

"Will you come back to Israel?" I asked.

"Mmmmm," she said, undoing my buttons, "if you ask me to."

"You would really if I asked you to?" I asked breathing heavily at her breast.

"Mmmm," her voice said, above me. "You'll have to help me with my dress."

Her body slipped into my arms and curled lightly on my chest.

"It's in the back," she said.

I unzipped the dress and she wriggled out of it, kicking away her high-heeled shoes. I put my hand on her smooth hips. Her soft breasts bounced gently against my face.

"You'll come back with me?" I murmured. "Really?"

"Sure," she said, digging her fingers into my hair, "I'm crazy about you."

Her dark nipples pressed against my head and then they slipped down.

"Now, shut up," she said, pushing her lips fiercely on my mouth.

My hands moved down from her hips to her thighs and again I felt a tremor pass through her body. She pulled her knees back and enveloped me with her long warm legs.

"Are you really?" I asked her afterward.

"What?"

"Crazy about me?"

She looked at me mischievously.

"What does it look like to you?" she asked.

I smiled.

"I like your new hair style," I said.

She frowned.

"It must be in a mess now. Took me a couple of hours to have it arranged."

"It makes you look like a movie star," I said.

"Is that important?"

"It is attractive."

"I should hope so," she said, arranging the pillow underneath her head. "They have nice beds in this hotel."

"Listen," I said.

"Yes. I am."

"We can go to Wales or Scotland. Drive through to the coast or something."

"Yes," she said, "sure."

"We could go for a few weeks, until we've had enough."

"Sure," she said, "as long as we want."

"And then we'll go back to Israel."

"Yes."

"And then."

"Yes?"

I looked at her. She had an amused expression on her face, as if she were watching a comedy she had seen before and knew that what was coming next would be really funny. She drew her hand from under the sheet and scratched her nose.

"Say listen," I said.

Her hand went back underneath the sheet.

"Yes?"

"I've been thinking."

"Good," she said.

"Why not?" I said. "Why not?"

"Who said not?" she said.

"Will you?"

"Will I what?" she said.

"Marry me?"

"Oh, of course not. I'd love to though."

I looked up at the ceiling.

"You won't?" I said.

Joy put her hand on my arm.

"Why should you marry me?" she said. "It would only complicate things for you. I'll live with you, if you want."

I kept staring at the ceiling.

"What's the matter?" she asked.

"It's the first time I've ever proposed and been turned down. I'm trying to get over it."

She played with my fingers.

"Do you really mind?"

"Yes," I said.

"Why?"

"I don't know. I guess I just want to marry you."

"Why?"

I considered the question.

"I just want to," I said.

"Why don't you say that you love me?" Joy asked.

"Well," I said, "I thought . . ."

"I think you do," she said, her upper lip twisting with amusement. "Does it embarrass you to say it?"

I shrugged.

"Do you love me?" she asked.

I passed my hand over my forehead.

"Yes," I said.

She laughed.

"Most people who have proposed to me before," she remarked, "mentioned that at an earlier stage, and quite voluntarily."

"Were there many?"

"No but enough to teach me the routine."

"Well," I said, "with a routine or without a routine, it seems we all got the same results."

"Some of the others tried harder."

"Yeah."

"What, for instance, would your parents say?"

"I have though about that," I said. "I don't care too much about their reaction."

"Oh."

"After all, it wouldn't be their wedding."

"Yes, that is a point."

"But I don't think they would be against it."

"I don't know," she said doubtfully.

"You see," I said, "I think I have told you, once. When I was small, I had the world figured out. It was wrong of course, but it was beautiful, and nothing turned out to be like it, nothing ever looked like my dream. But you would have fitted. You would have fitted into what I saw then."

I looked down at my side. She was lying with her face turned to me, and her eyes closed.

"That was a nice thing to say," she said softly.

I put out my hand and stroked the light hair that fell across her brow.

"The girl I saw in my imagination, I always thought of her as my wife. I'd like it to be like that, because it makes it more real. Then it isn't just a play. Do you understand what I mean?"

"Yes."

"Would your parents mind?" I asked her.

"I don't know," she said, "not much."

I looked at her toes peeking out of the other end of the sheet.

"Maybe you should try to ask again," she said softly.

"Will you . . . ?"

"Yes," she said.

"You mean it?"

"Sure."

"Well," I said.

She smiled.

"Are you happy now."

"Yes," I said. "I am happy now."

"I'm glad."

"Listen," I said, "so when do we do it? Tomorrow?"

She watched me, amused.

"You don't want a nice Jewish ceremony?"

"No," I said, "I wouldn't want you to convert. And anyway, I'd like to get married here. I don't really need anyone except you at the wedding."

"Two witnesses," she said vaguely, "and a registrar. I wouldn't mind converting. I don't care one way or the other."

"No," I said, "I'd rather you didn't."

"All right. Now I want a nice kiss for my efforts," she said.

I pulled her to me and kissed her.

"You should be careful not to break my jaw," she said, drawing back and pulling the sheet away from us. She moved her finger along my ribs, studying the scar.

"What happened to him?"

"He's dead," I said. "I killed him."

Chapter Nineteen

"I THINK you have to be residents at a certain address in the borough for two weeks or something like that," Lynda told us. "I don't really remember, but after that it's just a matter of a few minutes and a few shillings."

We were sitting in the kitchen having breakfast. It was around eight o'clock in the morning.

"Ahha," Joy said.

"John!" Lynda yelled.

His voice came through the corridor. "Yes, love?"

"Yes, love," Lynda complained to us. "Always his stupid football league. He never moves from that seat."

"How long do you have to wait to get married?" she hollered.

"Wait."

His long figure appeared at the door.

"Who do you want to marry?" he asked her.

"Not me. How long does it take?"

"I don't remember."

"All right. You can go back then."

"An awful husband," she remarked after he disappeared. "I can't imagine what I ever saw in him. I am joking, of course."

"We can go later and find out," Joy said. "It's practically around the corner."

"What?" I asked.

"The registrar's office."

We had to wait two weeks before we could get married. We had a good time. I booked a double room in the hotel and we moved in there. We spent the days walking around in town and seeing films and plays. I wrote to my parents twice during that period but I didn't mention Joy or any of my plans, I just said that I was feeling fine and hoped they were too.

Joy wrote her parents a long letter saying she was going to get married and settle in Israel. She said she hoped they were happy and in good health and would come to visit sometime in the future. She asked me to add a few lines.

I bought the Israeli papers in Piccadilly Circus three times a week. There was not much news. Secretary of State Rogers was expected to make a statement concerning America's position on the situation in the Middle East, but this statement kept being delayed. There were secret negotiations between Russia and the United States, but there was no announced agreement. The firing along the Israeli borders went on as usual.

Sometimes we went to parties or to discotheques with Lynda and John. Afterward, late at night, we would ride in the small Hillman I had rented through the near empty streets of the West End.

We got married on the twenty-ninth of July in the Hampstead registrar's office. John and Lynda acted as witnesses.

It was not as festive an occasion as I had expected. Joy wore a low-cut yellow minidress which was smart and fashionable. I wore a gray suit I had bought on Portobello Road. We repeated the few lines and the old solemn-looking registrar read to us and then he signed the marriage certificate and handed it to us.

"Well," he said, "that's it. Please accept my congratulations and I hope you have a long, happy life together."

That's all? I thought.

"Thank you," I said nervously.

I looked at Joy and then back at him.

"Maybe you'd like to kiss the bride, sir," he suggested finally.

Joy wrapped her arms around my neck and held her head back promptly. I kissed her briefly and she pulled away, laughing.

"I'll do a more thorough job of that," John said enthusiastically and grabbed her away from me, enfolding her in his arms. The registrar looked at me in a fatherly way, sticking his pen back into his breast pocket.

"I feel insulted," Lynda said, planting herself in my arms, "being the only one around who gets no kissing. Is she really prettier than me?"

"Yes," I said, bending to kiss her, "of course."

Right after the ceremony we left on our trip west, leaving John and Lynda standing on the sidewalk, waving.

"You'll have to look after me," Joy said shyly when we got into the car. "I'll have no one in Israel except you."

"I'll look after you."

"Let's go to Wales," she said, suddenly remembering to wave back at her sister and brother-in-law.

When we got to Gloucester I drove to the center of town and stopped the car.

"Won't be a moment," I said.

Joy looked around suspiciously.

"Who is she?" she said.

I pointed to the post office and jumped out of the car.

"Oh," she said, taking her make-up out of her bag.

I went into the post office and sent a cable to my parents. Afterward I returned to the car.

"Sent a cable?"

"Yes."

"Saying what?"

"Married Joy. Regards."

She shook her head.

"That's not nice."

"I'm not a nice guy."

"I know."

"You should have thought of that before you said yes."

"I think this is where Wales starts," she said.

We drove all the way up to Holyhead and found a small hotel near the beach. We stayed there for ten days, swimming and driving around. The landscape was beautiful and way up in the mountains it was really cold. We went for long walks there, climbing to the peaks through green fields that belonged to the farmers in the neighborhood. Occasionally we would come across a flock of sheep that would accompany us part of the way up in search of more grass. Sometimes we would approach the homely brown bulls and Joy would become jumpy because I always wore a red shirt. But the bulls only stared at us and went on chewing the grass with infinite peace of mind. In the evenings we sat down in the lounge with the hotel owner who loved to talk about his younger days when he had been a coal miner in the southern part of the country. When he was in particularly high spirits, he would sing us folk songs in his mother tongue because he claimed that every true Welshman was also a singer. We would sit close to the fire and drink the light beer he offered us until he got tired and dozed off in his armchair. Then we would go up to our room which had dark wooden walls and a large window overlooking the sea, and we would put on the electric heater and sit down and have another drink and talk. During the day, whenever it was not too cold, we went swimming, and when the sun was out and there were no clouds in the sky, we stretched out on the sand and lay on the beach until the breeze drove us away.

We usually had our meals in one of the small pubs, where the local people came to have a drink and a chat. We loved to sit quietly and listen to the strange melodious sounds of their speech, so different from that of the English.

A few times, we went dancing. There were only a few dancing places, and they were entirely different from the swinging discotheques in London. They were peaceful and relaxing. I was surprised to find that I could enjoy them.

We took our time and spent the days lazily, not talking about the future. The future seemed to belong to a different world. We didn't let it bother us.

Then, one night, when we were sitting in our room with two huge glasses of beer, listening to two happy drunkards singing in Welsh down on the street below, Joy said to me:

"It is so different here, isn't it? It's so cut off from the world."

"Yes," I said, "it's not much like the Middle East."

"What are we going to do when we get back?"

She was wrapped in a thick white woolen sweater. Her legs were stretched out close to the heater.

"I don't know," I said, "what do you want to do?"

"I'd like to try acting," she said, "sometime."

"I thought of trying to work this book of mine into a movie," I said. "Maybe I will. You could play the part of the beautiful girl. You would fit the part perfectly."

"But she dies in the end, brutally."

"I know," I said, "but it's a good part. The tragedy adds to the impact. I would really love to see you in the part. You could be a stunning success."

"I should study acting," she said. "I haven't been in a play since high school, and those don't count."

I nodded.

"But what about you?"

"I'd like to take my exams next month, so I won't lose the year, and my parents will be pleased. Then, I'll see. I'll have to see what happens with the book."

"It will still take quite a while, won't it."

"Yes, it should be out in six months."

"Did you send a card to Ram's mother?"

I looked down at my empty glass.

"No."

"Why not?"

I tapped my finger on my knee. I could see her motionless reflection in my glass.

"I don't know."

"I think you should write her."

"Yes. I suppose I should."

"Do you often think of him?"

I smiled bitterly. "No."

She came up behind me and put her hands on my shoulders. "Are you happy?"

"Yes," I said. "I am as happy as I can be."

Dead, I thought, dead. Ram, whom I had envied more than anyone else on earth.

"What difference does a postcard make?"

"I am sure she'd be happy to get one." Joy said.

"I will send one, then."

We were on our way to Edinburgh when we heard about the American peace plan. It was the first time since we had left London that we had heard news about Israel. We didn't usually listen to the radio.

Joy was worried about the news. I discovered that in certain ways she was quite a pessimistic person. She said the Americans were selling Israel out, and for a very cheap price. She said that the plan included practically all the Russian demands. It was a clear sign of the impotence of the leading country of the Western world. I wasn't sure she was right. I thought it might be the beginning of a serious peace move. In any case, I told the frowning Joy, Israel had come through worse crises. This wouldn't be the end of the story.

We stayed in Edinburgh for one day and then continued driving northwest toward the island of Skye. The scenery and the weather were bright and beautiful but we didn't have as good a time as we had had in Wales. Joy listened to the news constantly. I couldn't talk her out of it. She grimaced when she heard of Nasser's acceptance, too. She said she would like to think that some good would come of the plan, but she just couldn't.

We arrived in Skye in time to watch the traditional games and sports competitions. We stayed there for three days and then we returned south.

Arriving back in London, we found out about the three-month cease-fire between Israel and Egypt. The papers were

filled with the news and there were pictures of happy, celebrating Israelis in the streets of Tel Aviv. Joy looked at the photos
doubtfully and her brow wrinkled as she read the long articles.
It made me feel uncertain.

"My sister gave me a letter today," she said quietly. "It
came from my parents."

We were sitting on the big double bed in our hotel room.
The unpacked suitcases were standing on the floor.

"What did they say?"

"They said that they hope I'll be happy. They send you
their regards." She paused, staring at herself in the mirror
facing her. "They say they hope we'll come and visit them in
the States some day."

"Sound bitter?"

"I don't know," she said to the mirror. "Probably they are
not too happy, having their two daughters living so far away."

"But, you don't . . ."

"No," she said, smiling at me, "of course not."

"Maybe we'll visit them," I said. "Quite soon."

"How? On the way to Hollywood?"

"Maybe, who knows?"

I took off my shoes and stretched on the bed.

"Listen," she said.

"Yes?"

"What do we do next?"

"I don't know. Whatever you want."

She turned and stared down at me.

"Let's go back to Israel. I'd like to get started there and
anyway"—she grimaced—"from far away this cease-fire makes
me nervous."

I laughed.

"If a cease-fire makes you nervous you are becoming a real
Israeli."

We flew back the next day. Before we went to the airport
Joy insisted on checking at the American Express office to see
if there was any mail for me. We found a nice, long letter,

signed by both my parents. They sent their warmest regards and congratulations, and added that they were hoping to see us some day, if it wasn't too much to ask. Joy was visibly relieved as she read it for the third time and she decided we should go and buy a few small gifts for them. My telling her that there was nothing we could buy they didn't have anyway, did not dissuade her. We ended up with a few yards of silken material for a dress and three boxes of cigars. Afterward we went to the post office and sent a cable warning them of our imminent homecoming. Joy was very strict about such things.

We arrived in Israel on a hot August day. I found the white Triumph in the parking lot where I had left it a month before. While I was putting our suitcases in the back, Joy circled the car, inspecting it carefully.

"Not one single, solitary, miserable ticket," she announced finally.

"What inefficiency. You ought to report this."

I inserted the key into the lock and opened the door for her.

"Thank you," she said. "Do you think you have any gas?"

"Sure, I filled it up before I left."

"Oh, Christ."

"What?"

"I'm getting nervous."

"Don't be," I said. "We're home."

When we got near the house I pulled in behind the black Dodge and stopped the engine.

"Well," I said, "Mrs. Ryke."

"O.K.," she said. "Let's get the show on the road."

She got out of the car and waited for me to get the two suitcases.

"All right," she said calmly, "you lead the way."

My mother opened the door. My father was right behind her.

"Well, there you are," she said happily. "We just got your cable half an hour ago." She beamed at Joy over my shoulder. "Hello, dear, I am so happy to see you."

I saw Joy's tense expression relax and disappear. Her whole face brightened.

"Hello," she said.

"Well, come in," my father said. "We have the drinks ready."

"And the cake," my mother added, "and the flowers."

"Well," I said to Joy, "what do you know?"

We walked into the living room, leaving the suitcases in the hall. My father opened the champagne bottle and poured the drinks.

"I spotted a new case of Coke bottles in the fridge," he said, handing me my glass, "but it's not for this occasion."

Then he handed Joy her glass and a red rose.

"And that's for you, lady."

"Thanks." Joy said, smiling.

"Let's have a gulp then," I said, "I'm thirsty."

"Well," my father said, "to you."

"To your happiness," my mother said with glistening eyes. We drank.

My father put his glass down and walked around the table. He looked at Joy.

"I believe I have the right to kiss the bride," he said.

She bowed slightly, emptied her glass and put it down on the table.

"My pleasure."

I watched the scene curiously.

"And now," my father said, pulling back and breathing a bit heavily, "all I want is a bite of the cake."

"This sure is your day," I said drily.

"Then I can go back to my work and misery."

"They can't possibly go together."

"Be quiet," Joy said, picking up the huge piece of cake my mother offered her. "I'll have to educate him," she told my father.

Chapter Twenty

WE STAYED in my room for two weeks, until we found a flat. It was a lot pleasanter than I had expected. Joy seemed to get along with my parents extremely well. It took me some ·time, but I finally realized that they simply liked her. Late in the evening after our arrival I found my father sitting alone in his study and I walked in and closed the door behind me.

"Tell me truly," I said, "are you very much against this marriage?"

He put down his papers. "Not at all," he said. "Why should we be?"

He said I was too young, but that was not really important. Neither he nor my mother minded the religious difference. That didn't matter at all.

"I just hope Joy doesn't have any difficulties because of it," he said. "She shouldn't have to feel like a stranger if she settles in this country.

"For that reason," he went on, "it may be easier for her if she converted. This is the only country in which it is more convenient to be Jewish than not."

I shook my head slowly.

"I don't want her to convert."

"That's up to you."

For the first few days, Joy spent most of her time with my mother talking about the different possibilities for a young

woman in Israel and learning to cook. On Friday we had
gefilte fish for supper which she had cooked herself, under
my mother's supervision. I told her that if this behavior
continued I would divorce her within the month but my
mother told me to shut up. My father insisted he liked the
meal.

I spent a few days looking at houses with brokers until I
found a three-room flat for a rent of five hundred pounds a
month. It was in a pleasant area near Rehavia, and Joy and I
decided to take it. We didn't care too much where we lived.
It wasn't going to be permanent.

The apartment was furnished so we didn't transfer many
things there. Neither of us had a lot of belongings, anyway.
We rented it for a minimum of two months and paid the
money in advance.

I didn't think we would stay there longer.

The evening before we moved I sat in my room by myself
and tried to decide what to do next. My marriage came as a
surprise, quick and unforeseen, and I had liked it that way.
I thought it would put my mind at rest and enable me to
devote my time and effort to the work I wanted to do.

I received the galleys of my book a few days after we arrived
in Israel. There was still no indication from my publisher
of how they thought it might sell, but I assumed that it would
not be an absolute flop. Meanwhile, I intended to take my
exams in economics. I thought that maybe I would be able
to use that too.

After that there seemed to be a few possibilities. I could try
to write another book or work the first one into a movie
script. I could go to the States later in the year, and find out
how to get started making a movie, or I could try to ask my
father for money to produce a film. I gave the galleys to my
parents and they both read them.

I was pleased that my father liked the book. He said he
believed it showed real promise. Of course, it was not entirely
to his taste, but that needn't bother me, he said.

My mother said that she thought the book was good and

that she liked it, and I knew that neither statement was true.

I knew she wanted me to do work that would benefit other people and my country. She did not consider literature or show business within this category.

Joy had decided to take an intensive, two-month course in Hebrew. She said she hoped that by the time the course was over we would both have a clearer idea of our plans for the future.

A few days after we moved to our flat my parents threw a party for us to celebrate our marriage. They invited only a few dozen people because we did not want it to be a noisy event. The guests were mostly old friends of the family and relatives. They were all gathered in the living room where Joy and I, smartly dressed, stood by the door and received their good wishes and gifts. The only guests I personally had invited were Gad, Udi, and the straw-haired lieutenant. Joy invited one girl who had worked with her in the bookshop in Tel Aviv, and Muhammed.

"What a beautiful woman," my father's eighty-two-year-old mother shouted at me, pulling me down to her wheelchair, pointing at Joy with a shaking hand. She was an ancient-looking thing, nearly deaf and blind. She lived in Tel Aviv with my father's younger brother who was a surgeon. We seldom saw her and I regretted it every time we did.

"Yes, Grandma," I said into the old woman's ear.

"The main thing is," she shouted, "that she is a good Jewish girl."

"Yes, Grandma," I said soothingly.

"What?" she shouted.

"Yes, Grandma," I said and went to meet Udi who had just come in.

"I'm glad you could come," I said, meaning it.

"Hi," he said, "congratulations." He pushed a long thin parcel into my hands.

"Thanks."

"Mother couldn't come," he said. "She sends her regards."

"Thank you."

Joy came over to us. I introduced her to Udi and noticed their mutual curiosity as they looked a each other.

"I am very happy to meet you," Joy said. "Can I bring you a drink."

Udi blushed slightly. "Please," he said.

She picked up two drinks at the bar and walked back to him I watched them as they stood in a corner, talking.

"She is lovely," one of my aunts said, coming up behind me

"Yes," I said. "Excuse me."

I walked up the stairs and went into my room. I sat on the bed and wiped my head with the sleeve of my suit. Then I opened the long parcel that Udi had given me.

It was an old Arabic sword coated with silver. I had seen it many times before, sitting in Ram's room. It used to hang on the wall above his bed between two smaller bayonets. Ram had bought it in the old market in Acre, when he was fourteen. He had hung it on the wall instead of a picture. He had no interest in paintings.

I tried to draw the sword from its sheathe but it wouldn't move. There were small stains of rust where the silver coating had come off. I realized it needed oiling.

I studied the walls, trying to find a place where I could hang it. Then I remembered I was not living there any more.

"Where the hell have you been?" Joy asked me, about half an hour later when she found me there.

I put the sword on the bed.

"I've been here," I said cheerfully. "How is the party going?"

"People are looking for you." She sat beside me. "It's all right, I guess. I just felt a bit lost with all those curious people staring at me, and you vanishing without warning."

I took her hand and pressed it to my lips. "I am sorry."

She smiled at me.

"It doesn't matter." She looked down. "So this is Udi's present."

"Yes," I said, "it used to belong to Ram. Shall we go down?"

"We should, actually. A friend of yours just arrived."

"What does he look like?"

"Very pale yellow hair, just like . . ."

"Straw," I said.

"That's right."

We went downstairs and joined the guests again. I saw the lieutenant standing at the bar by himself, looking indecisively at the various bottles.

"Leave it," I said. "That's alcohol."

"You know," he said, not turning to me, "I feel a bit guilty about all this. I keep telling myself that if I hadn't intervened . . ."

"You see," I said, opening a bottle of Coke, "where your stubbornness leads you."

"You could have done worse though," he said, turning to look at Joy. "I'll take one of those too, if you don't mind."

I opened another Coke for him. Joy disappeared into the hall, and a moment later walked past us, accompanied by Muhammed. The lieutenant raised a yellow eyebrow.

"One of your relatives?"

"No, just a guest."

"An enemy?"

I nodded.

"Quite good-looking," he said, starting to drink again.

I left him and wandered around among the guests for a while, shaking hands and picking up an occasional piece of cake. My parents sat among a large group of relatives and discussed the chances for peace talks without much enthusiasm. My father was a pessimist. He didn't believe that anything helpful would come out of it. He had signed a contract with the government a week before, agreeing on a plan to build the aircraft motor factory. That was where his hopes lay.

The only non-relative in the circle of people sitting around him was Gad, who sat listening with interest, and smoking a cigar I had picked up for him earlier. When he met Joy he protested against my hiding her from him when he still would have had a fair chance. Then he drew up a chair and joined the discussion saying that after that disappointment, politics could hardly depress him more. He was constantly backing my father's opinions and I wondered whether he wasn't thinking about his own future. Gad believed that having the right connections was the most important factor in a man's success.

It was after ten when all the guests had finally left and Joy and I stuffed all the gifts we could carry into the back of the car and drove to our flat.

"Well," I said to her when we lay in bed, "now that that is over I'll start studying."

"When?"

"Tomorrow."

"My Hebrew course starts in three days," she said. "We'll have to start speaking Hebrew to each other. Imagine that."

I grimaced.

"We don't really have to."

"We will," she said. "I have to learn this bloody language once and for all."

"Our financial situation is not bad," I said. "I don't have to send you to work yet."

"That's reassuring. By the way, I think I'll get used to your family, eventually. They are not as bad as I feared, as long as we don't see them too much . . ."

"I guess my mother . . ."

"I didn't mean your parents," she said. "Just all those uncles and aunts and cousins."

"Oh, don't worry. You won't see a lot of them. We only meet at weddings and funerals." I looked at her, "I noticed your friend Muhammed left early."

"He probably didn't feel too much at home. He came out to be polite and left for the same reason. He is just very polite."

"My father chatted with him for a few minutes."

"So did your mother. They behaved rather decently. I really am beginning to like them."

I closed my eyes wearily. I wasn't looking forward to studying for my exams the following morning. I thought maybe I'd delay it for one day.

"Udi said we should come to visit," Joy said vaguely. "He said his mother would like to see us."

"Really?" I said sleepily. "We should go then."

Ram's mother took an immediate liking to Joy. It was obvious from the moment they met. She pressed her hand and smiled at her. It was one of the very few times since the death of her son that I had seen her smile. We sat in her small living room for more than two hours and most of the conversation was between the two women. Joy spoke about her reasons for coming to Israel, about her life in the past and about her hopes for the future. Ram's mother listened with open interest and from time to time nodded her approval. I chewed on my chocolate bar and watched them silently.

When we got up to leave, Ram's mother invited us to come for dinner. We agreed on two weeks from Friday.

"I was worried when I heard you had married," Ram's mother said to me as she accompanied us to the door, "but I didn't have to be. You have done well for yourself."

Joy bowed slightly and blushed a bit.

"I am glad that is what you think," I said.

"I certainly do. See you two weeks from Friday, then."

The next few days I spent at home reading books on economics. Joy went for her courses every morning. In the afternoons she was usually home, reading books about history or theatre, the two subjects she was interested in other than psychology. In the evenings we sometimes went to see a film, or to eat out, but mostly we stayed at home. There wasn't a lot happening in Jerusalem.

"This is no good," Joy said one afternoon.

I put my copybook down and looked up at her.

"What?"

"I've just been thinking, I have to start doing something. Except for this course, I feel like I'm wasting time. I should get a job, or study. I can't sit at home all afternoon and evening and watch you reading those bloody papers and drink-

ing those bloody Cokes. I get to feeling like a useless orna-
ment."

"It's only for three more weeks," I said. "I'll be through
with the exams and then . . ."

"Then what?"

"We'll see . . . maybe we can make a movie."

She didn't look enthusiastic.

"Do you think that is realistic?" she asked. "And even so,
it would take months, probably more than a year until we
could actually start with it. What will I do until then?"

"I don't know. You can do anything, everything. Get your
M.A. in psychology or study acting. Maybe we'll go abroad
for a while, I don't know."

"It'll be all right," she said. "I am not worried. It's just that
I never intended to get married so soon. Anyway, not con-
sciously. And so I'm not really sure what I want to do. But
I'll find out. There is no hurry."

"There is an acting group in Jerusalem which speaks English," I said. "They put on plays from time to time in different
places. I have never seen them but I've heard they're not bad.
Maybe you'd like to try and join them."

"What is the name of the group?"

"I don't remember, but it would be easy to find out."

"Will you find out for me?"

"Sure."

"Thank you, darling." She laughed and came from the bed
to the place where I was sitting. She hooked an arm around
my neck, pulled herself up and planted warm kisses on my
mouth. "I am in a good mood again," she announced. "See?"

"Yes," I said amused.

"Shshshsh," she said, putting a long finger in front of her
mouth. "Now you go back to your miserable studying while
I fix us some delicious strawberry ice cream."

She got to her feet and marched out of the room. The bell
rang.

I went over and opened the door.

"Can I come in?" my mother asked. She had a huge round cake in her hands.

I stepped aside.

"Sure, with that cake, you'd even be welcome."

"Hello, dear," my mother said to Joy who came out of the kitchen. She offered her the cake.

"Oohh," Joy exclaimed, taking it, "thank you. That will go beautifully with the ice cream. Here, put it in the kitchen," she told me. And turning to my mother: "Won't you sit down?"

I did as I was told and went to the kitchen.

"No thanks," my mother was saying when I reappeared in the room. "I just dropped in for a moment. What I actually came for," she added, turning to me, "is to tell you that your father received tickets for the premiere of a new Israeli movie. I forget the name, but it's about the Six Day War. He thought you might be interested in going."

"Certainly," I said. "When is it?"

"Tomorrow evening."

"That would be nice." Joy said.

"Well, here you are then," my mother said, taking two elegant-looking white cards out of her wallet. "Starts at eight-thirty, I believe."

"Thanks. Aren't you coming too?"

She shook her head.

"I think I'd rather stay home. Your father has a meeting tomorrow evening. You can tell me about it afterward."

It turned out to be a rather fancy event. The audience consisted of guests connected with the film industry, and people who could afford the costly tickets. The Prime Minister and some other celebrities were also there.

We sat in one of the first rows in the gallery. Joy wore her most elegant dress, a silver maxi, and her silver shoes and silver earrings. Every head turned when we passed through the hall. She looked stunning.

The film was called *The Dead and the Living,* and it was adapted from a novel of the same title that had been written by an Israeli author shortly after the war. I had not read the book but had heard a lot about it. It had been one of the most successful best-sellers in the country, the previous year.

Before the screening started the producer of the film made a short speech emphasizing the importance of this moment in his life, and tried to spice it with a few anecdotes. He finished by expressing his hopes that the audience would enjoy this work of art.

After the first ten minutes I lost interest in the movie. It was the usual sentimental, heroic story of gallant brave men and gallant women fighting for their lives and future with only God at their side. When the intermission finally came I told Joy I wanted to leave, but she wanted to stay. She said that if I ever wanted to make films I could also learn a lot from bad ones. I slumped down into my seat again.

"Pardon me. But you are a lovely young woman."

I looked in the direction the voice was coming from. A tall, dark-haired middle-aged man was standing next to Joy's seat, looking down at her with polite curiosity.

"Good evening," Joy said, gazing up at him.

"I hope I am not intruding." He spoke English with a distinct American accent. "Are you an actress?"

"No," Joy said, and then she smiled back at him, "not yet."

"I was sure you were," he said, raising his thick black eyebrows admiringly, "forgive me." He offered his hand. "I am Derek Bennett."

"Joy Ryke," she said, pressing his hand. "How do you do?"

Derek Bennett, I thought. I have heard the name before. Who the hell is he?

"Joy Ryke?" he was saying, still holding her hand, "are you by any chance . . ."

"I am his daughter-in-law," she said. "This is my husband." He turned and looked at me.

"Assaf Ryke," I said, offering my hand. "I am pleased to meet you."

"I am happy to meet you," he said. "I know your father."

"Oh," I said.

We shook hands.

"I am a producer," Derek Bennett said. "This is my first visit to this country." He looked around absent-mindedly. "I find it fascinating." He turned back to us. "Do you have anything to do with movies?"

"We are trying to get started," I said. "I write a bit, and my wife wants to be an actress."

A bell rang three times.

"I'll have to go back to my seat," he said. "Look, why don't I invite you for a drink after this is over and we can have a quiet talk."

"Why don't you?" I said, smiling.

"Right, I'll meet you at the exist." He turned away.

"Well," Joy commented.

"I've heard of that guy before," I said. "He must have produced a pretty important movie, but I can't remember which."

We looked at each other and then she winked at me and burst out laughing.

"You'd better watch your tongue then," she said.

The lights in the hall went out. On the screen, the young handsome heroes began dying again, saving their country in the process. I wasn't interested in their troubles.

"Shall we go to my hotel?" Derek Bennett asked, when we were standing on the sidewalk in front of the cinema. "We can sit at the bar there."

"That would be fine," Joy said.

"I've got a car here," I said. "It's a bit small, though."

He slapped me lightly on the shoulder.

"Oh, I don't mind that," he said, in good spirits. "Let's go."

I drove to the King David Hotel, careful not to have an accident on the way.

We sat in the bar and ordered scotch and gin and ginger ale. Bennett sat with his back to the corner.

"So what did you think of the film?" he asked.

"Lousy," I said.

"Why?"

"It's too sentimental and too heroic," I said. "It doesn't look real and therefore it doesn't involve you. A movie has to involve you in order to become a box office success. Plus, it's too common. It has been done and done before. People have already gotten the message that we are all heroes. An antihero would look much fresher and more attractive."

He nodded his head thoughtfully.

"What do you think?" he asked Joy.

She smiled at him over her ginger ale. "I agree with my husband."

Derek Bennett laughed and took a sip of his scotch. He had a pleasant laugh. It made him seem younger.

"So do I," he said. He turned to Joy. "You must be from New York?"

"Washington State originally," Joy said, "but I grew up in New York."

"And came here on your own?"

"Yes."

"When?"

"About a year ago."

"A Zionist family?"

"Not at all. Not even a Jewish family, in fact."

Derek Bennett raised his glass to his mouth. A flicker of interest showed in his eyes.

"What brought you here?"

"Curiosity, at the beginning," Joy said, "but I loved it from the first moment I came. It is a fascinating country."

"It is," he said. "I am here for the first time and I am addicted to it, completely. It fills my mind." He shook his head wonderingly. "Mind you," he said, "I was born a Jew, but it never meant anything to me. I lived completely without religion, and I liked it that way. I had even changed my original name to make it sound more"—he chuckled—"practical.

And now, after all these years, here I am and I am obsessed by what I see around me."

We watched him talk.

"Want another drink?"

"Please," I said.

Joy nodded, absorbed in her thoughts.

He raised his hand and signaled to the bartender to bring three more drinks. Then he turned to us again.

"How did you two meet?" he asked. "You don't have to tell me if you don't want to. I'm just curious."

"He picked me up on the street one Friday night," Joy said, squeezing my arm gently. "It was in the Old City. I used to live there."

"Oh."

"I was still in the army, then, on a weekend leave," I said. "Didn't have much to do so I was driving with a friend around town, bored stiff.

"It was nice," Joy said, looking at me.

"Listen," he said. "I've been in this country for only a week and I'll be leaving in two days, but I have made my mind up to make a movie about it." He paused. "I'd like to do that very much.

"I don't want it to be anything like the movie we saw to-night," he continued. "It should be funny and realistic and as contemporary as the two of you."

"I wrote a book," I said tentatively. "A novel. It's called *Running Out of Miracles*. It will come out in about six months. But I have the galleys at home.

"Oh," he said, visibly impressed. "Is it in English?"

"Sure."

"What about?"

"A contemporary Israeli story," I said, "about young people, with no heroes."

"Oh?"

For a moment no one spoke.

"You see," Derek Bennett said finally. "I would like to do

this movie in a way that would help the Israeli film industry as much as possible. I believe it needs encouragement, especially the young people who are trying to get started like yourselves. Money is not my problem, and this time, it is also not my objective. I have made lots of money on movies. This one I would like to do for more idealistic reasons."

"I see," I said.

"I'll have to read you book," he said.

"That would be great."

"Have you ever written a movie script?"

"Not really," I said. "I've written short ones, for myself. But I've read scripts and I've read books about scripts. I think I could do it."

"Well, we'll see," he said, "but first, I have to read your book."

"I'll bring it to you first thing tomorrow morning."

"Oh," he said glancing at his watch, "what's wrong with tonight?"

"Well," I said to Joy when we were driving back to our flat, "it looks like this is our chance."

"Don't get too worked up," she said. "We don't know anything yet."

"I think he means what he says."

"So do I," she said, "but we still don't know what's going to come of it."

"This is our chance."

"It would be beautiful."

"It will," I said, parking the car in the small street where we lived. We went up to the apartment. I took the galleys I had received from the publishing house off the shelf. Joy kicked her shoes off and sat wearily in the armchair.

"I'll go over to my parents' " I told her, "after I drop this off at the hotel. I have to find out from my father who this guy is."

"All right."

"I'll be back in about an hour."

As I walked out I looked at the calendar that hung on the wall by the door. It was Wednesday, September 16, 1970.

When I walked into the hotel, Bennett was still sitting in the bar, having his third drink by himself. I gave him the book, wished him good night and went out again. I drove slowly to my parents' house, going over the whole evening in my mind.

The last of my father's guests was leaving as I entered the house. I walked into the kitchen and helped myself to a bottle of Coke. After I heard the door shut and locked I got up from the table and went into the living room. Both my parents were there having a quiet conversation. I sat down on the sofa facing them.

"Hullo," my mother said, "Where's Joy?"

"At home. She was tired."

"How was the film?"

"Not worth mentioning," I said. "You were better off here." I turned to my father who was sitting in his armchair looking tired. "Do you know a man by the name of Derek Bennett?"

"A bit. He is a movie producer."

"Big?"

"I think so."

"Successful?"

"Richer than me."

"What is all this about?" my mother asked. "Why are you asking about this man?"

"I met him at the premiere," I said. "He is interested in making a movie about Israel. Maybe I can do the story."

"Oh," my father said.

"Is he reliable?"

"I should think so."

"You ought to be studying for your exams," my mother said to me anxiously. "You shouldn't waste time now."

I got up.

"No," I said, smiling at her, "I won't waste time." I walked over to her and patted her on the cheek. "Don't worry, Mother."

"I never know what you're up to," she said sadly.

"That's because I'm never up to anything," I said. "Well, I'll be on my way."

"Will you show him your book?" my father asked.

"I hope he is reading it right now."

"I see." He scratched his cheek and leaned forward to pick out a cigar for himself. "Just take it easy. It is a tricky business, films are full of disappointments."

"Sure," I said lightly, "but I can try. I'll have one myself," I added, taking a thick Havana, "if you don't mind. I'm beginning to feel like a businessman myself."

"Not a politician?"

"No."

"A good cigar never hurt anyone," my father said.

"So what happens next?" Joy asked me, half an hour later.

"He'll call sometime tomorrow."

"Think the book will do?"

"Do you?"

"I don't know. I like it. I think it might come pretty close to what he wants."

"In that case," I said, taking off my shoes, "perhaps you will play the part of the beautiful girl, after all."

"I don't know. I have no experience. There are hundreds of actresses who could play that role."

"I doubt that Bennett likes me," I said, "but I am sure he likes you. I think he would like you to be in the movie. Anyway, if anything came of all this talk, I would insist on it."

"Would you?" Joy said.

Chapter Twenty-One

WHEN the phone woke me at nine-twenty the following morning, Joy had already left the flat.

"I like it," Bennett said shortly. "If you can come and see me this evening we can talk the whole business over."

"What time?"

"Say eight-thirty?"

"I'll meet you at the bar."

"That would be fine. So long."

"I learned a lot of new Hebrew words today," Joy announced happily as she came in, around two that afternoon.

"Bennett said he likes it."

"I am really making progress. I can feel myself understanding people when they talk. It's great. I can say quite complicated sentences like . . ."

"Bennett called this morning," I repeaed. "He likes it."

"That's great," she said calmly, "but don't you want to hear a few samples of my Hebrew?"

I stood up and looked at her.

"Do you realize what this means?"

"Of course, darling," she said lightly. "He might make a deal with you."

"You're not excited?"

"Of course, I am. But that's not the only thing I'm living

for. I'm so glad that I'm actually beginning to understand the language. That is very important to me, too."

"Yes, of course," I said.

"Assaf?"

"What?"

"You haven't talked about anything in the last two weeks except our careers and now, this movie." She looked at me. "Don't let it become too important. There are other things in life."

"An opportunity like this doesn't come along every day," I said. "We could wait for years before we get another one."

"You have written the book."

"I know, but that's still not enough."

"What do you really want?"

"I want to make it big."

She shook her head slowly.

"Why? Do you think that is the most important thing in life?"

"No," I said, "not at all. But I want it. That's what makes it important. You've got to have what you want, otherwise why want it?"

"Yes. That's in your book."

"Please don't look so sad," I said, planting a kiss on her ear, "I'm not so terrible. Tell me what you learned in Hebrew and afterward I'll tell you about Bennett, but only if you want to hear."

"I am a girl," Joy said slowly, in Hebrew. "Every day I go to school to study my new language. It is summer now and the sum is shining and everyone is happy."

"Great," I said, "I don't know what to say; it's absolutely great."

"You're kidding."

"No, truly I'm not. I think you speak beautifully."

"I can write it too," she said proudly.

"You are going to be the most beautiful Hebrew-speaking girl in the country."

"Thank you kindly," she said and got up to her feet. "Right now I am the hungriest girl in this country."

"There are two steaks in the freezer."

"Come to the kitchen and tell me all about our producer while I cook a terrific meal."

I didn't study at all that afternoon. We passed the time making plans. I told Joy that after my exams we might go to the States and see the big studios in Hollywood. We could also visit her parents in New York and see the plays on Broadway. We could travel from the east to the west coast. It would be fun. Maybe she could take a quick course in acting while we were there, if such a thing existed. I thought Bennett could help us to find one.

At eight-thirty I left Joy and went to the bar of the King David. Bennett was already there, sitting at the same table as the previous night.

"Good evening," he said, "sit down. Gin, isn't it?"

"Yes, please."

I took the chair opposite him while he ordered.

"All right, then. Now we can talk."

"As I told you," he said, taking the galleys from the seat next to him, "I like it. That is, I like the style, and the spirit in which it's written. The end is no good for my purposes," he said. "He shouldn't die in the Six Day War, etc. and there has to be more about the girl. That is very important. She should have a bigger role, almost equal to his. The part about religion is good. It can be left as is."

He waited politely for me to comment, and when I didn't he continued.

"There is not much that needs changing, except what I have just mentioned. There should be a scene showing the night life in Tel Aviv, how the youth and soldiers spend their free evenings, and so on. Do you know what I mean?"

"I think so."

"Have you seen *Easy Rider* or *Midnight Cowboy*?"

"Yes, I have seen both."

"What did you think of them?"

"Good movies," I said.

"Yes, well those are the films that go now. You should have them in mind when you write. It will help you."

I nodded.

"The irreverence in your style is good, keep it."

I nodded again.

"Do you understand what I want?" he asked. "Do you think you can do it?"

"Yes."

He sat back in his chair and smiled.

"That's fine. I would like you to write a treatment on this theme, and send it to me. I won't pay you for it, but if I like it, I'll ask you to work it into a script, and if I like that too I'll produce the film"—he paused—"together with you, and you'll get fifty percent of the profits. It could be a lot of money."

"I see," I said.

"What do you think of my proposition?"

I smiled. "Terrific."

"It's a deal, then."

He reached for his breast pocket and pulled out a small white card. He handed it to me.

"This is my address and phone number in Hollywood. You can call me collect if you have any questions. And when you're through with the treatment, just mail it to me. O.K.?"

I looked at the card and put it in my pocket.

"I have a few questions right now," I said.

"Yes?"

"What kind of ending do you want?"

"That's up to you," he said. "Think of something. But he definitely shouldn't die in the war. That sort of thing is no good. You can't kill him, altogether."

"And her?"

"The story line is O.K.," he said. "Her part just needs developing. The audience abroad, especially the American audience, would get more involved if the heroine is an American girl. It brings the film closer to them. You just have to increase the number of scenes with her, and shorten the story after her death."

"All right."

"Just give it some careful thought," he said. "I'm sure you can manage."

"How long are you staying?"

"I'm flying to New York on Saturday. I am going on a tour of the West Bank tomorrow, during the day. I'll be back here in the evening. I'll probably go to sleep early."

"I'd like to try to write one or two short outlines," I said, "and show them to you before you leave. I want to be sure that I understood what you have in mind."

"I'll probably have supper here around eight," he said. "You could drop in then, if you want."

I suddenly remembered that we were invited for dinner at Ram's mother's. I hesitated for a moment.

You have to know your priorities, I told myself.

"All right," I said, "I will."

I got up.

"Thanks a lot," I said, "I'll be seeing you."

"Give my regards to your beautiful wife."

"Thanks."

I took two steps and then turned back to him.

"Could she play the female lead?" I asked.

"Maybe," he said. "We'll have to see about that."

"She could be good."

"I think so too," he said, "but there are screen tests and acting experience and such to be considered. There is not much point worrying about it now. We'll see about it when the time comes."

"All right," I said.

Chapter Twenty-Two

WHEN I came home I found Joy sitting in the armchair, in our small living room. She looked upset.

"What's the matter?" I asked.

"Nothing." She shrugged. "I am just worried."

I sat on the floor by her feet.

"What about?"

"I don't know where it will all end. The Egyptians and Russians keep moving the missiles and breaking the agreement all the time. And what does Nixon say? Just relax. It really makes you feel well-protected."

"The only dependence we can ever have is on ourselves," I said.

"That's what your father always says."

"He is right."

"I guess, but we still have to try to get outside help."

"Dayan says that we cannot remain inactive any longer. He says he would not stand by such policy."

"I know," I said.

"I'm afraid he'll resign."

"No. I don't think he'll be pushed that far."

"Aren't you worried?"

"You'll get used to it." I said, "in time."

Her face finally relaxed.

"Now we've even got cholera."

I laughed.

"That is a mess. But don't you see that this is what holds this country together—its innumerable problems?"

"Yes, I'm beginning to see that. What happened with Bennett?"

"I think we have a deal," I said. "I'll have to change the story a bit but that won't really be a problem."

I got up and pulled her to her feet.

"Let's go for a swim," I said.

"Where."

"Any swimming pool."

She laughed.

"Now? Do you realize what time it is? None will be open."

"I used to climb over fences in my younger days," I said, walking to the bathroom to get a towel. "Are you too respectable for that?"

The following morning I got up early and sat down at my typewriter. I typed two short outlines. One of them ended with the heroine's death in a road accident. The second ended with both main characters still alive but lying sick in bed with cholera. I tried to make this version as funny as possible without making it a comedy. I was already through with my typing when Joy woke up and came into the room. It was after eleven, but she didn't have to study that day. We had a small breakfast in the kitchen and read the morning papers. There wasn't any dramaic news for a change. The split between the factions in the government was sharpening and the hawks were pressing for more assertive action. There were a few articles analyzing President Nixon's statements and promises. Quite a few of them concluded that there wasn't anything behind them at all.

After thoroughly reading the English paper and the Hebrew paper for beginners she was receiving every day in the mail, Joy sighed and got up to take a shower. She came back after a few minutes dressed in one of her old white dresses, and said she had a lot of shopping to do in the supermarket for the weekend. I told her I would drive her there. I much preferred it to going back to my economics book.

We strolled around in the supermarket for about half an hour, buying all sorts of food. Finally we joined the shortest check-out line.

"I hope this will be enough," Joy said, handing me two huge paper bags. "Actually," she said, "we probably won't even need all of it. We're having dinner out tonight."

"I forgot to tell you," I said as we were walking slowly toward the exit. "I can't go this evening. I'll have to call Ram's mother and apologize."

Joy stopped walking and turned to me, surprised.

"You can't go? Why not?"

I took a few more steps but she didn't come after me, so I turned and walked back to where she stood.

"I have to go and see Bennett. He is leaving tomorrow morning."

"Why do you have to see him again?"

"I want to show him two outlines I've written. I've got to be sure I have it right."

"Why can't you show them to him this afternoon?"

"He'll be on the West Bank," I said patiently, "and later in the evening he'll be asleep."

"Oh." She shook her head in cold understanding.

"Send it to him in the States. You'd get an answer within a week."

"I don't want to lose time on this," I said. "He could find someone else or change his mind altogether. Anyway, I told him I was coming. I can't cancel it now."

Her mouth tightened into a thin, unpleasant line.

"Sometimes I just don't believe you," she said.

"Look, do we have to discuss it here? Let's at least . . ."

"We'll bloody well discuss it here," Joy said sharply. "What's your hurry? He isn't expecting you yet."

"O.K.," I said.

"One would have thought," she said, "that Ram would mean more to you than Bennett."

I stared through the glass at the street outside.

"Don't be stupid."

"Oh," she said. "Is that what I'm being?"

"What the hell has this got to do with Ram? Why bring him into it? For that matter, I don't give a damn about Bennett."

"Don't shout."

"Bennett can be dead and buried as far as I am concerned," I said calmly, "but I want to make that movie."

"I know."

"I don't intend to blow it because of one meaningless dinner."

"I wonder what you'd consider meaningful," she said bitterly.

"Don't you want to be an actress? He said you might get this role. Don't you want it?"

"I want it, but I wouldn't sell myself for it."

I waved my hand in exasperation.

"You're coming out with some really heavy thoughts."

"You'd really throw away anything just because of some . . ."

"Not some, this is a very rare opp—"

"Oh, for God's sake," she said scornfully. "If worst came to worst, you could always get the money from your bloody father."

We looked at each other silently for a moment.

"The whole point is," I said quietly, "that I don't want to get the money from my bloody father. I don't want it to be his money."

She looked down helplessly.

"Sometimes I wonder what the hell I see in you."

I put out my hand and touched her shoulder.

"Look," I said, "Everyone is watching. Let's get out of here."

She raised two mocking eyebrows.

"I'm sure you don't mind the audience. You're so keen on show business."

I bit my lip impatiently.

"Are you coming or not?"

"All right."

I turned and started walking toward the glass door.

"Oh damn, I forgot to get coffee," her voice said behind me. "I'll be with you in a minute."

I grimaced irritably and walked out.

I put the two packages in the back of the car and yawned.

A huge explosion knocked me sideways and threw me against the door. I was completely dazed for a few seconds, just leaning on the warm metal with my eyes closed.

By the time I turned around people had already begun screaming.

The glinting pieces of glass were on everything in sight.

I ran back through what had been the entrance of the supermarket and jumped over a few tin boxes and overturned stands. Then I stopped short. I could only see the white of her dress and the blood. There wasn't any face.

Chapter Twenty-Three

TWO weeks later, I sat in my old room in my parents' house and looked at the finished portrait of Ram. It stood on my bed, leaning against the wall. It had good, strong colors. They caught the eye immediately. I had painted the shirt and the background deep red. It fitted peculiarly well with the bronze color of the face. I loved to look at it.

It's strange, I thought, how alive pictures can look. Just a mixture of chemicals. And yet, there is so much vitality in the meaning you attach to them. There isn't anything there at all. It's just in you. It's all in you, and you choose in what objects to place it, and in what people. People don't matter for themselves. They matter because of the importance you add to them because you can't keep it all in yourself until it chokes you. It's because you want to make sure that they exist that you let it outside of yourself and lose it. But afterward you can't get it back because it disappears with whatever it was attached to. And the quantity is limited, that is probably why it hurts.

You lose part of yourself, when you let yourself out. It's safer inside.

But it chokes you. That's why you have to get out of yourself.

Memories, I thought. They're ugly things. They make you feel as though your life is over. One shouldn't have memories.

When you were small, really small, everything was beauiful, remember? There was no one else but you.

But then, there were other times, later. There was that evening in the hotel, when she said she would, and you hadn't expected her to because you had always known that she wouldn't, but she did. Remember?

And there was the trip. More than two weeks when there was no one else. She said it would be all right, it would only take time and you'll have to wait. Everything takes time.

And there was the first time you saw her when she was walking by herself on the sidewalk wearing her white dress and she looked like a little girl.

It's just that there is nothing to occupy your mind with, sitting alone in an empty room with a silent picure.

And remember how she came home only two days ago so happy about those new sentences she had learned and she said them with her funny peculiar accent "I am a girl, it is summer now, the sun is shining and everyone is happy."

My father knocked on the door and walked slowly into the room. He looked at me carefully and saw the thin smile on my lips. His face was tired and grim.

"Oh," he said slowly, carefully, "I am glad to see that you are feeling better."

"Yes," I said, "yes yes yes."